TAMING

ELLA JAMES

SEE WHAT OTHERS ARE SAYING ABOUT

TAMING Cross

BY ELLA JAMES

"Ella James has done it again. This is a really moving story about the power of love and redemption."
- *Paige Edward*

"Once again, Ella has woven a beautiful tale of love, secrets, adventure, and scarred (both physically and and emotionally) people who over come. I have such a book hangover this morning after having stayed up most of the night reading this book, but I simply could not put it down."
- *Delphina*

"Once again Ella James has crafted an edgy new adult romance featuring the darker side of human nature and their
I. consequences."
- *Gatosqueak*

"The chemistry between Cross and Merri sizzles and gives you butterflies as you race to finish because it's so great.."
- *Susie Q*

CHAPTER ONE

CROSS

SINCE THE ACCIDENT, I've had a sixth sense. I'm not even fucking kidding you. I think it started because of the pain. I don't remember much about the coma—most of it is sounds and smells and feelings stretched apart and pushed together like a dream under water—but I remember the pain. It was...different than the pain you feel when you're awake. The kind of shit that flows through every part of you. Sweeps you up and swallows you. And lots of times, I could feel it coming like you hear a train from a few miles out.

The day I had the stroke was like that. I had started to come around a little and my body knew its routines, even if my mind was still in Neverland. So I could tell something was off when they wheeled me out of my room and into the ambulance, moving me from the swanky ass private rehab where I started to a state facility for people whose families couldn't do better, or in my case, just said *fuck it*. As they loaded me up into the ambulance, I could feel that panic. I could feel myself slipping down, to somewhere dark you can't crawl out of.

1

Since I've come out of the coma, every time I get that panicked feeling, bad things happen.

Like when I got it two months ago, sitting in my friend Lizzy's Camry, waiting for her to come out of Hunter West's Napa Valley home. I woke up from a nap drenched in cold sweat, just as Priscilla Heat—my dad's former mistress, who sold her predecessor into the sex trade—walked around the house and rapped her long red nails on my window. And I knew, half a second before I saw the spark of her Taser, that I was fucked.

Tonight, I tell myself it's my parents throwing off my equilibrium. Making me feel *bad*. That weird kind of bad that I've come to know and fear. The fingers of my left hand tingle and my neck feels tight. I blink into the mirror and I squeeze my eyes shut. Grab a deep breath. Keep shaving.

I don't shave every day anymore, but my buddy Suri will be here in a few minutes, and if I don't get rid of my beard before she shows up, she'll know I've been holed up.

When was the last day I went out? Suri and Lizzy hauled me to The Napa Noodle…eight days ago? The night before they left for Paris. They got back yesterday—Friday—with Lizzy's wedding gown in tow. I left the house on Monday. Grocery run. So yeah, it's been four days.

I'm taking it slow on my neck—I'm a leftie, and since my motorcycle wreck, my left hand's pretty much fucked—but when I hear the bell atop the shop door ding, I speed up. Occasionally when I was in rehab, Suri shaved me, and if she sees how long it takes me, even after three month's practice, she's likely to try again.

My fingers sweat as I finish up my jaw. I hear the gentle clomping of expensive heels on cement stairs leading up to my loft, and— fuck! I feel a sharp sting under the razor, followed by a crimson bloom that quickly starts snaking down my neck. I'm muttering curses, tossing the razor into the sink, when Suri calls my name.

"Just a second," I call through the door. Damnit, I sound surly.

"Okay." Suri, as always, sounds like she belongs in the angel choir.

I pull open the swing-out mirror, revealing a shallow medicine cabinet that *doesn't* hold a shave stick. Shit. Through the door, I can hear Suri humming "Sympathy for the Devil." Guilt prickles through me, like I'm growing a cactus underneath my skin, and I feel it again—that dark tug that's just a breath away from panic.

I use my stupid but working right hand to press tissue against the cut while I ease my left arm into its shirt sleeve. A few of my half-curled fingers get caught on the inside of the cuff, and I'm trying to get my numb hand through when she calls, "C? You okay in there?"

"Fine." I'm trying for a more chill tone this time, but I don't really manage it. I still sound ornery. I'm probably the last person Suri should be spending her night with. Except, of course, my asshole parents—and they're the reason for this whole ordeal.

I smash the tissue onto my jaw and inhale deeply. This was a mistake, letting her go with me. I pull the tissue off my face. It's still bleeding, but it's slowed now, enough that I can get my shirt the rest of the way on.

The dress shirt is blue, which I happen to know makes my blue eyes look bluer, not that I give a fuck tonight. It feels like a lifetime since I tried to get a piece of ass—or thought about my appearance. I'm only looking myself over now to see what my parents will see: dark brown hair still a little shorter than I used to wear it; probably a good thing, because it makes me look more bulky. As I run my gaze down my shoulders, chest, and slacks, then back up to my face, I see myself clearly for the first time in a while, and I'm surprised to feel a sick pit in my stomach.

I look like shit.

Not as bad as I did a few months back—not nearly—but still, not like *me*. For starters, I'm too damn lean. I remember around the time Priscilla Heat and her lowlife partner in crime, Jim Gunn, hauled my friend Lizzy and me off to Mexico, hoping to dispose of us so we didn't spill their human trafficking secret, I was *really* lean. I could feel my hip bones and my ribs. The bones in my wrists and hands jutted out, and my face looked bony, like I needed to eat a motherfucking sandwich.

I'm not emaciated anymore, but I still look different. Muscle over bone, and not a whole lot else. Then there's the scars: on my temple, in my hair, under my collar, on my neck, on my hands, the creases of my elbows...and way too many underneath my clothes. I realize in this moment that I hate them. They make me feel... Fuck it, I don't know. Like a turtle without a shell.

I grit my teeth and rub my right hand through my hair. Tuck my bum left hand into my slacks pocket and shove through the bathroom door.

I don't bother faking it for Suri. No need for a phony smile as I step into the little loft space above my bike shop, where I keep my weights, my mini-fridge, two plastic bins of clothes, and my narrow bed.

Suri is perched on the edge of my mattress, wearing some kind of silky, pale green dress that's short enough to show off her legs and strappy over her sun-kissed shoulders. Goes well with her hazel eyes and brown curls and is completely Suri. She's as polished as Lizzy is natural.

"Cross! What the heck?"

I frown before remembering my jaw. "Oh." I cover it with my right hand, but it's too late. Suri's on her feet, gliding toward me in a haze of sweet perfume. With her chest only inches from mine, she catches my hand in hers and spreads her fingers over mine, so for a long second we're both touching my face. Our fingers tangle further as she pushes my hand away from the cut and makes a clucking sound.

Her subtly made-up eyes flick over mine. An eyebrow arches. "Shaving, weren't you?"

"Smart, aren't you?" I smirk at her, and Suri swats at me. "I am smart. Smarter than some of us, who hack themselves to pieces!" She sticks her pink tongue out, wiggling it in a way that tightens my pants. "I bet you hadn't shaved in days. Am I right?" She folds her arms in front of her slim waist, giving me a pointed, wifely look.

I shrug and shift my feet, putting a bit of space between us as I look her over. "What about you, Madeline? Paris treat you ladies right?"

Suri grins. "I'm surprised you know your kid lit."

I shrug. "Lizzy's house." I mean Lizzy's childhood home, where I hid out for a few months when the shit with my dad and the whole sex-slave mistress situation got real sketchy. "She said she got the Madeline books to give to

Martine or Marino or whatever her name is. Her little sister." As in, from Big Brothers Big Sisters. I shrug. "But they ended up in Lizzy's bathroom."

"Where you read them." Suri giggles, lightly touching my elbow with the back of her hand. Her eyes linger on mine half a second too long, and I can't ignore the emotion that I see in them: not just friendship, but something more akin to...adoration. Maybe I'm seeing things.

A second later, the look melts off her face, and she reaches into her purse for a little pack of tissue. I shuffle my feet as she dabs my jaw. Her thin brows pinch together as she draws it away, opening her purse again, this time to pull out a small bottle of water. She pours a few drops on the tissue. Instead of letting her wipe at my face again, I grab the thing from her and do it myself.

I can tell she doesn't like that. She tries to keep her face neutral, but I know her well enough to see the way her mouth pulls down just a little at the corners. Disappointed.

I don't get it. Am I supposed to let her mother me? Why would she want to? It's not like my own mother ever did. I ball the tissue up and toss it onto my bed, not caring if the blood stains my dingy gray blanket.

It wasn't always like this—things so complicated between Lizzy, Suri, and I. For years Suri's parents called us the Three Musketeers, and we were friends. Just friends. I fucked it up first by getting a hard-on for Lizzy. Then Lizzy met Hunter West, they got engaged, and I put a cap on my feelings. Around the same time, Suri and her fiancé, Adam, had a messy split, and I was laid up in rehab, still half dead. I think Suri needed the distraction of me. I'm not gonna lie: I love her for it. I will always love her for it. But I don't love *this*. The expectation.

What the hell does she want?

I'm looking into her eyes, trying to think of something funny to make her smile, when Suri leans in and puts her palm on my chest.

"Cross," she murmurs, looking earnestly up at me as her fingers move slowly over my shirt. "Did I do something wrong?"

I blink down at her. "No." *Yes*—and this is it! I look at her hand on my chest and think about how wrong it is: the way I'm thinking about her tits, freed from her bra, squeezed by my fingers. The way some wicked part of me knows, *I could fuck her if I really tried.*

And damnit, wouldn't I like to?

I can't jerk off anymore—not since the crash. At first I thought it was the stroke or something messing with my junk, but then I went to Marchant's perv ranch and some chick named Loveless got me off in less than twenty seconds, so I know it's not the hardware. When I'm alone it's just...not happening. But when I'm with someone like Suri...

Gritting my teeth, I move her hand off my chest. I lay my right hand over her shoulder, looking into her eyes again, like maybe mine will tell this story for me. Her frown deepens and I clench my jaw. *C'mon, asshole, grow some balls.*

"Suri," I say, my voice dipping low and deep, "be careful how you touch me." When her frown deepens, I heave a big breath. "Doing something stupid with you is the last thing I would want." I swallow, feeling like that shell-less turtle again. "You're one of my best friends. I just want to be careful..."

Her hazel eyes are large and earnest. "You're worried I might get hurt?"

I nod. "I'm…uh…I'm used to a lot of no strings sex. The problem is, right now, I'm not ready for any-thing...serious. Anything at all," I add. "And Suri, you're hot." It's just, it's all friendship and friendship boners. I don't want Suri in that way.

Suri's nodding like she's getting it, and I'm so relieved I feel like laughing. Then she wraps her arm around my neck, leans in close enough to kiss me, and lifts her delicate hand to stroke my cheek. My dick betrays me as she mash-es her breasts against me.

"There's nothing to worry about, Cross. I know you can't make promises...and that's okay with me. What I feel for you—" She looks into my eyes. "What I feel for you is unexpected, but I love it."

My lungs stop, mid-breath. *What?*

Suri takes my hand and tugs me over to the bed. I fol-low mostly because I don't know what else to do. When she pushes me down onto my back, I let her climb on top of me. Because I'm a bastard and my cock is cheering like a Red Sox fan in 2004. Because it feels so good to have a woman's body hugging mine after so long without.

Then she leans down, cloaking me in the curtain of her hair, and she kisses me like I never thought Suri would kiss. Holy blueballs, I can't help but kiss her back! I squeeze her hip and grab her ass. I try to grab her ass. Both arms raise, both hands move to cup her taut ass-cheeks. But as my right hand grabs her through her silky dress, my left just hangs from my arm—dead weight.

That's all it takes to break the sex spell Suri has on me. I blink up at her, and the wrongness of it hits me even harder.

"Suri." I'm panting as I crawl back toward the headboard. She crawls after me, but when she gets close enough that I can smell that damned perfume, I hold my right hand up. "Suri..."

Her lips part, and it's weird as hell to see her like this—like a vixen. She scoots a little closer, and my cock throbs painfully against my slacks.

"I told you Cross, I don't care about the details. I just..." She makes a funny little face—her shy face—but it's quickly transformed into something surer, something fierce. "I just want you, Cross. Is that really a bad thing?"

Jesus Christ.

I push myself up on my elbows, trying to think past the throbbing in my pants. "Suri, I'm not saying that it's *bad*." I flick my right hand at her. "Look at you. You're gorgeous. Any man would want, you know. I'm a man, Suri, so yeah, I want to fuck you upside down and sideways. But you're my friend."

I clench my jaw, because I'm imagining the upside down and sideways, but the fantasy disintegrates as I watch her eyes fill with tears. Somewhere in the last few months, Suri got a thing for *me*.

Lizzy tried to tell me once, but I didn't take it seriously. Now I really wish I had.

Surri tucks her chin, looking down at the blankets, and I can see her lip tremble. I feel awful, so I reach for her. She crawls off the bed and steps back, toward the bathroom, and I feel slightly dizzy as I think, *I knew this night would suck.*

How the fuck did this happen? *It doesn't matter, Cross. Just deal with it.*

I get up off the bed and grab her hand. "Suri, you're my best friend. You and Lizzy." She won't look at me, but that doesn't mean I'm going to quit talking. "But that's all that it should be. Do you think I want you to be just another fuck?" Her eyes widen, and she tries to jerk away, but I tighten my grip on her wrist and hold her gaze. "That's just it—you *wouldn't* be. But I'm not ready for this, Suri. It would be bad. It would end up being bad for *you*."

Her gaze flicks up to mine. Her eyes are red and wet. "I don't know how I read this all so wrong."

I grit my teeth. I don't know how, either. "I love you, Sur, you know I do, but we're friends first."

More tears drip down her cheeks as her chin trembles, and I feel like a steaming pile of dog shit. "You want to be more with Lizzy," she whispers.

"I don't," I grit my teeth as my heart pounds. It's true, I got distracted by Lizzy a few months back, but that's long over. "I don't want anything with Lizzy."

She shakes her head, then turns on her heel and marches into the bathroom.

For the next few minutes, I stand by the door, feeling helpless and heartless and frustrated. I consider knocking, but I can hear her sniffing and I wonder if she'd rather have her privacy. I rub my neck, which is still too tight.

I'm mulling that one over when I hear the door creak, and Suri steps out, looking calm and gathered. I reach for her hand, touching it for a moment before she draws away.

"Suri, I'm really fucking sorry."

She holds up both hands. "I know, Cross. And it will be okay. I still want to go with you tonight, just as a friend. You really shouldn't have to face the firing squad alone."

I shouldn't face the firing squad at all, but I've got things to settle with my dad. "I appreciate it. You'll never know how much. But I think it would be better if you just go home tonight. We'll talk tomorrow."

I can see the moment that her eyes go cold. The moment that I lose a friend—just as surely as I lost Lizzy to Hunter. "Okay." Her lips press flat. "Whatever you want."

She walks briskly from the room, and I can't think of anything to stop her.

CHAPTER TWO

Merri

IF YOU'VE NEVER eaten ant eggs, you haven't lived. You only think I'm kidding. They taste...buttery. Buttery and crunchy and almost the texture of a boiled peanut. For not the first time, as I sit at one of the ragged picnic tables inside our little cafeteria, I think about Alec, the self-styled food critic who wrote columns for my college's newspaper. His favorite word to use in conversation was 'copious'. He broke his leg junior year, and for weeks afterward, Alec was laid up in his king-sized love nest, reviewing take-out food. Copious amounts of pepperoni pizza and greasy burgers. I smile a little at the memory. Like so many things from my past, it seems light years away from day-to-day life at St. Catherine's Clinic for Sick and Needy Children.

It's a weird place. Most of the time I'm here, taking care of children in this poverty-stricken Mexican neighborhood, nothing else exists. That includes memories.

I finish my rice and chicken, topped with the ant eggs that were a gift from Señora Maria, the mother of a little boy with cystic fibrosis. Victor's family has more money than most we see, which is probably the only reason he's alive today, at three. He had a rough winter, with a long hospitalization during which I couldn't give him any of his favorite 'pequeño Victor' back rubs.

Those are the worst times, I think as I walk my empty bowl over to a row of garbage cans with tubs for dirty dishes on the top. The times when the kids I love the most stop coming here for one reason or another, and I can't go visit them. Some of the nuns do house calls, but I can't. I can't ever leave St. Catherine's Clinic.

A lot of times, it's not so bad. The building is short but wide, with several different areas so when I pass from, say, the clinic quadrant into the living quarters, I feel like I'm going somewhere. But I'm not. When I think of how long it's been since I felt the sun on my skin, since I cranked up the music as I sped down an empty highway... Since I browsed the internet or read a book I chose for myself or got my hair done at a salon... I kind of want to scream. Okay, I do scream. Sometimes at night, I scream into my pillow. Then I remind myself I'm lucky. My story could have had a harsher ending. Actually, it probably should have. This life I have here, with the sisters, with the kids...it's a fairy tale, compared to what could have been.

I place my metal spork atop the nearest trash can, in a little plastic bin of silverware to-be-done, and put my bowl in a bin for plates and bowls. I glance up at the clock on the wall over the self-serve bar, where cheap grub rests in brassy bowls that are either kept cold on ice or hot on electric plates. It's almost four o'clock, which means I have one more client before the day winds down and I prepare for evening prayers. I glance at one of the big, vertical windows that span one side of the room, wondering how hot it is outside right now. Wishing I could smell the sun-steamed grass.

I don't peer out the windows or even step close to them. Instead I head into the dingy, one-stall bathroom with its meager supply of toilet paper and take the three squares allotted for each use. When I first took refuge at the clinic—which is located in the same building as St. Catherine's Convent, just inside the city limits of Guadalupe Victoria—I was appalled by the scarcity of supplies, but after more than half a year, I've learned how to make it work. As I do my business, I wonder how many squares I'd allow myself to use for a 'number one' if I were to make it back into the States. Maybe four, I decide. Anything more than that would probably feel wasteful. I wash my hands, and as I dry them on a rough rag, I tell myself to be thankful for what I have. Even if I never make it back to the U.S., I have a good life here.

You can't be grateful and bitter at the same time. So says Sister Mary Carolina. So what am I grateful for? I stare at myself in the mirror, ticking things off inside my head. I've been blessed to learn massage therapy from Sister Mary. I've been able to make a difference in the lives of children. And, almost more importantly, I'm accepted here. Cherished, even. Which is so much more than I expected when I arrived.

I'm smiling as I step back into the empty cafeteria, already looking forward to my session with little Alexandria Perez, a one-year-old with a severe case of congenital torticollis. I'm passing by the garbage cans, glancing toward he windows, when I see a mirage from my past: Juan and Emanuel, eleven and twelve year olds the last time I saw them. What the heck are they doing here in Guadalupe Victoria.

I don't get to ask.

Light engulfs the room, and a sonic boom throws me back toward the wall.

CHAPTER THREE

CROSS

WITHOUT SURI'S LAND Rover, I'll have to ride one of my motorcycles. No big deal, I tell myself as I unlock the heavy metal door between the showroom and the garage. I've been putting it off, yeah, but once I'm straddling one of my favorite hybrid bikes, it'll feel like old times. Has to. I've been riding since I was fifteen. Haven't owned a car in four years, since I dropped out of Cal at nineteen and sold my Beamer to buy a 1963 BSA Rocket Gold Star Spitfire Scrambler.

I step from the glossy urban expanse of the showroom into the dingier garage, inhaling the familiar scent of gasoline and metal, then turn around to lock the door between the garage and the showroom. I set the alarm for the whole place, giving myself a generous eight minutes to be out the garage doors on the back of the building, and I jiggle my key ring until I find the electronic key to the security system I keep for my favorite Cross Hybrid, the first prototype of my custom Anomaly job, with an engine that runs on part gasoline, part water.

She's a beauty. Started out as a 1974 Kawasaki H2 B

750 Mach IV MK4, but I've changed her a lot. Gave her steel frame a sea blue and black paint job, emblazing my "CH" symbol on the tank. Added a slightly roomier, gel-filled seat, so both Lizzy and I could fit on it in a bind. Put on some Sunrim 6000 series aluminum rims with Dunlop Arrowmax tires. And of course, I re-worked her insides so she's hybrid.

I bought her two years ago off a seventy-something-year-old collector in Laguna Beach. My plan was to sell her at one of the shows I do each quarter—in either New York or L.A.—but once I rode my renovated, gas-and-water powered Mach, I knew I couldn't part with her.

These old Kawasaki Triples make for a comfy ride. Lots of leg room. Easy turns. It'll be like getting on a nine-year-old roan after being thrown from a stallion, I tell my-self as I wrap my hands around the handles. I *try* to wrap my hands around the handles, but I'm going on muscle memory, and the muscles of my left hand don't do shit. I look down at my half-curled fingers.

"Fuck."

Chill out, dude.

I grit my teeth, then pull a small steel bar up from the spot where it's locked against the left side of the Mach's neck. On the end of the bar is a black leather band, sized just right to slide about halfway up my left forearm. My fingers don't work, but if I'm right about this, I can jam my forearm into the band, and since the steel bar holding it is welded in two spots between the left handlebar and the dash board, I can effectively hold the handle by using the weight of my left shoulder to press against it. My right hand will be doing most of the work, so it's risky business, but it's the best that I can do.

I lock the steel bar into place, curl the fingers of my left hand, and push my wrist into the thick leather band, sliding it halfway up my forearm as I lean down over the bike's handles. Usually I'd push a bike out of the garage before mounting, but I need to be on the bike to be sure I've got my arm in place.

With a deep breath, I throw my right leg over. It feels awkward as shit, because I'm a leftie and I used to get on with my left leg first.

Now it's wobble time. I get up on the tips of my toes, scuffing up my old John Lobbs, and hit a button on my key chain that makes one of the garage doors open. I barely make it down the slight incline leading onto the cement slab behind the building. I scoot, on my toes, over the oil-stained cement, over the spot where I've worked on so many bikes along with Wil and Napo, the other two members of Team Cross Hybrids.

Guilt nags me. I've heard from both of them and I know they'd like their old jobs back, but I haven't offered. Shop's closed—for now, at least.

I'm scowling as I balance on my left arm, using the fingers of my right hand to poke at the garage remote attached to my key chain. I can hear the warning beeps of the alarm, telling me I've almost taken too long. Nearly eight minutes to get a bike out of the garage. This is why the shop's still closed.

I stare out at the field that stretches behind my building, then turn to my right to look at the backside of the row of shops next door to my freestanding building. Downtown Napa, California, is quiet and peaceful, which makes me want to fucking scream. My neck is tight and my hand feels weird and the panic is just below the surface. I remember when Napa used to seem to tame to me. I could do anything. The roads and the shops all seemed so small. Even the vast vineyards in Napa Valley seemed small. I wonder how long it would take me to get down to the valley now, driving the Mach one-handed. Probably forever.

The garage door closes behind me, and there's nothing else between me and the road. I look down at the band around my left forearm and suck back a few deep breaths. Like this is the fucking Sturgis Rally. Like I'm green as grass.

I don't have a watch, but I can tell I'm late already, and I'm annoyed that it bugs me.

I hear my phone ring. "Satisfaction" by the Stones. Lizzy. Great. I look down at myself, and I feel like such a helpless freak. There's no way I can answer the phone in my pocket. Not if I want to keep this bike upright.

I wonder why the hell she's calling and I tell myself I don't care. I can worry about Suri and Lizzy later—and I know I will, when I get back to the shop tonight. I wait another second for another burst of the tingling pain that starts in my neck and shoots down my arm. Neuralgia, they call it. Otherwise known as a 'suicide headache'. But at the moment, I feel okay.

I bite down on my lip and jam my forearm as tightly as I can into the little leather band, straightening out my elbow so I can lean into the band with the full weight of my left shoulder. Without anymore stalling, I white-knuckle the handle with my right hand and ease my thumb onto the accelerator.

The ride to my parents' house is short and heart-pumping enough to make me worry that in addition to all the other shit, maybe I lost my balls in the accident as well. By the time I glide through the massive, black iron gates and slow the Mach in their tree-lined, semi-circle drive, I'm drenched with sweat and gritting my teeth.

I wobble a little as I try to balance the bike using my toes. I hiss another curse as I squeeze my eyes shut, wishing I was the kind of guy who could just let things lie. But I refuse to let them off so easy. I refuse to let my father get away with what he did. I refuse to be complicit any longer.

I glance at the massive gray stone, built to look like an English manor house. My gaze tugs in the direction of the regal double doors, and at that moment, one of them swings open.

My muscles freeze as I wait for the familiar combed-over black hair, laughing blue eyes, hook nose, thin lips. Renault is the man who raised me, a Frenchman who introduced me to classic rock, bought me my first box of condoms, taught me how to puff on a cigar. He drove me to junior high school dances and showed me how to loop a tie. I feel breathless as I wait to see his face—and then the shadows flicker and instead there is a stern-looking woman with tightly up-swept gray hair and sharp blue eyes. It takes me a long, baffling second to realize it's my mother.

Well of course it is. Dark blue dress—Dior, her favorite—paired with silver heels and diamond-pearl earrings that sparkle in the porch light. But her face looks tired and her posture sucks, like she's forgotten how to play the part of Derinda Carlson, governor's wife.

I get off the bike as smoothly as I can, parking it in the

flawlessly manicured lawn, and don't allow myself to look away from her as I step slowly up the porch stairs. I wonder briefly where Renault is, but once I'm close enough to take in the full context of my mother, the only thing I can think is *why*. I wasn't a model kid, never did great in school, but I don't think I was unusually difficult. For most of my childhood, I did whatever they asked, went wherever they went, usually decked out in a mini tux or a little suit, my hair clean cut, my mouth stretched into a big fake smile.

Even after I dropped out of school and opened my shop, I played the dutiful son, waving at campaign stops. Smiling at every camera. Giving perfect quotes to newspaper reporters.

My mother reaches out to...I don't know what—pat my shoulder or something?—and all I can think is: *WHY?* I know the answer: I found out about Missy King, the Vegas mistress my father had sold into sex slavery in Mexico, so my father gave the order to sever ties. But how could Mother follow it?

She tries to embrace me but I step aside. There's something on her face, and I think it's contrition but I just can't care.

When I fail to meet her eyes and accept her hug, she drops her arms down by her sides and wears her campaign face—phony, through and through. She smiles a little, tilts her head so those stupid earrings sparkle, and she sweeps her hand back toward the foyer.

"Cross. You're looking well."

It's so ridiculous, so utterly crazy, I'm not sure what to say. But when has that stopped a Carlson? I nod. "Likewise."

I walk through the door she holds and the foyer seems smaller than it did a year ago. The chandelier doesn't sparkle, just reflects the glow of gaslight; the floors don't gleam; the imported rugs look faded. As I follow my mother down the hallway, past the parlors and the library, I'm surprised to find it doesn't look like she's redecorated anything. When I lived here—even when I lived in the guest house, before I fled to Lizzy's mother's house—my mother changed the décor weekly. A new pillow here, a new rug there. Even when she and Dad were spending most of their time in the city house in Beverly Hills, there was always an event to host or a party to throw. The lack of change now gives me the impression that no one's been here this last year.

I hear the clearing of a throat, and I notice the stiff set of my mother's shoulders just before she turns to look at me. She regards me like a stranger. "Delphina Fieldman told me your shop is still closed. How are you getting buy?"

I press my lips together. Not straying far from the script, of course. She's always tried to buy my loyalty. "Fine," I half-growl.

I rotate my left shoulder, digging my hand more deeply into my coat pocket, and I wonder why they invited me tonight. I assumed it was so Dad could get his ducks in a row. Mom's involvement…it bothers me. Almost as much as her abandonment.

"I'm fine," I lie more smoothly. "The shop will reopen soon."

She smiles, and I can't read anything in it before she turns back toward the hallway, leading us past an alcove filled with bookshelves and leather couches, closer to the formal dining room. "I'm designing a restaurant in La Jolla."

Just a few years ago, I would have asked questions and had an interest in her answers, but that was before my father kicked me out. Before I found out he let a porn star—the infamous Priscilla Heat—talk him into selling his former mistress as a sex slave. When my mother chose to tow his line, she lost me.

We near the end of the hall, so I can see the candlelight flickering in the massive, formal dining room, and suddenly I just want to turn and run. Instead my temper flares, and I stop walking.

My mother turns, wide-eyed, and I relish the startled look on her face.

"What's the point of this, Mother? Why invite me into your house? Was it Drake's idea?"

Her brows narrow, and her face bends into a scolding look. "Don't call your father by his first name. You're not sixteen, Cross."

I twist my face into something between a smirk and a scowl, and she folds her arms over her chest. "It was your father's idea. He'd like to make amends. And we want to...explain what happened while you were unconscious."

"Explain what happened?" I cross my arms—another habit—and I notice my mother's eyes fly to my left hand. I drop both arms to my sides. My face feels hot. "Well I'm here right now. Why don't you tell me—what happened?"

She squares her shoulders, giving me a prissy, defensive kind of look. Then her eyes flicker to my hand again and I grit my teeth. "You better get on with it, or I'm leaving."

"Your father has spent us dry, Cross. That's why we had you moved from the nicer facility at NVIR."

I raise my brows. I'm surprised she even knows the name—Napa Valley Involved Rehab. After all, they never visited.

"Let me guess: too many hookers."

As soon as I say the words, I want to take them back. My mother recoils as if I've slapped her, and I open my mouth to say something to appease her. But I can see in her eyes that she's still denying it. Pretending he's not a philandering dickhead who cheats from coast to coast. And that pisses me off.

"You know he has mistresses. Everybody does. You think because he's the governor that you can't leave him? Damnit, Mom. I don't know what he does to make you drink the Kool-Aid." I shake my head. "Does he have something on you?" That's how things in this family seem to work.

My mother locks her jaw. She looks furious enough to hit me, and as I stand there with my heart pounding, I almost hope she does.

"I stay with your father because I was raised Catholic, Cross Evangeline Carlson, and despite his flaws, he's my husband. Don't you dare disrespect me—"

I bark a laugh. Disrespect her? I cock one of my brows. "If you think I give a damn about respecting you, you're wrong. You don't deserve it. Either of you." I clench my jaw so hard it pops. My head feels hot, the way it used to when the Dilaudid would first kick in. "You deserted me. You didn't even visit me."

I watch a vein pulse in her forehead and I know I've gotten to her when her face screws up and she tosses her hands into the air. "It was too painful!"

Bullshit. "You were a coward."

She whirls and then she's gone, stalking through the dining room and in the direction of the stairs. I hear a low murmur, followed by my father's voice at regular volume, followed by my mother's strangled sob.

Fuck her.

I stride into the dining room, my heart pounding despite the cold, detached feeling that's taken over my chest. A second later, I'm staring my father down from across the massive Georgian table. He's wearing a Zenga suit and the same clean, in-control expression that got him elected, and I'm surprised to see that, unlike my mom, he looks better than the last time that I saw him.

As soon as he meets my eyes, his voice rings out. "Did you come here just to upset your mother?"

I grit my molars. I can ruin him. I can turn him in. I really can.

When I find my voice, it's soft. "Do you think that's why I came?"

"Is it?" He arches one black brow.

"I came to talk to you."

He spreads his hands before him, like he's got nothing to hide. "Let's talk."

"Are you sure you don't want to go into your office?"

Without missing a beat, he motions toward the hall. "Anything to make you comfortable, son."

Anything to make me comfortable. For half a heartbeat, I'm going to slam my fist into his phony face. But before I can, he turns and walks into the hallway that runs behind this room. His caviler, unaccountable, uncaring attitude is so stunning that it takes the steam right out of me. I couldn't punch him if I wanted to. Then I almost laugh as I remember I'm a leftie. I'm not even sure I can take a swing with my right hand.

For a weird moment, as my legs stride after him, the hallway spins and I feel like I might fall down. I can feel the awful burn of gravel in my forehead. I can feel the roar of pain that starts in my neck and runs from the ruined spinal discs down my shoulder, exploding in an inferno through my hand. And, oh God, I can feel my fucking hand.

My neck's so tight I think it might pop off my shoulders, and as we step into his office I can feel the curtain falling, the curtain of badness that always leads to darkness, fear, and pain.

I knew this would happen.

My father steps past me to shut the door. I hear the click through the agony of my pain. I feel his hands on my elbows as he thrusts me down, into one of his leather chairs, and leans over me.

"I hope you didn't come here to threaten me."

I shove him in the chest and he slowly wraps his hand around my neck, somehow finding just the spot where the vertebrae were crushed and wired together. Just where all my pain begins. Fucking surreal. I blink up at him, breathing so hard I can barely find my voice. "You gonna finish the job?"

He loosens his grip, steps back. I'm pleased to see his shoulders are heaving just like mine are. "What do you want from me?"

"Did you know about it?" Ignoring the pain, I stand.

"Know about what?" He's rocking on his heels.

I swallow, using all my energy to focus on my words and not the pain that's still lighting up my neck and arm. "Did you know about what they did to me," I rasp. "To my bike."

"No," he snorts, "I don't know the first thing about your bike."

"Jim Gunn—" one of my father's former body guards and Priscilla Heat's partner in crime— "loosened the oil filter so oil got all over my back tire and fucked the steering."

"The night of your accident? When you were drunk?"

"The night Jim Gunn fucked up my bike."

His hands come up, palms out, like he's flabbergasted. "Do you think I would murder my own son?"

That's rich, coming from a man who just had his hand around my throat.

I had to move, in secret, into Lizzy's childhood home because Jim Gunn had some rough-looking motherfucker follow me. That was *before* what happened with the bike, at a vineyard party last November, but after my father told Priscilla Heat that I'd found out what had happened to Missy King.

"I don't know what you would do," I tell him bluntly, "but I know what I'll do." I burn him with my gaze, as if my arm isn't roaring with pain, and I tell him, "I'll tell everyone. I'll tell the world what I know."

I watch as my father's eyes narrow to slits: a monster cornered. "What do you want from me, Cross?"

I stand there, just breathing, thinking *what do I want?* I'm surprised to hear myself say, "I want you to find her."

"You're serious."

I nod. "Find Missy King. Whether it was your idea or Priscilla Heat's—" and I know it was Priscilla's— "the girl got sold as a sex slave, Dad."

He waves a hand, like it's no big deal, and then he says something that surprises me. Shocks me, really. "Cross, there is no Missy King."

I frown, having trouble following; the pain in my head and neck and arm is getting worse. "Don't bullshit me. I want to know where she ended up. I want to find her. Help me or I'll talk to the press. Unless you really would kill your own son."

He regards me for a long moment before reaching behind him and grabbing a small flask. He takes the top off and I want to jump him, steal the liquor, douse my pain.

"Missy King is just the name she used as an escort. Her real name was Meredith Kinsey," he says quietly, "and they sold her in Mexico. Same place you were when Priscilla lost her mind and hauled you and Lizzy down there a few months back. Sold her to a tall guy by the name of Cientos. It's all drug-runners down there, Cross. Cartels. There'll be no point. She's probably dead already."

"You're sick," I whisper.

He looks defensive, then annoyed. "She wanted me to leave your mother. When I refused, she wanted money. She threatened to go to the papers with our relationship. She wanted to ruin me. Priscilla offered to take care of the situation. I didn't ask how. I ended up finding out, but by then..." He takes another drink, then shrugs. "It was too late."

I almost believe him, but I know instinctively there's more. My father is an excellent liar, but I can see his nostrils flaring; that's his tell.

"Mom deserves better than that shit." I stare at him for a moment, at his regal features. He is handsome. This is the face of a governor, and looking at him that way—as the son of a bitch politician I know he really is—I can't even summon disappointment over what an awful father he is.

I'm turning to go when suddenly I remember an important question. I'm panting as I turn back around, but I take deep breaths and try to take advantage of the way my mind zones out when the pain gets this bad. When I speak, I sound almost normal. "What did she look like? Mis— Meredith Kinsey."

I'm surprised when he opens a mahogany cabinet and scoops up something, holding it out in his closed palm like a butterfly. It's a picture—wallet-sized. It looks like a mug shot, the kind TV reporters use. It's worn. He snatches it back and uses a Ray Bans sunglasses cloth to wipe it of his fingerprints before handing it to me.

His face is stern. "Keep this to yourself, Cross. And don't ask me for anything else—ever."

"Whatever," I mutter as I walk out.

I make it down the front porch steps and to my bike before the pain is bad enough to bring me to my knees. Sometime later—minutes? hours?—I feel a gentle hand on my back and look up, praying for Renault. Instead it's a Southeast Asian man with kind eyes wearing a butler's suit.

"Can I help you, Sir?"

I take the hand he offers and use all my willpower to

get back to my feet. I grab onto my bike's seat. "Where's Renault?"

"Renault DeFritsch?" The man's eyes widen. "He died four months ago."

That's the last thing I remember clearly before waking up on my bed a day and a half later. I lie here for a moment, breathing deeply, wondering if there's anyone on this godforsaken planet more miserable than I am.

One name comes to mind: Meredith Kinsey.

CHAPTER FOUR

Merri

THE SISTERS DON'T think the bombing was for me, but I know it was.

I know Jesus Cientos, and I know his tactics. The man is a pyromaniac. He has a love affair with hand grenades. He has half a warehouse filled with nothing but grenades, manufactured for the U.S. Military, smuggled into Mexico by Jesus's soldiers. I've seen the explosions before, a few times. I've watched them from behind the bullet-proof windows of Jesus's silver Escalade. I've watched them rip apart half a house, even seen the massive fireball from an exploding gas station.

Juan and Emanuel are the surprise. That Jesus would his nephews out so young. That they would agree to target me. I should know better, but my heart makes it hard to accept.

The explosion on the west side of St. Catherine's killed a woman. Her name was Henrietta, and she was walking on the gravel path beside the clinic, toward the market on Flag Street to buy food for her twelve-year-old son.

I think about her, about Juan and Emanuel and Jesus,

as I lie on my cot at night, in the wide, hot, high-beamed attic where I sleep beside Sister Mary Abalitta. The sounds of Sister Susan snoring, of Sister Daniella turning the pages of a paperback under the covers, of the box fans spinning in the two pushed-open windows...they ought to be familiar, soothing, but after what happened yesterday, nothing can soothe me. I clutch my rosary and pray to Mother Mary for strength. I should talk to Sister Mary Carolina again; she didn't believe me the first time. She is too good to give me up, and I'm too afraid to leave the clinic.

I wonder, as the sun comes up, what Jesus will do to me if he gets his hands on me. It wouldn't be sex—that much I know for sure—but it could easily be something worse. I hurt his pride and his reputation when I ran, and I guess it's still hurting, even after almost nine months. That's the only reason he would strike now. Here. At the one place in the state of Durango_that all of the cartels have promised to protect.

I curl over on my side and listen to the thunder rumbling in the distance.

CHATPER FIVE

CROSS

I HAVEN'T SEEN Suri since three nights ago, but Lizzy's been here twice. The first time, I guess I was in my pain trance, the one I learned from Akemi, a Zen master in downtown Los Angeles, during my fight with Dilaudid. The second time was a few minutes ago. She left a note on the door and texted me the same thing: *Cross, quit hiding from me. I want to talk.*

I feel like an asshole for not calling, but I know I won't—not yet. I don't want to talk about what happened the other night with Suri. I don't want to talk about what happened with my parents, or about Renault. Don't want to talk about Cross Hybrids or Hunter West or the wedding.

I have enough conscience to feel guilty for neglecting both my longtime friends. Suri deserves an in-person apology, and Lizzy deserves some face time. I just don't know what to say to them. Suri, for all the reasons anyone would guess, and Lizzy because...fuck, I don't know. She's living in some wedding fairy land, while I'm in bike shop purgatory. It's not that I'm not glad for her. I am. I'm glad she's getting the happy ending she deserves. I just don't feel like I have a lot to offer anyone right now, and besides that, it's too much effort.

I wait around the house another twenty-four hours to see if I get another pain attack. Another neuralgia episode, as they're really called. When nothing new happens and I don't feel quite as tired, I get back on the Mach and ride over to the local library. I'm glad that I'm at least having an easier time of it today.

I used to have wireless internet at the shop, but I didn't pay the bills while I was in rehab and since coming home, I haven't felt like getting it turned on. What's the point? I pretty much know I have a pile-up of work orders, people wanting custom jobs, and I also know I'm not open for business at the moment.

I feel a little tug of guilt as I get off the bike and stride up the stairs of the two-story brick building. It's true, I miss working on bikes—and the money—but I can't do it one-handed. Not without some help. And help would lead to pity.

I pay one dollar for a temporary library card and sit down at one of the black plastic computer desks on the back row. I pull my little photo out and put it on the table. I haven't looked at it but once or twice, just for a second or two as I loaded and unloaded it from my pockets, but here under the fluorescent lights, something about her face strikes me, like a chime inside my chest. Missy King. Meredith Kinsey. The mistress. The whore.

Her smile looks genuine. It makes her green eyes tilt up at the edges. Her pinkish mouth looks innocently happy, slightly playful, and very familiar, as if she knows the photographer well; as if they're friends. I scowl down at the image. This girl looks young. Eighteen at most. I wonder, not for the first time, if my father made up the name he gave me. This girl, with her prim white button-up blouse and straight white teeth, is probably the daughter of a California senator.

Pecking at the keys with the fingers of my right hand, I search the name. Within milliseconds, links appear. The first one grabs my attention: Meredith Kinsey – Managing Editor, *The Red & Black*.

I squint. Clearly, that one's not my girl. Missy King was a high-priced prostitute, not a journalism student.

I click on the second link and find 'Meredith Kinsey' on a list of University of Georgia, Grady College scholarship recipients. She's there not once, but three times: William Dale Tichenor Scholarship for Excellence in Journalistic Writing, Sean Love Scholarship for Dependability and Service, Gloria Stamps Scholarship for Excellence in Academics.

I snort a little, drawing a glance from the punk ass kid beside me. Yeah, this can't be her.

Back on the main page, I try a few other links, wondering why the hell I didn't ask my father where the girl was from. Couldn't have been Georgia. I find another Meredith Kinsey: award-winning quilter from Salt Lake City. Her web site features a picture of a gray-haired woman with a bowl cut.

The next link takes me to Meredith Kinsey, singer/songwriter. I get excited about this, but then I notice she's in Ireland—and just updated her blog with new lyrics today.

I sift through Meredith Kinsey, freelance writer for an

Atlanta home brewery magazine (probably the college kid after college); Meredith Kinsey, high school gymnastics star in Boise, Idaho (photo shows a girl who can't be older than ten); Meredith Kinsey, harpist in Knoxville, Tennessee (tall with a bird-like nose, which my father would hate); Meredith Kinsey, dead at age 86 in Kansas City, Kansas, and another dozen or so Meredith Kinsey's before I get to almost an entire page of links that direct me to *The Red & Black*: award-winning college newspaper at the University of Georgia, operating independently without the use of student funds since 1980.

Woop de freaking hoo.

I sigh and click on one of the links, because it's dated two years before my Meredith Kinsey disappeared, and it looks to be a rant about the horror of beauty pageants. I skim the piece, finding that this particular Meredith Kinsey objects to pageants on the grounds that they objectify women; she compares the women in their swim suits to cattle at an auction. Another snort, followed by a rub of my eyes. Definitely not my Meredith.

Except...there's a small square picture in the middle of two columns of text, and the face is identical to the one in my picture.

Meredith Kinsey, college feminist.

Holy shit.

I SPEND THE next hour looking for more information, trying to figure out how a college student with strawberry-blonde hair, twinkling green eyes, and a wide smile turned into Missy King, governor's mistress and small time extortionist-turned-sex slave.

I click on every link I find, reading through a couple of her news stories and one more opinion piece ("Holiday Celebrations Can Be Inclusive And Traditional") before the timer on my screen flashes, and I'm forced to give my computer to a woman who's wearing a skirt suit and typing on her Blackberry. I pay three dollars for a permanent card, which will buy me unlimited time tomorrow, and head out into a drizzling rain.

The photo my father gave me is tucked into a little pocket on the inside of my beat-up jeans, but I can see her face as I roll down the streets of downtown Napa. The bike's tires make a *shhh* sound, tossing up a spray of rain-water that makes my ankles cold and chills my feet through my boots.

I don't get it. Is this some ruse my father cooked up? Why would a girl with a college degree—and no student loans—turn to a life of prostitution?

I know what they say. People like Lizzy. *"The girls choose to be escorts. It's their* choice, *Cross. Smarter than giving yourself away for free, huh?"* Marchant fed me even more cliché lines: They're stakeholders, some of them have stock portfolios, working on college degrees through the University of Phoenix, la da da.

I bet most of them don't have college degrees. I bet they didn't get into the whoring business just for giggles.

As I fumble for the garage button with my elbow, pressing into the pants pocket where I keep my keys, I feel the familiar sting of guilt. Whoever she is, Missy King de-served better than what she got. And as far as bullshit goes, I'd have it coming out my ears if I didn't admit that it's my fault nobody went after her. I could have told somebody. I should have.

Instead, I tried to forget about her. I told myself it wasn't my business. That she was already out of reach.

It might have stuck, if I hadn't been taken to Mexico myself and watched as my best friend was on the auction block. Ever since that day, it's been under my skin like a bad rash. Missy King was just as helpless as we were.

And for all my lofty thoughts about desperation and how escorts have no other options, I want to believe that Missy King is *not* Meredith Kinsey. I want to believe that Missy was a slutty girl who wanted to drive a shiny red Porsche and wear expensive jewelry. A girl who, just like me, was giving it away to anyone who asked and figured, why not charge?

If I let myself believe that this girl—the one inside my pocket, with the happy eyes—is somewhere down in Mexico, I'll go fucking crazy.

THE NEXT MORNING, I wake up early, take my time shaving, and ride back to the library. I take the third-to-last seat in the computer lab, and by the time I'm ears-deep in a story Meredith Kinsey wrote about date rape, a pair of teenage lovebirds come in and take the seats on either side of me. As I lean in to the computer, they lean around me, laughing about something they saw on Facebook. For some reason, their whispers piss me off. I glance at the dude, giving him more of an evil eye than I intended. He looks like a kid: seventeen, eighteen? If Meredith started college at eighteen and that was almost eight years ago, that means she's twenty-five or twenty-six now. That means the year that she was twenty-three—my age, Suri's age, Lizzy's age—she was on her way to becoming a sex slave.

My desire to know what happened to her amps up a notch, so much so that my hands feel sweaty and my temples throb. How did she get to Vegas? After another hour of searching, plus some credit card fees paid to various databases, I find a missing person's report filed a little over four years ago—or rather, I find her on a list of missing people. I can't get any information about her specific report unless I travel to Georgia, and that would waste too much time. A few minutes later, I'm surprised when I come across a news brief in the *Atlanta Journal-Constitution*. It mentions that police are looking for twenty-two year old Meredith Kinsey of Albany, Georgia, for questioning in relation to the arrest of Sean Tacoma. This makes me feel almost sick with curiosity.

As I print off a few more of her stories, it dawns on me that maybe it's not just curiosity that makes this feel so urgent. So...personal. From the looks of things, Meredith Kinsey had a pretty violent fall from grace. I had a fall, too, didn't I? Went from the only child of California's governor—charming and wealthy, with a world as wide as Hargrove Day School and the privileged, sheltered social circles of Napa—to disabled, disinherited fuckup who can't even work.

It makes me feel weird about myself. Like I don't even know who I am. And for some reason, that makes me want to understand who Meredith Kinsey is. I want to know what happened to her. Maybe I just want to see someone else's route to ruin.

I shove her stories into my back pocket and speed back to the shop. On the way there, I picture myself in a police station, ratting out my father. I grit my teeth. I'd probably get prosecuted for sitting on what I knew this last year, but I could do it. I still have some of the e-mails I found on my father's computer, between Priscilla and Jim Gunn, and between Priscilla and my father. Not all of them, but enough that even if he avoided prosecution, he'd be ruined.

The question is: Should I? If I were to tell the cops, would anyone actually go rescue 'Missy King'? As far as I know, there's no organization actively sending people out to look for sex slaves. Some of the authorities investigate, yeah, but that seems to be it. Nobody's going to jump onto their bike and just go searching through Mexico. Not for a former escort. Not for a married man's mistress. The legal system is fucked up, and people like 'Missy King' usually don't get justice. People like Meredith Kinsey: pretty, educated, scholarship-getting girls whose families file missing persons' reports… Now that's another story. But I can't actually prove that Missy King *is* Meredith. Not yet, anyway.

As I wait at a red light under the dim midday sun, I tick off the verifiable information I know about 'Missy'. Former Vegas escort, working at the Starry Sky Brothel on the Strip and rumored to be the governor's mistress. This 'Missy', mentioned in only one gossip column on a local, Vegas blog, was supposedly "exclusive, in a Kingly way", which I assume was meant to allude to her relationship with my father. I know, based on what the Love Inc. shrink told Lizzy, that Missy King was liked, and that some of the

Love Inc. girls missed her, and felt like not enough had been done to find her.

Jim Gunn's cousin was a detective in Vegas; still is. Hunter West told me one of the detective's buddies pulled the Missy King case. I'm not sure if it's true, but I wouldn't be surprised if it was.

I roll into the garage and lift my left arm out of its leather band. And for the first time since the wreck, I feel shitty about my hand for a reason that has nothing to do with me. If I wanted to go look for Missy King, or Meredith Kinsey, or whoever the hell the missing woman really is, I'd probably get my one-handed self shot.

I swing off the bike and feel the curtain of darkness drop around me, enclosing me inside a box of dread. Then I look up and spot Lizzy in front of the door that divides the shop and garage.

"Fuck."

Lizzy grins evilly and holds up a garage remote. "Bet you forgot who watched over the shop while you were sleeping, bro."

"I didn't forget," I mutter as I bridge the gap between us. I reach for a strand of her long brown hair and tug it, out of habit. "Just didn't figure you'd go sneaking around like a cat burglar."

Lizzy curls her hand. "Meow."

I brush past her and open the door to the show room. She follows me inside, but instead of going upstairs, to the site of the Suri disaster, I slump down into one of the leather chairs beside a restored, hybrid-ized 1967 BMW R 69S. I reach into an old-school Coca-Cola cooler beside the chair and pull out a glass bottle of Sunkist, which I tuck into the crook of my left elbow. Then I grab a Dr. Pepper.

Lizzy stands in front of me with her hands on her slim hips. She reaches out and grabs the Dr. Pepper, but she doesn't open it.

"You know why I'm here, C."

I widen my eyes in feigned drama and hold out both hands. "Let me guess: It's an intervention."

"You could call it that." She nods, looking shrewd with black Aviators propped up on her head. And hot in tight blue jeans and a jade green t-shirt, with diamonds winking in her ears.

I push up the sleeve of my battered button-up, so she can see the permanent skid mark scars inside my elbow. "Too much H?"

She shakes her head. "Too little C." She narrows her eyes. "I can see you've shaved, and I support that. You went out somewhere, on a bike no less, and I support that, too. But seriously, Cross, I want to know how you are, be-cause Suri's worried about you and I am, too."

Right—so this is about Suri. I rub my eyes, but I can't complain much. I should have known a long time ago she was getting too...caught up. Lizzy even told me that she was, on the drive to the vineyard on the day that we got hauled off to Mexico. But I didn't believe her. And after that day's adventure, I kind of forgot about it. Selfish, thoughtless Cross. I let Suri get and stay close to me, and then I let her lay it all out on the table before I sent her away with her tail between her legs.

Through the web of my fingers, rubbing my eyes, I see Lizzy sink down to the polished cement floor and cross her legs. Looking up at me, she says, "It's not your fault she didn't see straight. She shouldn't have thought you felt the same way just because she hoped you did. She's not upset with you. She's upset...with herself, I guess."

I cross my arms loosely over my chest. "That why she hasn't called?"

Lizzy nods.

"She ever gonna call?"

She nods again. "Sometime. Probably soon. I think she's just embarrassed."

I snort. "No need for that shit. We're all friends, aren't we?" The question comes out sounding kind of like a jab. I feel like a five-year-old, but the truth is, it bugs the shit out of me that Lizzy's just a few weeks away from walking down the aisle to marry Hunter Player West. Instead of being my friend, she's going to be some other dude's wife. I know it's immature and patriarchal and whatever else, but it rubs me the wrong way.

Lizzy makes a tsking sound. "I sense some bitterness." And then, in all seriousness: "Really, Cross. You still don't like him, do you?"

I stand up and start pacing like a caged lion. "You tell me he's a fine guy."

"But you don't believe me."

"So what, Lizzy? I'm gonna forever hold my peace. Isn't that what matters?"

She stands up, coming over to me, but instead of hands on hips this time, she wraps her arms around her waist. "You know that's not what matters. Cross, we're family. I don't want you to be unhappy whenever you think of me. I want our friendship to stay strong." She exhales, looking miserable. "If there's something I can do, something that will make you feel more open to—"

I toss my arms out. "There's nothing you can do, Lizzy. You've done nothing wrong. Neither has West, at least not to me. And before you ask, I'm fine about the money thing."

Lizzy sold her virginity at a brothel in Vegas so she could help pay my medical bills after my motorcycle wreck. Don't worry, the story had a happy ending—for her, at least. Hunter West, her soon-to-be hubby, was the highest bidder.

She did this while I was in my coma. When I first woke up, I was pissed, but I've gotten used to it now. I can't change it, so I tell her, "I will always love you for it, end of story."

Lizzy comes a little closer, and I can smell her lotion: gardenias and maybe roses. I stare into her face, so different than it was before my wreck. She looks thinner... Less like the grown up Lizzy I knew and more like the girl I knew in high school.

"It's okay, Liz. I'll learn to like West. I can even show him how to fix that banged up Roadster he's got in the garage." I paste a smile on, hold my arms out, so she comes in for a hug. "BFFs?"

"BFFs," she says warmly, pressing her cheek against my chest.

I open my eyes and pull away first, then walk back to my Sunkist and ease down on the floor. I motion to the chair. "Sit down and stay a bit."

And Lizzy does. We talk for two hours—longer, I think, than we have since before the accident. We talk about everything but the pain attacks; she doesn't ask, for once, and I don't tell her that they're getting worse.

I wait until she's almost out the door to drop the bomb: "Wanted to mention I'm going down to Mexico."

Her eyes pop.

I shrug one shoulder. "Biker thing."

I can see the approval on her face—the relief that I'm finally living life again.

I shut the door behind her, grab my soda and head up to my room to read the folded papers in my pocket.

I surprised myself, too, with that little revelation. I'm going to motherfucking Mexico.

CHAPTER SIX

Merri

"BLESS ME, FATHER, for I have sinned. It has been more than three weeks since my last confession."

I press my butt more tightly down against the backs of my shins—my legs are folded under me—and glance through the curtain of my strawberry hair at the sheet of thatch that stands between me and the priest. I can't see his face, but I assume because it's the second Tuesday of the second week of the month, that it's Father Mendez, the traveling priest from Fresnillo.

"Yes, child." The gravelly voice confirms my suspicions. Definitely Father Mendez. His advanced age— eighty-one, the nuns say—means he's one of the few I trust not to have ties to the Cientos Cartel. So I shut my eyes, inhale deeply, and try to really pour my heart out.

"I must confess many sins," I whisper in soft Spanish. "The first is envy." Another breath to rid myself of my embarrassment—the embarrassment of being totally open and honest with a virtual stranger—and I plunge forward. "I envy the nuns who are able to leave the clinic when I can't. I feel like a prisoner, and rather than being thankful for the second chance I've been given, I'm...frustrated. I know I have no one to blame but myself, so I just keep praying for forgiveness and hoping I'll find a way to feel more grateful." I'm silent only long enough to clear my throat. "I definitely need to feel more grateful for what I have right now. But sometimes... I miss certain parts of my old life."

I close my eyes, and I can see Katrina, with her sparkly nail polish and kind smile, rubbing my calves and painting my toe-nails in the beauty parlor in Jesus's mansion. Sometimes when I'm eating rice here at the clinic, I can taste bell peppers and that yummy cheese dip that Arman, Jesus's chef, used to whip up. "I miss seeing the sun, but I miss other things, too, like taking a long bath with soap that smells good."

I also miss the more forbidden things—like the feel of a man's mouth on mine. That particular desire tosses me all the way back to eleventh grade, the year I lost my virginity to my high school band's assistant director, Sam Kline. Sam was only twenty-two, and he ended up transferring schools at the end of my senior year because he felt so guilty about what we did every afternoon in the instrument closet. But I can still see his brown eyes. Read the feeling in them. When he clung to me after we both got off, he held me tightly, like he was desperate to feel my body against his.

I press my lips together until they sting, because I'm not going to tell Father Mendez any of this; but sometimes when I remember Sam, my chest feels like there's a fire inside of it. That's how much I crave that closeness. After Sam...

There were half a dozen others after Sam, but God is only holding the last one against me—because it's the only one I'll never confess. It's the only one that really feels 'sinful'. So I skirt it, going as close as I ever do to a confession: "I'm an impure woman," I murmur, lifting my head and looking at the thatch.

"I know I'm not cut out to be a nun, but I love being here and helping. And that leads me to my worst sin since I've been in this place."

I hear the rustling of robes on the other side of the thatch, and I push myself to continue, even though I feel like I can't breathe. Father Mendez knows a little bit about me—he knows all my confessions over the last nine months—but he might have heard more. He might know exactly who I am and where I came from. The thought fills me with shame, but not as much shame as I feel for the sin I breathlessly confess.

"I'm afraid some people from my past have tracked me down. I'm afraid the explosion that blew up the cafeteria was a warning. A warning that I need to leave. I've told Sister Mary Carolina but she either doesn't believe me or she refuses to make me go." I hesitate, trying to think of how to explain, in case he doesn't remember my story or never really knew it.

"Before I was here, I was in...a bad place, with people who were bad. I managed to run away," I say, frowning at the horrible memory—which is so much more than merely running away.

"I selfishly sought refuge here, and the nuns were kind enough to take me in and train me to do massage therapy for the children. But I'm afraid that if I want them to be safe, I need to leave. But I can't make myself leave. I'm afraid of death." My voice cracks, surprising even me. "I'm afraid to die without ever falling in love or having children. I wanted a good life, one that wasn't complicated or full of pain, but I ruined everything." I press my hands over my eyes, trying to compose myself. I take a few long breaths and find my protective shell again, and along with it, my rationality. My sense of responsibility. "I know that this mess is my fault. I didn't use good judgment and I wasn't living my life in a way that would please God."

Silence eats my words, and I wipe my eyes with the palm of my hands. My heart is beating hard, and for some reason I think of walking out of my second grade classroom to Aunt Britta's van, of how my backpack felt so heavy, and I disliked being stuck in that school building all day so much. I want to cry some more, but I manage to hold it in, because I'm not a girl who cries.

Finally, I hear the slight rustle of Father Mendez's robes, and his low voice travels through the thatch.

"The Lord hears you," he says. "I don't want you to say Hail Marys. Close your eyes and see your past and understand that you have paid these debts already. Sister Mary Carolina—she wishes to shelter you. St. Catherine's offers shelter for all people and if there is danger we will trust our Lord to deliver us."

And now Father Mendez leans forward, so close to the thatch divider that I can smell a whiff of coffee. When he speaks again, his voice is nothing but a hiss. "But if you want to ensure that God keeps these children safe, I have a message. Walk out the door nearest the site of the explosion Thursday at ten o'clock in the evening."

He leans back into his seat.

"I cannot promise that the Lord will preserve your life.

but I have heard your confession and I believe your heart is pure. If you perish, you will join our savior in Heaven."

CHAPTER SEVEN

$C \mathcal{RO} \mathcal{SS}$

ONCE I DECIDE to go looking for Meredith Kinsey, I feel like a weight has been lifted off my shoulders. It's my fault she's still in Mexico. If she's dead and gone, that's my fault too. I could have told someone. Shown someone the files I saved on a USB. Copies of e-mails that showed my father conspired with Priscilla Heat and Jim Gunn to sell one of his former mistresses as a sex slave.

When I found out, last May, Cross Carlson had his own shit going on. He was busy making money, tweaking bikes, fucking around.

He's done fucking around.

I have to drive to Vegas before I do anything else. I leave early Wednesday morning, armed with my trusty leather bike bag, plus my passport and a fake I bought last night from one of my high school buddies, a civil servant who specializes in fake documents for illegal immigrants. After making a pit stop at a bookstore, for a road map of Mexico, I adjusted the Mach's arm band for extra mobility and steering accuracy. Right before bed, I called my mobile phone provider and got the internet turned back on; I've emailed both Wil and Napo, plus my old receptionist, Martha, informing them that I'll let them know something about the shop in the next two weeks. It's a small step, I know, but it feels good.

The air is cool and crisp at 6 a.m. as I head down I-680 toward Walnut Creek and Dublin, which will get me close to I-5 South. The sky is caught between shades of blue, the grass glows yellow-silver with the sun's first rays, and on my bike, I feel okay. Capable. Good.

I got a voice mail in the wee hours of this morning from my father. He sounded drunk and said some vaguely threatening shit about the situation between us deteriorating further if I stirred up any trouble regarding 'the situation we discussed'. If anything, it was the final affirmation that I'm doing the right thing.

I make good time through Walnut Creek, past Livermore; then my route veers eastward, then South on I-5 toward Bakersfield. I make a couple of stops to stretch my arm and shoulder, but I've got PB&J and water, plus some jerky and a couple of apples in my bag. It's enough to tide me over until I get to Vegas.

The nine hour drive is surprisingly enjoyable. I haven't felt the wind on my face the way it hits you on the highway in a long, long time. I know I must be hard-up for this when I feel my throat get thick outside L.A. It's not the most beautiful place to ride—far from it—but it just feels so damn good to be back on the road.

By the time I roll to a stop at a gas station in Vegas, it's mid-afternoon and I'm sweaty, stiff, and tired. Still, I grin when I pull my helmet off and rub a hand back through my sticky, matted hair. I unzip my leather jacket and fish a map of the city out of my bag.

I'm looking for an upscale suburb on the west side of town. It's called The Woods, although I can't imagine there are really any 'woods' in Vegas. I find Birch Street pretty quickly and, again, feel surprised at the ordinary name.

For Priscilla Heat, I'd imagined something more exotic—and maybe she *was* living somewhere more exotic, before what went down in Mexico two and a half months ago. She and Jim Gunn tried to make Lizzy and I the latest victims of their budding business. While Jim Gunn got arrested right out of Mexico and charged with multiple counts of abduction, human trafficking, and murder, Priscilla didn't re-surface until March, when she got caught crossing the border with some drug runners near Nogales.

Somehow, both she and Jim Gunn got out on bail. I guess my father's not the only powerful friend they have. I don't think there's any way Jim Gunn won't get put away for life, but rumor has it Priscilla is planning to turn state's witness, so she could still come out okay.

I know for sure she's hidden in this little corner of suburbia because Hunter West told me—and he's got a P.I. on her ass. Now that she's here, she can't leave. She's got a tracker bracelet, or something like that. I guess I'll find out.

The drive to The Woods takes me about forty minutes, and as I suspected, there's hardly a tree in sight. The neighborhood is gross: a bunch of three-story, Spanish style homes that sit on half-acre lots in between near identical three-story, Spanish style homes on acre-sized lots. There's a sidewalk lined with bushes. Tennis courts. Grass and flowers meticulously maintained by the HOA.

Nothing marks Priscilla's house as different from the

rest. One nineteen Birch Street is a patterned stone mon-
strosity with a gaudy leopard fountain in the front and huge
cement balconies on all sides, as if it was built for someone
under a "no leaving the house" rule. The grass is so green it
hurts my eyes, and as I roll closer, I can see the spray of
sprinklers embedded here and there, making little rainbows
in the fading sunlight.

There's no gate, so I can drive right down the winding
driveway. I park the Mach between the large, circular fountain and her front porch. As I take off my helmet, I notice
the porch is pink-tinted cement. Classy.

I brush my hair down with my fingers, then think of
who I'm visiting and pull it back up sideways. My shoulder
is sore, so I roll it before putting my left hand in my jacket
pocket. The jacket is heavy, and it's not cold here, but I
can't bring myself to take it off. Now that I'm here, I feel
weird. I feel naked. Exposed. I guess it's because she got
one up on me that day at the vineyard. Or maybe I'm just
nervous. I ring her bell.

I pull the little picture out of my jeans pocket and look
down at Meredith's face while I bang on the door. It sucks
being here—having to go to Priscilla Heat for anything—
but I remind myself that I'm doing this for one of her victims. One who didn't escape her like I did.

I slide the picture back into my pocket and I lift my
hand to knock again. Before my knuckles hit the wood, I
hear a second of static, followed by Priscilla Heat's snippy
voice. "What do you want?"

I spy a discreet speaker on the wall to my right; it's
maybe the size of a wallet, and painted to blend in with one
of the slabs of stone. Facing it, I say, "This is Cross Carl-

son."

"I can see that." I glance up, then left, and there's the camera. I need to be more observant. I tilt my head back at it and shove my right hand into my pocket. "Look—I want to talk to you."

"Not interested."

There's a noise, like the connection was cut, and I say, "Wait! Are you there?"

No answer.

I ring the doorbell eleven times before I hear the speaker come on. "This is harassment." She sounds annoyed. "I can have you arrested."

I snort. Yeah, right. I direct my gaze back to the camera. "I'll stop if you let me in."

"You'll stop when I send my body guards down." She sounds intent, but something in her voice makes me think she's lying. Probably the knowledge, also provided by Hunter West, that she's almost broke.

Regardless, I try another angle. "Your trial's coming up, right? Sometime in July?"

There's a pause. When she speaks, she sounds bitter. "What do you want, Cross Carlson?" She drags my last name out, like it's a curse word, and I wonder if my father has really severed ties with her this time.

"I said I want to talk." I roll my eyes at her through the camera. "There's something in it for you. After you hear me, if you don't want to help me, you can tell me to go fuck myself. I'm not interested in spending more time with you than I have to."

Another pause, during which I can practically see her face pinch into a frown. "Come inside. Third floor, second bedroom on the right. If you see the bunnies, don't be loud or stomp. It frightens them."

The intercom goes dead and the front door clicks open. The foyer is gaudy emerald marble, but obviously expensive, so I guess she's not completely out of money.

I'm about halfway up the highway-wide sparkling stone staircase when I notice something dart past me. It's small and dark, and the shock of it zipping between my legs almost makes me lose my footing. I climb a little faster, and that's when I see its ears wiggle.

Bunnies...

I see a second set of ears, and a third.

Holy shit, does this lunatic have a McMansion full of rabbits?

CHAPTER EIGHT

CROSS

AS IF IN answer, when I get to the third floor landing, a large, brown rabbit approaches. His ears twitch as he sniffs my boots. I spot more rabbits roaming the lush red carpet. Most of them are white, but some are brown and others black. One is gray. I'm so shocked by them, I almost don't notice that I'm heading left instead of right. I turn around, almost squishing a really tiny white rabbit with my boot, and I hear a squeal echo through the sound system.

"BE CAREFUL!"

I turn a quick circle, looking from my feet to the ceiling, where I see more cameras. Damn. I've gotta get better at this shit.

I roll my eyes again and make my way to her bedroom door, hyper-focused of how big and dirty my boots are on the thick carpet. Or, at least I am until I see three more of the little critters huddled together farther down the hall. Black and brown and white. I shake my head at them and knock on Priscilla's door.

It clicks open with the same magic as the front door, and I step inside what can only be described as a shrine to

Priscilla Heat...and rabbits. I don't even spot Priscilla herself at first, because I'm lost on the custom, heart-shaped bed (topped by a framed portrait of Priscilla in nothing but thigh-highs); the sunken sun-shaped tub a few steps from the bed; the wall of Priscilla Heat posters (oddly, signed by Priscilla); the red, pink, and white décor; and all the rabbits. Jesus H. Christ, there are a lot of rabbits in this room. I sniff the air and am stunned to find it smells like overstrong perfume and not rabbit shit.

Then Priscilla steps in front of me, wearing a plush pink robe with her hair piled on her head, and I realize I didn't see her sooner because she blends in with the room.

"Holy shit," I breathe. I look around the room again, trying to get a number on the rabbits.

Priscilla smiles, revealing her freakishly bleached teeth. "There are twenty here with me in my suite. Twenty-nine more are in the house." She frowns, looking troubled. "We lost one yesterday. Prince Albert got electrocuted when he chewed through a lamp cord."

I blink. Then I focus on her eyes, checking for pupil size. If she's high, they'll be big, the way mine always were back at rehab.

She looks lucid enough, though. Perfect tanned skin, flawless red lips, shiny blonde hair. Her breasts force the too-small robe to part, so I can see almost everything but her nipples. My traitor of a dick twitches once before it realizes who she is.

Priscilla spreads her arms wide. "Take a seat, Cross Carlson. Anywhere is fine." She says it like a sigh, but there's some theatrics there. She's happy that I'm here. I'm sure she is.

I wave at a nearby fluffy white love seat, which ironi-cally looks like it's made of rabbit fur. "Why don't you? I'm okay standing."

She arches a brow, giving me an exaggerated expres-sion that falls somewhere between a pout and feigned con-cern. "I see you're looking better. Less like death."

She sinks into a wing-backed chair and I curl my lip. "Disappointing I'm sure."

She looks down at her blood red nails, rubbing one with the fingers of the opposite hand. I feel a streak of an-ger that she can use both hands.

When she looks up again, she's all business. "What do you want, Cross Carlson? I'm not interested in buying wrapping paper."

She extends her legs out in front of her, and I catch the glint of her state-issue ankle monitor.

"I'm looking for Missy King. I know you know where she is. If you tell me, I'll help you."

Priscilla snorts. It's the girliest snort I've ever heard. Her nostrils flare a little, and she makes a high-pitched noise somewhere in the back of her throat. "And send my-self up shit creek even further? No can do, señor."

I fumble for the plan I should have polished back on my Mach. Nothing comes to mind, so I have to settle for, "I can help you if you help me."

Another snort. "You can't even help yourself."

I roll my eyes again. It's not something I do a lot, but Priscilla brings it out of me. "Who's walking around and who's stuck at home with a police tracker? You need as much help as you can get. Being tied to Jim Gunn is poi-son."

ELLA JAMES

She puckers her lips, saying nothing because she knows I'm right. I don't speak, wanting to make her ask me what I can offer her. I need to hear her ask.

She spreads her arms theatrically. "What can you do for me, Cross Carlson?"

I press my lips together as the obvious answer comes to me. "It's more what I *won't* do. I won't turn in the evidence I have against you, Jim Gunn, and my father. E-mails that you sent to each other about a year ago. I have them in my inbox, and I also have them printed, hidden in a few spots." One of which is Lizzy's mother's house.

"I don't believe you," she says, but her words are an angry hiss.

I pull out my cell phone, and in half a minute, "I've got one up now." Within a heartbeat, Priscilla is on me, legs and arms wrapped around my hips and torso like an over-sized koala bear. Her rock-hard breasts punch into my chest, and her fingernails scratch my neck as she grabs for my phone. I accidentally backhand her in the struggle, and I cringe as she falls back against the white couch. She is a terrible person, but obviously I would never intentionally hit her.

"I'm sorry." I step back, sliding my phone into my pants. "I take it you believe me?"

Priscilla arches her left eyebrow in a way that reminds me of a Disney villain. "I want to see one of the e-mails."

I shake my head. "I'm not handing you my phone again. But I'll give you some details. In one of them, you and Jim Gunn mentioned something about your diamond-studded cunt." I smirk at her, and Priscilla actually colors a little. It's quickly followed by an unabashed grin, which I

60

feel sure is just for show. "I'm pierced, darling."

I'm not going to dignify that with a response. "Obviously there's lots of damning stuff in there too. Jim Gunn isn't very smart. He actually mentions Ceintos by name in two of the e-mails."

I slide my phone into my jacket and fold my arms as Priscilla pales.

"That may be, but *I* never did."

"You're disgusting, Priscilla. Not any better than Jim Gunn—"

"This is his business, not mine!"

I shake my head. "That doesn't change what you did."

Priscilla's red mouth twists into an ugly pout. "She was a little bitch. She fucked your father behind your mother's back. You should be glad she's gone."

"No one deserves to be gone that way." I want to add, *except maybe you*, but bite my tongue. I need her help. "All you have to do is tell me where you think she might be."

"Why do you care?"

I don't see why I should lie to her, so I don't. "I feel like shit for just leaving her there. I found out this happened a year ago, and—"

"If the police find out, you'll be in trouble too."

"I don't care." It's true—I really don't.

Priscilla rubs her forehead with her manicured hand, and her eyes meet mine. "Believe it or not...I do feel guilt at times. It was a mistake, getting involved with Jim. He brought me down. Made me worse than I really am."

I nod solemnly, event thought I'm not buying any of it.

She stands and steps close to me. Close enough that I can barely breathe for the scent of her toxic perfume. She runs her finger down my jacket, almost like she's seducing me. I step back.

"I'm sorry about you, too, Cross. We were covering our asses, and we made a terrible decision that night."

"Well this is your chance to undo that. Start making better ones. Tell me what happened to Missy King."

"That Mexican you saw in the barter house that day, the one whose gun you stole—that's Guapo. He works for Jesus Cientos." She pauses, scrutinizing my face, like that name might mean something to me. It doesn't. She smiles. "He's big-time. The leader of the Cientos Cartel. Usually he just sells the girls, but he kept Missy. He liked the lit-tle— he liked her. During the...time I spent in Mexico—" she must mean when Guapo and his guys ran off with her— "I found out she ran from Jesus. He treated her very well, I heard, but she wasn't grateful. Some months ago— almost a year maybe; I'm not sure—she ran to...some church." Priscilla wrinkles her nose, like the word tastes bad. Hell, it probably burns her tongue. "A Catholic church. It's supposed to be neutral ground for the cartels."

Priscilla sits back down and drops her head into her hands. "Sometimes when I think about this, I feel ill. It was a bad decision. Very bad."

"How can I find this church?"

When Priscilla looks up, I'm surprised to see tears in her eyes. "I know someone who might be able to help you, but...it might be dangerous."

"I don't care. Tell me."

"His name is Carlos. He's a hustler in Mexicali. Most nights he's at a seedy little strip club called La Casa del Amor, off Boulevard Islas Agrarias."

I pull out my cell phone, jotting down what she said, then cut my eyes up at her. "Seedy by American standards or Mexican standards?"

"Mexican." She fans her face.

I slip my phone back into my pocket. "And if I want to talk to Carlos, I should...mention you?"

She nods. "Mention Priscilla sent you."

"He'll know where the church is?"

She nods. "It's hardly a secret."

I think this over. Figure it's the best I'm going to get. "Thank you, Priscilla."

I start walking to her door, and she grabs my arm. "You're not going to tell, are you? You're not going to share the e-mails? I'm repentant. I'm helping you."

I nod. She is helping me. But I'm leaving the decision to Missy King.

CHAPTER NINE

CROSS

I WANT TO drive toward Mexico as soon as I leave Priscilla's house, but that would put me crossing the border at night. And I know that's not a good idea. I exit her neighborhood the back way and spend some time driving around the city, trying to be sure she didn't put a tail on me. For all I know, my father warned her I might pay her a visit.

When I feel reassured that no one's on me, I stop at a Target in the burbs and stock up on supplies. Some are for Meredith, some for me. Maybe I go a little overboard with the girl stuff, but if I find her, and I can get her to leave with me, I want to have everything she needs. Everything she hasn't had this last year—or however long it's been.

It seems possible to me that we might have to hide out for a little while, at the shop or maybe somewhere else when we get back to the States. I think I've got the essentials covered (I am NOT buying tampons or any of that other stuff), but I'm reminded again that I really don't have a plan, and what little I'm going on comes from the mouth of deviant porn star.

I wonder, as I cross the parking lot to the Mach, if a year or a year and a half—I don't know exactly when they sold her—is long enough to ruin someone for good. I hope not.

I check into the Hampton Inn and soak my shoulder in a hot shower. It's stiff and sore from the way I'm riding the bike, but I don't feel a pain attack coming on, so I'm fine.

The next morning I'm up before the sun is. Just can't sleep. I pull on the jeans I wore yesterday, my scuffed up boots, and a long-sleeved ringer that's got a grease stain near the collar. I think of Suri as I clomp down the stairs. She still hasn't called me but I called her last night and left a message.

I use an old rag I grab out of a janitor's cart on the first floor to scuff the Mach up some—more inconspicuous that way—and check my map again. Almost six hours to Mexicali, and La Casa del Amor.

Thoughts of the strip club bring up thoughts of Marchant Radcliffe and his whore house, the ridiculously named 'Love Inc.' I've gotten to know the guy, and he's decent, but I can't get over 'Love Inc'. I think he should call it Blow Jobs for Big Money.

I only got to know of the place because Lizzy sold her virginity there. To pay my medical bills. She even opened a savings account for me, which I haven't been able to get her to close yet. I'm not touching the money, and I think she knows that. It's not like I was penniless when I had my accident.

Sometimes, when I think about it too long, I hate her for it.

And the two million dollars—yeah, two million—just

sits there. I thought about investing it and giving it back to her with gains, but realized the first time I tried to read the *Wall Street Journal*—even the front page—that I'm no investor.

Her groom to be, on the other hand, could probably double it before the wedding.

Hunter West.

His name still leaves a sour taste in my mouth, and I know I have no right. I was a whore just like good Mr. West, so who am I to judge his past?

Speaking of pasts: Missy King. Meredith Kinsey. I torture myself, imagining her fate. Wondering, for the thousandth time, if Meredith really is Missy King, or if this is some elaborate plot my father cooked up to throw me off the trail.

And if she is, what happened to her? How did she go from crusading college reporter to sex slave?

People like you happened to her.

As I weave between a Mack truck and a van, I think about how true it is. The guy arrested on drug charges back in Georgia was probably her boyfriend. Maybe she fled to Vegas, where she didn't have any money, and she met my father, who probably promised to take care of her.

I used to think of myself as one of the good guys. Sure, I slept around, but every woman I was with wanted to be there, too. They wanted the sex as much as I did, and when it was over, we usually parted as friends. I try to stay away from anyone who might want something else.

See? One of the good guys.

But for almost a year, I knew what happened to Missy King and I pretended I didn't. I believed she deserved what she got. Innocent women don't fuck married men, right?

The thought makes me feel nauseated.

I let fate stay its hand while I sat on her secret. While I protected my father. I let him get away with something abhorrent, and then, that night outside Hunter West's house, I paid for it. Jim Gunn, evil fucker that he is, was doling out justice in my case. I still want to kill him—preferably after feeding him his balls—but I know by the time this is over, I'll see just how much I deserve what I got.

I take a sharp curve around a clump of cacti and my body tenses at the feeling of off-balencedness I get from steering. I've got a fucked up left hand, and I can't even ride a bike without losing my damn nerve. No way I'll be saving anybody.

And for the first time yet, I wonder if I'm really going to Mexico to die.

ALMOST SIX HOURS later, I cross the border at Mexicali, the capital of the state of Baja California, Mexico, with my passport and a story about motorcycling through the country. In the bottom of my bag is a second passport, for 'Meredith Carlson'.

It's my hand, I tell myself. Because I'm disabled now, I need to feel like I can actually do something. But doing something is telling the cops. Not riding into a drug cartel's turf.

As I get into the bustle of Lazaro Cardenas Boulevard, with its half-dozen lanes of thick traffic baking under the hot sun, I take a very stupid risk, balancing with my left shoulder and hand and sticking my right into my pocket, where I grasp Meredith's picture and throw it out into the wind.

The second after, I'm wrenched with regret. Just another sign that I'm pathetic. A lump of emotion rises in my throat, but I swallow hard and navigate the traffic. I focus on finding my way to Islas Agrarias Boulevard, which will take me to a little side street—Av de Los Serdan—where I should find La Casa del Amor.

I'm in shoulder-knotting traffic for almost an hour, feeling the sweat drip through my hair and down my neck, wondering what will happen when I get to the strip club, when I finally spot the turnoff onto Islas Agrarias. My phone isn't working like my provider told me it would, so I'm relying on visual memory of the map as I look for Calz Tierra something, the smaller street that will take me to the even smaller Av de Los Serdan.

The roads here are paved but it's been a while. Small, square business signs, nothing but colorful paper plastered over plywood squares, line Islas Agrarias, advertising party spots, a lawyer's office, free colas. There's no grass anywhere—just piles of sand that sprinkles across the road as a dry wind slaps me in the face.

I squint through the sweat in my eyes, pass an old brown Jeep, and get into the right lane, where I think I see Calz Tierra. Yeah, that's it. Calz Tierra…something. I can't read the words. My eyes are too blurry. I make a slow turn onto it with my heart hammering in my chest, taking in the few food shops and businesses that, to me, look like little more than roadside stands. I pass a fruit vendor and someone selling something that looks like lottery tickets, and then I'm here: Av de Los Serdan. La Casa de Amor.

Merri

IF THERE'S ONE thing I've learned from spending time at St. Catherine's Clinc, it's that I lived a mostly selfish life before. It didn't start off easy, but that doesn't mean I wasn't a selfish girl with dreams and desires all centered around myself.

My mother died in childbirth—her labor came on too fast, and I was born in the car—and after a month nursing bottles from my father, I wasn't gaining weight, so my Aunt Britta and Uncle Walter took me in. They had a one-year-old, my cousin Landon, but still, they made time and space for me. I saw my father on the weekends until I was four, when he was involved in a one-motorcycle wreck on a lonely Georgia highway outside Albany. Just before I started kindergarten, my aunt and uncle adopted me and made me Meredith Kinsey.

Aunt Britta always made sure I looked nice and knew the things a girl should know. Cross your legs when you're wearing a skirt and don't talk to strange men. Don't go close to big vans with dark windows. That kind of thing. I did okay, I guess, until I hit puberty, and by then I'd started feeling...left out. Maybe it's because Aunt Britta was dark-haired, with brown eyes, and I'm so fair, or maybe it was because she used to introduce herself at teacher conferences as my aunt. I wanted a mother and a father. My childhood was consumed by wanting to be normal. A normal child with a mom and a dad. Not an orphan.

When one of Landon's friends kissed me on a fresh-man/sophomore class trip to the aquarium, I felt so good...and it wasn't too long before kissing boys became my thing.

It made me feel brand new; alive and wanted. Usually I'd go to bed and hug my pillow and I'd dream of marrying whoever I was kissing at the time. I would marry my crush and we would have a baby, and when I got six or seven months pregnant I would just go to the hospital and stay until I had the baby. No dying in the car. After that, we'd be a family. I wouldn't be the left-out little girl. I would be the mother. I would have a daughter with strawberry-colored hair just like mine, and when I took her to the grocery store, our outfits would color coordinate.

I started writing stories in high school and it was around that time I met Sam, the band director. I learned how much I didn't know about what men and women did, and for a while, I relished the pleasant things he taught me. The world was worth being in, because someone wanted me.

I was upset after Sam left town. Devastated. I had this crazy idea that I would get a job in Alpharetta, where he had transferred, and I would marry him, but Aunt Britta (who had no idea why I wanted to move to Alpharetta), in-sisted I go to college. I got a scholarship to UGA and went for something I thought would be easy: journalism.

I was pretty much just like I was in high school, in col-lege. I dated a few guys and we did more than kiss. I didn't sleep with all of them. My roomie, Carla, used to call me a kissy whore, and I guess I was. I was looking for the hugs and cuddling, and the kissing and other things—the hand-jobs and the blow-jobs and doggy style—were just a way to get there. To a place where I felt loved and cherished.

And then I found another rush, another passion, and strangely enough, it was the student newspaper. For about a year and a half, part of junior year and all of senior year, I stopped dating completely and just worked. I loved it.

I would go to the bar every once in a while, or smoke pot at a friend's house. But the rest of the time I was working, chasing my buzz. It wasn't a bad life, and I never even thought about my lack of parents.

So, when I met Sean the weekend before graduation—when I finally met the infamous Sean Tacoma, the weed dealer I'd never met (because I was always left in the car while Alec ran in)—I couldn't help but be smitten.

Sean was cute, with bright green eyes and reddish blond hair, and all I could think about was what pretty babies we would have. They would be cuter than all the other kids in preschool. Better-dressed. And they would have the perfect family with a mother and a father.

Stupid, I know. Stupid, selfish Meredith.

I squeeze my eyes shut thinking about how stupid I was. I didn't know where my choices would take me, and if I had... I could have joined the Peace Corps. Been a missionary. Nowadays I think that I would like that. Volunteer work. Work that helps people. Now that I don't have any choices that don't suck.

Sometimes, since coming to the clinic, I think about the pretty kids that Sean and I would have had—if we hadn't gotten into trouble in Atlanta. If I hadn't fled to Vegas. Sometimes I think about the children I've met here who were born without arms and legs, children with cleft lips, children who can't afford clothes, and I feel sick with my old self. I wish I could send a note back to my past.

"Señorita Merri, you look sleepy!"

I'm holding four-year-old Maria in my lap, and we're working on her hand coordination. She has a rare condition where she's missing a part of her brain—the corpus collosum—so she has trouble with fine motor skills.

I lean in and kiss her on the nose, then snap my teeth near her cheek. "Grrrr! I am a dragon! Dragons never sleep!"

Maria giggles and snaps her teeth at me, and in seconds we are rolling on the floor. She flops onto her back, still giggling, and points to my hair. "You have a barrette. It looks like a diamond. I like diamonds."

It's not a real diamond. I found it on the ground one day and only kept it because I really needed something to keep my hair out of my face. Pretty soon, I won't need it anymore.

"Can you get it out of my hair? If you can, you can have it."

I feel her little fingers grip my neck as her other hand delves into my hair, and I can't resist tickling her underneath her arm.

"No fair!" she cries, but she's laughing.

I lean my head down and wait for her to free the barrette.

If only I had known how nice life is when you're focused on something besides yourself.

When Maria gets the barrette, I clap and kiss her cheek. I hold her close for just a second, telling her a silent goodbye. Tomorrow, I'm leaving. I hope she wears the barrette for a long time. I hope that she's the prettiest girl at preschool.

CHAPTER TEN

CROSS

THE CLUB IS less than fifty yards ahead: a box-shaped, white and red building framed by a parking lot that's surrounded by dirt. As I come up on it, I realize it's not quite as small as I thought—maybe about the size of a roller skating rink back home. The parking lot isn't empty but it isn't full, either. I count maybe fifteen or so cars and one ragged out white Honda CB500F.

I notice, as I park beside an old Maxima, that on the wooden porch there's a girl with long, bleached blonde hair wearing nothing but a sombrero and a black string bikini. I wonder how seedy a place has to be for Priscilla to call it that.

It takes me a minute to get off my bike, because my body is so stiff and sore, and after that I have to dig through my bag to find the one source of protection I was able to take across the border: a small, palm-held Taser. I bought it for Suri years ago, when we were all starting college, but she refused to carry it, and somehow it ended up at my house. I slide it into my pocket, check for my wallet, and lock my bag onto the bike.

The whole time, this girl is dancing for me. As I cross the dusty parking lot, where the air smells of sour liquor and fried foods, she rubs her palms over her tits. I try not to ogle her, but her breasts are huge and she won't let me break eye contact. When I get to the door, she holds out her hand for me, like she wants me to take it and pull her inside. I don't take it, and she makes a pouting face. A second later, a short, broad-shouldered bouncer comes out the door, trailing a cloud of bar smoke. Mexican party music booms behind him.

He gives me a murderous look, but the girl laughs and says, "This one is okay, Pedro."

The guy flicks his fingers at the door, and I step into the thickest cloud of smoke I've ever seen. I can hear the clink of pool balls before my eyes clear enough that I can see. In every direction, there's a pool table, and on my left is a long bar where girls in short shorts and skirts are talking to guys in grungy, baggy clothes and sometimes baseball caps. Like inside most bars, the patrons are mainly in their 20s and 30s, but I think I see a few teens.

I choose a booth near the back of the room and pull my phone out of my pocket, pretending to text someone while I get a better look at things. I rest my hands on the table top and cringe at the sticky filth that coats it. I lift my hands, and that's when I notice the filmy curtain on the wall a few feet to my right. Beyond it, I can see women's bodies in various states of undress, gleaming in stage light. If I strain my ears, I can hear the cat calls.

After few minutes of pretend texting, a waitress comes over, wearing nothing but a lacy hot pink apron and a g-string. She turns her body to the side, giving me a good view of her ass. Then she bats her fake eyelashes and smiles at me. Her teeth are crooked. "Can I get you something to drink, sir?" she asks in Spanish.

While I order a bottle of Corona, she looks me over—slowly. I must be really off my game, because it makes me feel uncomfortable. Like she can see all the scars under my clothes. Like she knows my hair is short because I had my skull sawed open less than six months ago.

When my beer arrives, the uncomfortable feeling magnifies. I look around the club and realize I have no idea what to do next. I take a few swigs, discreetly searching the room for someone I could ask about Carlos. I see a few bouncers—one with prominent acne scars, one with a permanent scowl, and one surrounded by flirting women—but none of them is nearby, and none looks in charge.

I finish my drink and order a second. It's been a long while since I drank regularly, so I feel a little lightheaded, but it works for me. Makes me looser. When the waitress brings my second Corona, I lean in and ask her if she knows Carlos.

She hesitates for half a breath, then nods toward the sheer curtain on the other side of the room. "He's there. In the club."

I guess the curtain separates the strip club from the bar. I slide the waitress a twenty. "Thanks."

I want to get to Carlos before she can tell him that I'm coming, so I get up almost right after she saunters off. Unfortunately, she senses me behind her and turns around grinning, probably thinking I'm coming after her.

She waves at herself, as if displaying the merchandise. This is when I know I've definitely lost my game. I can't even come up with something smooth. Instead I hold my hand up and lamely shake my head, and the girl huffs off, shaking her ass like she's got a hula hoop around her waist.

I pass a cluster of American frat bros, heehawing and guzzling beer from a funnel. The old Cross would have stuck out just like them, so I feel grateful for my dusty clothes and sweat-rumpled appearance. Nobody seems to notice me as I cross the room.

When I go to duck through the curtain, the womanizing bouncer grabs my left arm from behind. I whirl around, snatching my arm away from him on instinct.

He holds his hands out like he meant no harm. "Two hundred," he says smoothly.

I frown.

"Two hundred dollars."

Is he serious? He doesn't blink, so I pull the money out of my wallet and press it into his palm, and he waves me in.

"Carlos," I say before he slips back onto his bar stool.

"Right there."

He nods at one of the dozen round tables set in the room, this one nestled in a shadowy corner, and I glance quickly around the room before I start that way. It's smaller than the bar and not quite as disgusting. It doesn't smell like stale urine inside a beer bottle, and the lights are more than just bare bulbs. The girls swaying around poles on stage are nothing to scream about, but maybe I'm just not feeling the whole working woman thing these days.

I pick Carlos out before I get to the table. He's sitting with three other men, and he's the smallest one, but he's wearing an expensive looking red silk dress shirt with a diamond-studded pin on the lapel, and the other men at the table are all listening intently as he speaks with broad hand gestures. His longish black hair is slicked back with gel, and even so, he has the shine of wealth that no one else in this place has. Like he has his own personal strippers scrubbing him down in his Jacuzzi every morning.

I dread approaching the table, but I don't let it affect my mannerisms. When I'm within spitball-tossing range, I catch his eye. I step closer, placing one fist on their table: casual but firm. "Can we talk for a minute?"

I realize this might sound threatening, but I'm not sure how else to put it. To my surprise, he looks almost glad to see me. His eyes roll over my body and I shake off the self-conscious feeling that's new to me since the wreck.

He sends the men around him to another table near the stage, and as they leave he motions for me to in the chair one leaves out, across from him. I slide in, taking my time so he doesn't notice my left hand.

Carlos lights up a cigarette and exhales to his right, so it doesn't go into my face. "What can I do for you?" he asks me in English.

"I'm told you're a man who can find people."

Carlos smirks. "It depends on the people."

"I'm looking for someone." I heave a deep breath. "An American who's been in Mexico for a year or two." Based on the e-mails, I think Missy was sold around September 2011, making it almost a year and a half ago—but I don't know that for sure.

"You think I can help you find this girl."

I nod. "The girl I'm looking for is named Missy King. I've heard she's at a church."

My neck feels tight, and my upper arm is aching. I grit

my teeth and ignore it, focusing on Carlos's face. He seems to be considering what I've told him, with his palms pressed flat on the table.

"You know…I have heard that a little bird is staying with the Sisters at St. Catherine's Clinic in Guadalupe Victoria."

My heart leaps. Guadalupe Victoria is where Priscilla and Jim Gunn took Lizzy and I. "You've heard of her? You're pretty confident she's there?"

He shrugs. "Most people have heard of this Missy. The Cientos Cartel is nothing to play with."

I nod, trying to match my expression to his reverent one, but I'm too worked up. I tap my foot under the table. "Can you tell me anything about the convent?"

Carlos glances behind me, and then he slowly smiles. "Yes. You are never going to see it." I grunt as I feel the air shift behind me, and something glass breaks over my head.

Merri

SOMETIMES I THINK about writing a book.

How to Wreck Your Life in Two Years or Less, by Meredith Kinsey.

As Wednesday afternoon shines hot and sunny down on the convent, and I do my paperwork for the last time, I can't help but think about what happened to me. What I did to myself, and what other people did to me.

How much of the blame is mine, I wonder. If I die tomorrow, will this fate be one I chose, or was it chosen for me? I remember the quandary from high school Sunday school class. Predetermination. If God knew our lives before he made them, how can a good and loving God choose only some people to be his chosen ones, the ones who go to Heaven when they die? And if he didn't choose, how is he all knowing? All deciding?

It just can't be.

I only know one thing for sure: I wasn't chosen. There's no way I am. So if I die, I guess I'm on my way to Hell. It doesn't matter how many Hail Marys I said here.

CROSS

THE PAIN OF the blow shoots me up out of my seat. I round on the guy behind me as I reach into my pocket for the Taser. Before I can pull it out, the goon socks me in the jaw, and I see stars. I feel hands on my shoulders, the hardness of the bench under my ass. Something glints in the low light, and Carlos's face is stretched into a big grin.

"Priscilla told me to expect you."

I blink my eyes a few times, still clutching the Taser, and I realize the glint I saw was Carlos's gun. He's holding it out toward me, his hand resting on the table as he points the nose at my chest.

"You can come with me to meet Jesus, or I can kill

you now."

I cough a little, tasting blood. "You'd really kill me in the middle of a club?"

"It's my cousin's club." He shrugs. "Sometimes people die here."

My heart speeds up like I've been hit with an epi pen and I glance around behind me for the other guy. He's gone.

I can't see where, but I bet he'll be back. For now, it's just me and Carlos and his gun. I'm probably going to die here, I realize. Then an image of my last few months flits through my mind, and I vow that I won't. I didn't suffer all that shit to die in a sleazy Mexican strip joint.

Carlos is giving me his poker face, still pointing his gun my way, when I lunge forward and smash my Taser into his throat. As I move, I twist out of the line of fire, but his fingers jolt along with the rest of him; he never even pulls the trigger. He slumps face-first over the table, his gelled head landing in an ash tray.

I grab his gun, then glance around. No one seems to have noticed. The girls are still dancing. Men are still smoking, laughing, and cat-calling.

Carlos twitches once more.

Fuck.

I inhale, exhale. Focus on the feeling of the floor below my feet and try to ground myself, the way Akemi taught me during that long, long week when I first learned to meditate. Then I stick Carlos's gun and its huge magazine into my pants and glance around again. No one watching me. Carlos is still twitching a little, moaning. He looks like he drank too much, not like I just shocked the shit out of him.

I need to get out of here, fast. There's an exit over to my left, beside a bathroom sign. I could run right now, but first...I kneel under the table, heart pounding in my ears, and reach inside Carlos's pockets until I feel something hard and square. My hand is shaking as I work it out, then drop the phone in my pocket beside mine.

"Thanks," I mutter.

I get up and walk quickly to the exit door. When I feel a rush of dry air on my face, I lunge into a run and don't stop until I mount the bike—left leg first, the way I do it fastest. For once, it actually works.

The entire time I'm trying to get my left arm in that damn band, I'm sweating bullets. I glance up once more before I gas the bike, going almost sixty before I even leave the lot. I don't slow down until I'm near Ejido Choropo, a rural area south of Mexicali. I pull over in the shelter of a small, scrubby tree and ask Carlos's map app how to get to Guadalupe Victoria.

I wonder if Missy King is even there.

In less than two hours, I'll finally know.

CHAPTER ELEVEN

Merri

SEAN WAS AMBITIOUS, but he was raised by a drug addict father and he didn't have any money when he got to Athens Technical College. I think he planned to try school, but it wasn't long before he realized he could exercise his entrepreneurial spirit dealing pot.

Sean and I started dating around the time I graduated, and at first I thought what he did for a living was awful. It wasn't especially dangerous—he was selling to college kids, after all—but when I stayed at his place at night I used to have nightmares about the police kicking his door in and shooting us as we startled awake.

After a few months, I got used to it. I even started to think of myself as some kind of outlaw by association. He enjoyed the way I saw him: some renegade/freedom-fighter mash-up. When Sean insisted on paying for my apartment in Atlanta while I tried to get my freelance writing career going, I let him. The job market sucked, and my aunt and uncle were already helping Landon. By the time Sean needed to move in because there was too much heat on his place, I had started to get weary of his lifestyle. But Sean was paranoid, and he needed me. That's what I told myself.

A few weeks later, Sean decided he wanted to move to Vegas and deal drugs there. I thought of Vegas as a sleazy, gross kind of place, but I knew I would go with him if he asked. I thought I might get some good freelance stories out of it. Maybe I could do something on some of the girls. Something for a national publication. Or if worse came to worse, one of the Atlanta-based magazines that I had worked with.

Finally, at the end of February, we decided it was time to try Vegas. I had packed his car, a brand new black Corolla with shiny rims. He was in one of his paranoid moods, convinced the cops were coming to get him, and I remember I had offered him a handful of my Skittles as we got into the car.

"Everything is fine."

I can still hear myself saying that, half a second before the squeal of tires.

They shot him with rubber bullets and came for me, but Sean had another car, a sleek white Mustang he kept parked two streets over, as a getaway car. I had the keys; I was going to drive it to a trucking company that would ship it across the country.

As I raced away, clutching Sean's key ring and aiming for the Mustang, he was screaming for me, screaming my name like the selfish jerk he was, I guess—but I kept running. I got the keys into the ignition just as a rubber bullet hit the side of the car. Somehow I made it off the one-way side street, out of downtown, onto the interstate.

I got some money at the first ATM I saw and drove straight to Vegas, only stopping for bathroom breaks and gas. I wasn't sure where else to go. Later, on the AJC online, I read about the bust. The police were searching for me. They wanted to ask me questions.

I ditched Sean's Mustang immediately. He had ten thousand dollars in a gym bag, plus two bricks of marijuana. A lot to have in a gym bag, but not enough to last me. I ended up at the Starry Night Brothel and pretended to be reporting. I guess I didn't know what else to do. I liked the girls, and they liked me. It was a reputable-seeming place. I met the owner, a woman named Tess, and I told her what had happened. She offered to sell the weed for me, but she wanted something in return. She wanted me to service a client of hers. Drake Carlson—the governor of California.

"He only does blow jobs," she told me. "Thinks it's not really cheating if it's not sex, but they say he's impotent."

I remember sitting on the leather couch in Tess's suite, looking at my hands and wondering if I could give a blow job to a total stranger. To someone kind of...old.

But Tess thought she could get a lot of money from the weed, and I needed money. I was terrified of going back to Georgia, terrified of prison—even though I'd never done any drug dealing myself—and terrified that maybe Sean was crazy enough to try to pin the whole thing on me. I didn't know what else to do, so I agreed.

It was weird. Not what I'd imagined for myself, but I tried to pretend I was a character in a book. We had dinner. Wine. Drake was charming. Funny. Even protective, in a way that Sean had never been. I felt an element of safety for the first time since landing in the city. He said he wanted to see me again, and proved it by pre-paying the brothel. It was a lot of money—and he hadn't been so bad.

The next time he was in town, I went down on him. He wasn't impotent, but it was hard to get him off.

The third time, a hot weekend in May, he wanted to touch me. After that, he always touched me, but he never asked for anything except blow jobs.

Soon I was going to dinners with him. He started introducing me as his mistress. I was living there, with Tess, and I wasn't an escort. I was a blow job queen. He named me Missy King, and that's who I was on Tess's roster.

Months passed, and I was making more money than Sean had with his pot. And I was saving every penny of it. Once I got a hundred thousand dollars, I wanted to move to California, to San Francisco, and start a new life.

I didn't get there, obviously.

Drake's Las Vegas body guard started dropping by to see me sometimes. His name was Jim Gunn, and I always thought he was a creeper. He used to stare at me like he wanted to eat me for dinner. But the first time, he told me Drake wanted him to take me out to dinner, to see how I was doing. It had been three weeks since the governor was able to make it my way, so I took Jim at his word. He was on Drake's payroll, after all.

After that, Jim took me out to dinner once a week, every week, always asking me personal questions and questions about my past. So the governor could "do damage control" if anyone ever found out he was seeing me. I hated going out with Jim, but I did what I was paid to do. Not once did Drake ever mention my outings with Jim, and it wasn't my job to mention things to Drake.

One week in August, just after Drake had been in town for a 'celebrity' poker tournament, I starting hearing things about this porn star named Priscilla Heat. How she wanted Drake. How she thought I wasn't worth his money. Just a few days later, the rumor started that I was cheating on the governor with Jim Gunn.

Drake never asked me about it. He came to Vegas one more time, and we went to a fancy casino restaurant with some of his friends. He went home on a Sunday, but on Monday, Jim Gunn called and told me he'd decided to stay. He wanted me to meet him at his penthouse at the Wynn.

Jim picked me up at six sharp in a big, black SUV I'd never seen before, but I didn't question it. When I got into the back seat, Priscilla Heat was there, and then I started freaking out. The two of them wanted me to quit seeing the governor. Priscilla told me he was hers, and I needed to go back to Georgia. I wondered how she knew I came from Georgia, but then I remembered: I'd told Jim.

"Are you guys working together?"

Priscilla laughed, and they explained how I was going to call Drake and ask him for more money.

"He already knows your plan, my dear." Priscilla grinned. "How you're actually an undercover reporter. How you'll tell everyone about what a lying, cheating bastard he is if he doesn't pay your price."

I was so young and stupid, it took me a minute to understand: This was blackmail. We were on the highway, then, and when Jim Gunn turned around from the driver's seat, he held up a pistol.

"I think you want to do what we're asking, darlin'. We've got some fun things in store for you."

I was so young. So stupid.

I never even had a chance.

Hopelessness washes over me now, as I think of walking out of here to meet Jesus.

Maybe I should run. Maybe running would be better than walking into yet another trap.

Instead, I pack my bags in the attic—where no one will find them for a while; so they will assume I ran away—and when the sun comes up, I'm prepared to face my last day of freedom.

I go to breakfast. Eat my rice and beans as if it's not the last time I'll ever spoon them out of these metal bowls. The hardest thing, I think, is Sister Mary Carolina. She pulls me into a hug after my first appointment and whispers in my ear, "No worries. God will take care of you."

It's all I can do to hold back tears.

I'm sitting in a tiny office, filling out paperwork to order more menthol back cream for a little boy named Fernando, when I say the only prayer I will ever say for my own fate.

Whatever happens, please help me to bear it. Please don't let any of the children get hurt—or anyone at all. Please don't let the Sisters see me walking out tonight.

That's the last thing that I pray before the door swings open, and Sister Mary Carolina tells me that I have a visitor.

CROSS

I'M SURPRISED BY how pretty Guadalupe Victoria is. It's a small, flat city surrounded by rising hills that might be mountains, and in comparison to the dusty haze of Mexicali, it's green. Not so much of a waste land, even though I know that technically, it's got to be poorer than shit.

By the time I stop at a small, two-pump gas station on the outside of town, my shoulder is aching and my neck feels really tight. I sit on my bike for a minute rubbing the tendons in my neck before going inside to ask about the St. Catherine's Clinic.

"The sick kids' clinic?" the man asks.

I shrug, then nod. "Yeah."

He gives me directions to the north east side of town and tells me the building was burned.

"Burned?" I put my hand to my chest, where my heart feels like it might have stopped. "So it's gone?"

He shakes his head. "Only part of it."

Shit. "What happened?"

He leans close to me, so I can smell the food residue in his moustache. "The cartel," he hisses.

"They went after a kids' clinic?"

"They went after a woman. She belonged to Jesus Cientos. She left him and went to the convent. He wants her back."

I clutch the counter. "But he didn't get her?"

The guy makes a fish face and shrugs his slim shoulders. "How would I know? I work at a petro station."

Fuck.

I think him and speed toward the area of town he mentioned. I was thinking of buying a hat or maybe even ditching my bike, but I'm so impatient, I just drive right to the clinic. It's not the only building in town that's half burned, but it's the only half-burned building that smells *just* burned.

What if she's not here?

Then I'll find her somewhere else.

What if I get shot when I walk through the door?

I swallow. I'm not backing out now.

I park my bike beside the charred remains of the left side of the stout, wide, stucco building and pull my bag into my lap, cursing myself for not doing this sooner. I slide Carlos's gun—a black 9 mm Beretta—into the bag and check the clip. Completely full. That's good.

She's probably gone, I tell myself as I situate the gun in my pants. What kind of self-respecting Mexican drug lord would blow up half of a clinic and not claim the woman he came for? This is probably just a pit stop for me. I might have to chase Missy King all the way to Jesus Cientos's doorstep.

Damn, that makes me feel tired.

I pull off my helmet and look around. If anyone's expecting me, I'd like to know before I get off my bike; but the parking lot is still and calm. There's no sign of a threat. Beneath the helmet, my hair is matted damply to my head. In some spots, it's dried and sticking up at weird angles. I run a hand over my face and wonder if I still look like hell. The look that was so convenient for the club last night will probably scare the pants off everyone in here. Assuming the place hasn't been claimed by the cartel.

With my teeth gritted, I stride toward the clinic. A willowy woman is pushing out the door with a tiny baby in some kind of sling. I give a weak smile, just to let her know I mean no harm, and she holds the baby a little closer.

Two more steps and I find myself inside a tidy, worn-down waiting area, outfitted with your basic metal foldout chairs and a round wooden table piled high with dog-eared magazines. Beyond the waiting area, only a few paces behind the last of the chairs, is a simple school-style desk. A petite girl with braided hair sits at it, thumbing through a day planner and looking surprisingly prim in a plain navy blue dress with a large, brass cross necklace.

When she sees me, her brown eyes widen. She audibly swallows, and I notice her left hand is clenched around a bunch of peanuts.

"Did I interrupt your snack?" I ask her in Spanish.

She smiles a little, but it's a nervous smile. She looks down at her hand, like maybe she's going to offer me some of her peanuts, but instead she draws the hand into her lap and looks me up and down.

"Welcome to St. Catherine's Clinic. How may I help you?"

I reach into my pocket for the photo I'm so used to carrying around, and I guess the girl thinks I'm reaching for a gun, because she jumps up, tossing up her hands. Her mouth is stretched wide in a scream I never hear. Instead her lips pinch shut and with a frenzied shake of her head, "I'll go with you! I won't make any noise! Please, don't harm the children!"

Holy shit.

"You think I'm here to kidnap you?"

She lowers her eyes, as well as her hands. "Y-you're not?"

"I'm not with a cartel." I had thought that didn't need saying, but clearly I don't know how things work. "I'm only here to find someone."

"You came here for…an American?"

I nod slowly. I didn't really plan on having this conversation with a kid. "I'm looking for my sister." My fingers twitch in the direction of my pocket, but of course, the photo I had is gone. "I lost my photo of her—" and the video in my inbox on my phone, of Missy King wearing a baseball cap and a heavy coat, is next to worthless if I even have service— "but she's got red hair and green eyes. She's not very tall, but she is pretty. Close to my age," I say.

I can tell I've hit the jackpot. She's chewing on her lip.

"What is her name?" she says, cleverly biding time. She fiddles a bit more with her necklace, and I feel sorry that I've put her so on edge.

"Her name is Meredith Kinsey, but she once went by Missy King. She was kidnapped, more than a year ago, but she escaped. I've been told she took refuge here." The girl doesn't confirm my story, so I add, "Sometime recently, the cartel came looking for her. That's what happened to your building, isn't it?"

She clenches her eyebrows and shakes her head, and at that moment, I hear the clicking of a woman's shoes.

"Alexandria." I hear an older woman's voice before she rounds the corner. When she does, I note a nun's habit and a face that's stretched wide in alarm. Her eyes narrow as they run over the girl's slim form. "Alexandria," she says, relieved, "go into the back room and help Sister Rita with her reports."

The girl's eyes hold the older woman's for a moment, and the older woman nods. The girl clutches her necklace, and I realize it must have been some kind of alarm.

A second later, the girl is gone, and the nun is standing stone still, looking stern, and I feel like I'm about to get thrown out of catechism class. "What is your business here, sir? Do you have a child that we can help?"

I shake my head. "I'm looking for someone. My sister, Meredith. She once went by the name of Missy King. She was kidnapped and sold. I heard she might be here."

I'm searching the woman's pretty brown eyes for some hint, but she gives nothing away.

Instead, she folds her arms across her chest and sighs. "Whether she is here or whether she is not, it makes no difference. We have no business with those who seek to do harm to others."

"I don't want to hurt her," I make the sign of the cross. "I was reared Catholic."

She arches a brow, and her eyes move from my sweaty head to my dusty toes. "And what are you now?"

"Looking for someone." I lean in closer and let my urgency show. "And I don't have much time. If she's here, I'm her best shot at getting out. But it has to be now."

More like I'm her only shot, because it really does have to be now, and the sister seems to get it. Her thin lips press together. "Follow me." Two men come around a desk and she says, "They need to check you for weapons."

I hand her Carlos's Beretta, plus the giant magazine tucked into my pants. "I want it back when I go."

"Of course," she says smoothly.

They have scanning wands, and I'm slightly shocked when the one on my left goes off around my hip. The one being wielded by a dude on my right goes off around my neck. The men, both of them muscled enough to be imposing, grabbed me by my arms, and the woman holds up her hand.

She comes around behind me, runs her fingers along my neck, and presses something at the base of my skull that almost makes me purr.

"You hurt your neck," she says simply.

I nod, turning to face her once the men drop me. She nods at my legs. "You hurt your hip?"

I nod again.

"You have a slight limp. Only slight. It must have healed well."

"Observant."

She shrugs. "My job."

She holds her hand out, and when I don't take it right away, she grabs my left one from my pocket. When I recoil, she says, "That's what you are hiding in your pocket."

I exhale. "Yeah."

She opens the door to a small office and I step inside. "Tell me about the woman you are looking for. I want the whole story." I hesitate again, and she puts her hand on my shoulder, urging me into a fold-out chair. She walks around to take a seat at her faux wood desk, where she sits her hands on the table and nods at me. "Go on now, the whole story."

I find myself giving it to her. Not the abridged version, but the whole story, leading to my wreck, to the conversation I had with my father, and finally—when I can tell she knows where Meredith Kinsey, or Missy King is—my hunch that I need to keep my real name quiet at first. Because Meredith might not leave with me if she knows who I really am.

"If she's in danger, I want to get her to the States, where I can help her. It's the least that I can do."

"And your father?"

"I would never give her back to him. I'm going to get in trouble for it, but I plan to turn him in."

She nods for a long time before standing up. "Come follow me, Mr. Carlson."

CHAPTER TWELVE

Merri

I'M PRETTY SURE if I have a visitor, it's not one I want. My heart pounds so hard I can barely draw a breath as I follow Sister Mary Carolina down the hallway in the direction of the prayer rooms.

Why is this happening today? Is this Jesus? I decide as I walk briskly behind the woman who's been most influential in my life, that if this is one of is Jesus's guys, I'll go willingly. The Sisters have said over and over that they won't allow that. That we all stand together; that's the only way it can be. But I can't let harm come to them.

The only thing I can't figure out is why Jesus would send someone to kidnap me after the message Father Mendez delivered.

Sister opens the door to a small reading room with green carpet and white bookshelves, and we pause before going in. All at once she pulls me to her chest and kisses my head.

"Be brave, Merri, my love. You must do what you must do. We only want what's best for you."

And then she...leaves. She leaves me here, before I

even see who's in the room.

For the longest second, I stay on the threshold, staring at the man who is facing the bookshelf. My eyes run down the length of him, expecting to find Jesus or one of his sicarios, but that's not what I find.

I don't know who this man is. He's tall, with dark hair and large bones. Long legs, wide back, big shoulders. He looks lean, almost sick, because I can tell he should be bulkier. He reminds me of a starved lion I saw once in a documentary.

He turns toward me slowly, and as he moves I'm frozen, like in those nightmares where you're being chased but you can't run.

At first I'm not looking at his features—only the expression, which is somehow both solemn and surprised. And I feel like I've been struck dead, because he has an angel's face. It's not just the flawless blue of his eyes or his celebrity-perfect bones. It's not his perfect, straight-line nose or that lush, cherubic mouth. It's not his smooth skin. It's what I see inside his eyes. Something so intense, so sad, so ecstatic, so relieved, that I know he must be God's answer to my prayer.

For the longest moment, he just looks at me. I feel like I'll unravel in the brilliance of those ice blue eyes. I'm so thrown off I whisper exactly what I'm thinking.

"Are you here to take me?"

His lips curl slowly, into something that's not at all a smile. My heart stops as he steps closer.

"Rescue you." His eyes. They're still on me, burning through me. Holding my gaze like his hand is under my chin. His throat works and he seems to struggle with his words. "Meredith Kinsey." His chest heaves. "You're her. You're really her."

I wrap my arms around myself as my throat constricts. Nobody here in Mexico knows my real name.

He strides closer, close enough so I can smell his sweat and see his stark white teeth. And his skin: I can't see a single pore. His lips aren't chapped. His nose isn't crooked. His eyes are even bluer this close. Tall, dark, and handsome, I think dizzily. I'm gawking at my killer.

I back into the bookshelves, holding out my arms. "Who are you?" It's embarrassing, the way my voice comes out a croak. I flail behind myself for a heavy book and hold it out like that might keep him away.

His blue eyes widen. "You don't believe me."

"No joke!" I'm shrill. My chest is heaving now. He starts to step closer but I wave the book. "Don't do that! No! I want to know who you are, right now!"

He's from the U.S. Government. He must be. Sean really did pin everything on me and I'm a wanted woman. Wanted for dealing drugs. *And they found me down in Mexico! I have ties to Jesus Cientos!*

Mother Mary, I'm going to go to prison.

My eyes fill with stinging tears, but I'm not sad. I'm angry. "Do you know why I'm hiding here? Because a Mexican drug lord wants to kill me. Because he bought me as—" my voice cracks here— "a sex slave! I was sold as a *sex slave*! I don't know what Sean told you but I didn't do those things. I have my flaws, I have my flaws but I was just his girlfriend!"

I burst into tears—angry tears; my lifelong nemesis— and it's not a second later that his hands are on my shoulders, squeezing gently but firmly. I'm terrified and out-raged, but his right hand moves to the crown of my head, smoothing down my hair, cupping my neck, and God help me, it feels really good. Too good. Maybe he *was* sent by Cientos. I jerk back. Look up into his eyes. Again, the shock: This guy is seriously hot. I shove it away and side-step toward the door.

"Why are you here?" I hold my arms out. "What do you want?"

"I told you already. I'm here to help you escape."

"Who says I need help?"

"I do. And I know you don't have much time."

Does he know about tomorrow? How, unless he *does* works for Jesus? But why is he here if he does? "If you're a sicario, just be straight with me. I don't like suspense."

He's confused, and growing frustrated. "I get that you have a lot of questions, but we don't have much time. I got into it with one of Ciento's guys—"

"So you are with the cartel!" I jab my finger at him, and he groans.

"Noooo. I'm trying to get you back to America."

My heart starts pounding so hard I think I might pass out "D-do you want me because of Sean? Because I know him—*knew* him."

"No. I don't even know who that is." That seems to be the truth; I feel a cold rush of relief. "I only want to take you back."

"Who are you?"

He smiles a little, lopsided. "I'm your guardian angel, Meredith Kinsey."

I'm not buying it. "I go by Merri."

"Merri." He says it with so much relief. "Merri, we don't have much time. I got in an altercation with one of Cientos's guys, so by now Cientos knows I'm coming for you." I try not to shake as those blue eyes blaze. "We need to leave ASAP."

"I— you can't." I stand there, breathing hard, struggling to explain why to him and myself why this thing I've wanted so bad can't work. "If I were to leave with you, they'd find us." My heart aches at the thought of what might happen to the clinic. "And plus I can't be sure you're not with them. How do you even know my name?"

He leans back against a bookshelf, looking weary. "You're a missing person, Meredith."

Missing. No I'm not. I've been right here. It feels to me that the rest of the world has gone missing. I lean against the bookshelves, too, because my legs are giving out.

CROSS

"WHO DO YOU work for?" Her green eyes, still bright from tears, are dancing, angry now. Her strawberry hair, tied into a bun behind her head, glints in the fluorescent light. Her cheeks are pink. Her lips are tight.

Meredith Kinsey in the flesh is super hot, so help me.

I grit my teeth and try to focus on what she said just now. *Who do I work for?* Right.

I don't have an answer for that. Preparation never was

my strong suit, so I just bullshit. "I find sex slaves and people sold on the black market and bring them back into the U.S."

She blinks. "For what agency?"

Uhh...what?

"What agency are you with? FBI? The State Department."

Fuck. I clear my throat. "We're a group of bounty hunters. We do contracts for the government." That seems plausible—or maybe not.

"Which branch of the government?" she asks.

I scratch my head. "I've only been with the outfit for not even a year. They just send me on jobs." My dad always said I was good at looking dumb. He also taught me how to lie.

She folds her arms under her gorgeous breasts and looks me over. "How did you get here?"

Flailing... "I rode a motorcycle."

She doesn't like that. I can tell, because her lips pinch and she lets her breath out slowly. While I fumble for something to make it better, she fires again. "Why do you look familiar?"

My throat tightens. Is it possible that I look more like my father than I thought? I blink, then shrug, like I haven't the slightest. "No idea."

She brushes a stray strand of hair off her forehead and sighs. "I'm not used to American faces anymore. That's probably it."

Whew. "Probably."

"How do you plan to get me away?"

You'd think she found me on the Internet. "Uh, I've arranged for you to cross the border. With me." Well, no shit Sherlock. Damnit, I'm striking out, but Merri is shaking her head. She doesn't seem to notice.

"I can't leave." She closes her eyes briefly. When they open again, they're wet. "The people here would be made to pay. They'd get hurt. I would need protection for them."

"What happens if you don't leave? Do you think that was the last bomb?"

She nods. "I do."

"Are you crazy?" Her eyes widen, and I nod. "Yeah, your intentions are pretty clear. You know the nuns here want you safe. You *should* be safe."

Merri's eyes squeeze shut, and when she opens them, she looks bleak. "I'm sure they do, but I just can't. I can't risk innocent lives."

This floors me. "Aren't *you* innocent?"

She brushes her palm over her cheek, like she's wiping away a tear. "We work with children here. I can't leave. It's just...not safe." A strand of hair falls from her bun as she lowers her head, looking at the floor with wide, wet eyes.

"I'm sorry," she says, jutting her chin up so our eyes meet. "Thank you for coming to find me." Her delicate mouth trembles. "Just tell them that you didn't."

CHAPTER THIRTEEN

CROSS

AFTER A STUNNED moment, I follow Merri out of the door, but she was in a hurry, and she's nowhere to be seen. I start wandering the halls. I have no idea when the cartel will come for her—for us—and I don't think I can risk finding out. I don't want to force her to go with me, but I've got to figure out something.

The first thing I do is return to the waiting area to see if I can find my gun. The young girl from before is helping an older kid sign in on a clip board, and I don't see either of the guards or the older nun...I forgot her name. I turn around in a circle, and that's when I see it: the bottom end of the magazine, sticking out from between the leaves of a droopy, flowy plant sitting atop some filing cabinets.

Checking to be sure the girl is still helping the kid, I grab the gun, attach the magazine—just to be on the safe side—and stick it back in the belt of my pants. I hope by the time they notice it's missing, Merri and I will already be out of here.

After maybe twenty minutes of searching, I pause in the middle of some hallway and let out a deep breath. Meredith is here. Missy King is Meredith Kinsey. I almost can't believe it. I wonder again how she came to this fate—but does it matter? Am I still trying to ease my guilt? I pick up my pace and keep on the lookout for nuns, for anyone who can direct me to Meredith.

The building is actually four buildings: one that was apparently the old cafeteria, and was all but decimated by the bomb; another in the front that serves as the clinic; another pod serving as the sanctuary; and still another unit with the dorms. I've wandered into the church pod.

The carpeted halls are dark and smell like old Play Doh. I pass a young nun who is busy cleaning; she glances at me, then hurries by. An older nun chases a little girl who laughs ecstatically as she rushes past. I just keep moving, reminding myself that I'm doing nothing wrong. Another hall, a sharp right turn, and I see signs for the sanctuary. I peek inside, hoping to find Merri praying, but it's empty. The painted porcelain crucifix on the far wall glows under two weak lights. It kind of creeps me out. I cross through a hall at the back of the clinic, and I'm pretty sure that this will lead me to the dorms. Where I hope to find Merri.

I'm feeling more and more stressed thinking of where the cartel is right now, when like an apparition, I see a swatch of reddish hair flying down the hallway right in front of me.

I pick up my pace, and I'm about to shout Merri's name when she ducks her head, and I notice the way she's dressed: black sweatpants and a grey t-shirt, plus sneakers. And she's creeping, like she doesn't want to be seen.

Interesting.

For a half second I hope maybe she's looking for me,

but then she goes down another hallway, pushes through a door, and disappears.

By the time I finally get the nerve to follow her into the room, at least a minute has passed. It's dark when I walk in. Then I notice movement, and I realize a window is open. A window is open, revealing a small swatch of the deep pink sky, and Merri is halfway out of it.

I don't think before acting. I close the distance between us in half a second and wrap my hand around her upper arm. "What are you doing?" I have a sick feeling in my stomach when I ask this. I've built Merri up to be innocent—the opposite of everything I'd thought about Missy King—but what if she's really some kind of drug runner or something?

Then she looks up at me, and I know I'm wrong. Her eyes are huge, her mouth a worried twist. And when she speaks, her voice is barely more than a rasp. "Are you here to take me to Jesus?"

"What? Fuck no! I already told you that I'm not." I tighten my grip around her soft, warm arm, trying to tug her gently toward me, but her hands cling to the window frame.

"What are you doing, Meredith?"

"It's not your business!" Her eyebrows pull together, like she's worried, but then her face twists angrily. She jerks against me. "Let me go!"

"I will," I say evenly, "but I'm coming with you."

"No you're not!" She jerks again, this time hard enough to throw me off, and in a heartbeat she's sailing through the window.

It takes me a second longer, because I've got to push

my body through using only my right hand for balance. My booted feet hit sand about three feet below me; a dust cloud puffs around me, blocking, for a second, my view of a row of scrubby bushes and beyond that, a quiet rural road topped by a fading sunset.

Merri is moving through the bushes, sticking close to the building, hunching down low to the ground. My legs are so much longer than hers, it's not hard to catch up. Only this time, instead of grabbing her arm, I throw both arms around her back.

I whirl her around to face me, gritting my teeth as she claws my neck. "Where are you going?"

"Let go!" Her eyes are dancing. Furious.

"No! Are you going back to Cientos? That's crazy!"

She flails against me, trying her damnedest to get away. "A lot of things are crazy!"

"You need to—"

"No," she hisses. Her chest is heaving, her hands now locked around my forearms. "They'll kill me, here or there. Anywhere. I'm dangerous to everyone. That's why I'm doing this."

What the fuck?

I guess I give her a look that shows her just how crazy I think she is, because she looks triumphant.

"See?" She pulls back a little, so I can see every inch of her stubborn face. "I told you to go away and forget you found me. You think you can go up against the Cientos Cartel?"

I notice movement behind her as I say, "I think I *will*."

Then I see the glint of light on metal, and I realize there's a gun to Merri's head.

Merri

I KNOW SOMETHING is wrong by the look on my stubborn angel's face. In the dim light of dusk, I can see him blanch. Then I feel the gun against my head and I just let the breath seep out of me.

So this is it. This is how my life will end.

I clench my right fist against my angel's arm and pretend that I'm holding my rosary. I left it in my luggage, in the attic, along with a long letter to Sister Mary Carolina; if I were to bring the rosary anywhere near Jesus, he'd accuse me of trying to manipulate him.

I say a silent Hail Mary and pray that the Sisters here are right. That God forgives; that He's forgiven me.

For what seems like too long, none of us move. It's quiet, so I can hear the heavy breaths of the man behind me. It's Guapo, I think—one of Cientos' lieutenants. He manages the sex business. He's tall, always wears black, and he smells like the vanilla tobacco he loves to smoke.

If Guapo has his gun to my head, there's no way I'll make it out al—

A gunshot bursts my eardrums and I wait to die. When I see my angel jump from his crouch, I just assume he's been shot.

I'm blinking, wondering dully why God would send an angel to me only to have him killed, when hands grab me. Not Guapo's, the angel's.

I don't get a chance to orient myself before we're running alongside the stucco wall, feet kicking up the sand nestled around the building's base. Despite having spent my entire time here on the *inside* of this building, I'm pretty sure we're moving toward the front. I didn't climb out where Father Mendez told me to, near the cafeteria wing that got burned, as it's not Thursday evening.

Is this another full-on attack? Are they going to burn the whole clinic this time?

I try to communicate my worries to my angel, try to tug on his arm and tell him, "I have to be sure they're okay!" and for a second I think he's heard me. He drops back, but instead of addressing my concern, he gets behind me, shoving me forward with his right elbow.

"What the hell?"

For a second, as I'm shoved along, I worry that he's with some other cartel. Or at least hired by one. He could even be freelancing—taking me hostage so Jesus has to pay to get me back.

I throw my arms out, wanting to stop and think before I just go with this guy, but I hear men's voices shouting somewhere nearby, and my feet are moving too fast for me to slow down. We round the corner, to the front of the building, on the side where it's charred, and I'm shocked to see Juan, plus Malcolm, one of Jesus's lieutenants, on the pebble path in front of the building. They're both pointing guns my way.

I hear shots, and then I'm on the ground. Evan's knee is on my back, and he's firing over me, BAM BAM BAM. I strain my neck in time to I see Juan crumple to the ground. I guess I scream. I don't know. I hear a woman screaming, and I'm on my feet. "No don't, no don't." I'm crying, bullets are whizzing by, and BAM BAM, Malcolm is down. Oh my God, there's so much blood.

My body trembles violently as I hang onto the angel. "What are you doing? I don't know what's going on!" This isn't even Thursday...

He shoves me behind him and runs a few paces forward, firing again and again. All my senses are sluggish I hear tires screech, and look up in time to see a familiar silver Escalade crash into a telephone pole.

A second later, I hear a woman's wail. *Katrina's* wail.

Angel is back, pushing me again, toward the clinic parking lot. Katrina is wailing like a mad woman, and like a frame from a disjointed film reel, I see her tall, round form stumbling toward us.

"You killed him! You killed him you stupid bitch!" She fires a .22 right at my face, and I can feel the heat of the bullet as it travels just to the left of my ear.

Whoosh, whoosh. Whoosh. The bullets wiz by, but none of them hit. Katrina is a lousy shot. She does fingernails.

WE'RE OUT OF town before I hear the roaring engines of Jesus's crew, on our tail. They're not right up on us yet, but it doesn't matter. We'll still be dead by morning. My only prayer is that my angel didn't really kill Jesus. Katrina wouldn't know. She probably over-reacted. Once before, Jesus got shot and came home bleeding, and she had to be sedated more than he did before Dr. Marino dug the bullet out.

As I hang onto my angel's waist and clutch the bike—and the angel's butt—with my thighs, I think of how weird it is that I'm this calm. Someone from the United States came here to take me back. Then he killed Juan. And Malcolm. And probably Guapo. And maybe Jesus. And Katrina, my old BFF, tried to kill me. And now the Cientos Cartel is coming after us. *Me.*

I spin through my mental, cartel rolodex, wondering who's in charge. If Jesus is really indisposed and Guapo is as dead as I think he is, who will be behind the wheel of Jesus's battered Escalade?

Probably Christina, his twenty-year-old sister.

I close my eyes against the sting of the dry wind and wonder why Jesus was at the clinic anyway. It's not his style to come in person. But he was coming for me. Maybe he thought it was something a lover would do.

For some reason, I picture the nightgown-clad body of a young girl who got caught one time in Jesus's crossfire as he tried to kill her father. Then I picture Juan and Emanuel, in their slouchy blue jeans and designer shirts and boots. How I would ride with them to school in the back of one of Jesus' many cars. How I used to think of myself as their substitute mom.

I'm so stupid.

I'm so very, very stupid.

The engines roar behind us, and the guy who rescued me—probably not an angel, after all—juices the bike. I wonder how long till they catch up. I haven't moved my body in miles; it feels cemented to the bike seat. But now I lean around the guy's arm to see the road in front of us. We're on 490, heading north toward Torreon; it's one of the largest roads around, probably one the cartel would expect us to take. I frown as I peek out at the dark, cracked road again. My angel isn't holding the handlebar with his left arm. I can't tell *how* he's driving, but I know I don't see fingers around the handlebar. Did he get hurt?

Lots of people got hurt...

One of them was Juan.

How can a kid that young be dead?

It's disgusting. It's horrible, a shame, and I wish it wasn't real. I start to cry, and I'm ashamed because I'm crying for myself. I'm going to be lying in a pool of blood, too. So will my "rescuer." I wonder if he has any idea what they'll do to us. Especially if he killed Jesus. Gory images fill my head, and it's everything I can do to raise my arm and tug his shoulder.

I lean closer to his ear and suck in the dusty air so I can yell, "Pull over!"

"WHAT?" The wind carries his deep voice, slaps it against my ears.

"Pull over, now!"

It's a long shot, but it just might work. In the world of the cartels, you don't turn tail and run—ever. And by the logic of this hot, dry, barren place, you definitely don't pull off on the side of a highway in the middle of nowhere and hunker down with a big, shiny motorcycle. But that doesn't mean we can't try.

I see a farm house up on the right and jab his back.

"PULL OVER NOW!"

He veers sharply off the road, kicking up a cloud of dust as we fly behind a quaint brown house.

Crap, the dust cloud! I'm praying for a strong wind to blow it away when the sound of roaring engines explodes behind us and we go toppling off the bike.

CHAPTER FOURTEEN

CROSS

I COME AROUND lying on my back, staring at the moon, which has a triple halo that smears and stretches in time with my pulse. I blink a few times to clear my vision and realize my mouth is stuffed with grass and dirt. There's something hot and wet on my lips. Damn. I bring my shaking hand up to wipe at a hot smear of blood.

I roll over, push up on my elbow, and look around the junk-strewn, dirt lawn, but I don't see her. "Merri!" I'm on my feet fast enough to make my head spin, striding toward the house. There's not a light inside it anywhere; everything is quiet. Where the hell is she?

"Merri!"

She hits me from behind. Hits me so hard she knocks me down, and I realize as we land in a heap of tangled limbs that the buzzing sound I thought was ringing in my ears is really the cartel catching up to us.

I see their headlights and Meredith jerks me toward the back porch.

"Come on," she hisses. "Hurry!"

I glance at the Mach, dusty and scuffed-up, lying on its

side beside the porch stairs, and I wish I could run and grab it, push it up the stairs and out of sight—but I can't. Not with one hand.

Merri jerks me along behind her, leading me through a sea of broken children's toys and rusted car parts, and I wonder what the odds are that she knows the people who live here. I've got my mouth open to ask her what the plan is when she drops to her knees on the wooden porch. As the motors roar closer to us, she lifts a hatch door. I'm thinking it's not even big enough for a dog to climb inside when she jabs me in the abs with her elbow.

"Get in there!"

"You first."

I watch her ass disappear into the darkness and see her hand jut out. "Come on!" she hisses.

I'm not sure I can fit, but I'm leaner than I used to be, and anyway, it sounds like our pursuers are in the driveway now, so I don't have much choice. I go in feet first, giving Merri a front-seat view of my ass. When I'm in up to my armpits, I feel her arms yank around my waist and I topple back against her. She mutters something.

"Sorry," I hiss.

I'm clawing at the boards that make up part of the porch and also our little shelter's walls, trying to take some of my weight off her, when I hear a car's motor yards away.

Motherfuck. I pull the gun out of my pants with my right hand. I feel Merri move behind me and I want to tell her I've got this, but I'm too afraid to break the silence.

The motor dies. It sounds like just one car. The rest of the cartel has driven on; once their noise fades, a deathly quiet settles. Then I hear a man's voice. He sounds winded.

I figure he's excited about spotting my bike, but instead I realize he's talking into a phone.

"Yes, he is really dead. Yes." There's a brief pause, during which I hear the click of a cigarette lighter. With the gun still in my hand, I train my eyes on the boards to my right, the part of the porch that separates us from our pursuer, but I can't see him. Can only hear him. "Yes, we are hunting them like dogs." Another pause. The man laughs. I smell cigarette smoke. "I don't know about the clinic. It's supposed to be the Virgin's place."

I'm going cross-eyed trying to look through the boards when all of a sudden, I feel Meredith's body shaking against mine. I wish so badly that I could reach my arm back and hold her hand—or something—but it would be stupid to let go of the gun. I turn my body slightly sideways, trying to lean into her, but it doesn't work. We're too cramped. I can't move.

Damnit, she's starting to cry. I can hear her small, wet breaths.

"I got to do a walk around this house," the guy is saying. Pause. "Oh, you want to blow me instead? How about I come over as soon as I'm done here and bring some of my tar?" Another pause. Merri's body is shaking so much now I decide to tuck the gun into my boot. "Then we plot how we will get the power." The man laughs as I turn, with effort, to face Meredith.

"From my cock," I hear the guy say with a chuckle.

With a final glance above me, at the hatch door, and just a breath of nervous hesitation, I wrap my right arm around the woman crouching behind me and bring her head to my shoulder.

She's still shaking. I lean against her, just a little, and she wraps an arm around my waist and buries her face in my throat.

It's okay, Merri. It's okay.

Beneath my concern for the woman I'm supposed to be saving, I'm tense with wondering if the dude will come and find us, but then I hear him say "fuck it," and I hear a stomp that I assume is hombre putting out his cigarette.

Hail Mary, that would be some f-ing awesome luck.

And then his car door slams, the engine purrs, and he drives off.

Merri

I'M STILL SHAKING minutes after Tito drives away, and my savior's arm is still around my back. I squeeze my eyes shut and take a big, deep breath, grateful that I'm not alone in this. I'm grateful for all of half a minute, and then I shove the stranger away.

I reach around him to throw the trap door open, and as soon as the moonlight beams down on us, my terror and fear bubble up, and all of a sudden I'm furious.

"Do you know what you did tonight? You *killed* Jesus!"

The guy frowns, looking pensive as he holds onto the walls to keep his balance in the cramped space. "It's been mentioned."

"Do you know what this means for me? It means I'll never, ever, ever get out of this country in one piece! Neither will you! We're fucked! I'm sorry I don't curse usually, but when there's only one word that works you have to use that word and we are *fucked*! Royally fucked!" I storm up through the trap door and fall onto the porch, belatedly realizing that I'm crying again.

The guy is right behind me. His hand is on my back. I swat it off and stumble to my feet.

"What's your big plan? I hope it involves a helicopter or a tank because otherwise we're going in an unmarked grave!" I cover my face, crying again, almost hysterical. "And the clinic..."

It's my fault. It's all my stupid, selfish fault.

I shove him in the chest. "What's your plan?" Before he can answer, I throw up my hands. "What's your fracking name?"

"You said fracking." His eyebrow arches.

"Yes, I did. So the frack what?"

"I love *Battlestar*."

"I don't see how that matters."

I turn away from him, because all I can think about in this second is that if I'd just gone with Jesus, probably no one would be dead. There's a chance he might have killed me just to make a point, but there's a chance he might not have. Jesus liked me. He might have forgiven me, and there would have been no blood shed. No dead kids. No one in danger.

"It doesn't matter," the guy says with a shrug of his shoulder. "But it's cool."

"Who are you?" I put my hand on my hip. "I want to know, for real this time."

He reaches down into his boot to get the gun, pointing

it at the ground as he raises up to face me again. "Evan. Does that help?"

"Not at all." I slump down on the stairs. "Who do you work for, Evan?"

"I already told you—a company that finds missing people."

And at that, he turns away, scanning the yard for something, then cursing. He lopes down the stairs and through the mess of junk, and I realize as he reaches the bike that the metal piece that holds the front wheel onto the rest of the frame is bent.

"Motherfucking hell."

I'm right behind him, not sure if I'll cry this time or sock him in the nose.

"Can you fix that?" I snap.

I want him to say 'no', to tell me that we're screwed. That we're fracked. I want to give up hope, because it would be so much easier to just give up when I know there really isn't any hope.

Instead, he crouches beside it, running his hand along the metal rod. He flicks a glance at me. "I'm sure I can."

"Of course. What can't you do?"

He grins a little. "Nothing. Actually," he says, as he stands the bike up, "I couldn't slow us down a little while ago without knocking us both off. I'm sorry about that." He looks like he might say something else, but instead he opens a big, leather pack attached to the back of the bike and starts to pull out tools.

That's when I notice something: he doesn't use his left hand—at all. He spreads his tools out on the ground, laying each one down with his right.

The night breeze plays through my hair and my eyes fill up with tears again. How long has it been since I've felt a breeze? Since I've seen the moon without the barrier of a window? I look up at it, feeling so many things, and wondering how long do I have to see it now, before the cartel finds us?

"They'll find us, you know." My voice is barely loud enough to be a whisper. "With Jesus dead, Christina will take over. His sister. She doesn't like me very much anyway, and she won't like you."

"That right?" He glances over his shoulder, holding a tool between his teeth, and I nod.

"You think I'm not likable?"

"You think this is a joke?"

He doesn't answer me. Instead, he looks over his shoulder, at the house. "How did you know about the porch?"

I zip my lips. I know about it because the elderly woman and teenage boy who used to live here were gunned down by Jesus. The teenager robbed one of Jesus's country homes, and the old woman tried to protect him when Jesus came. I was in the back seat of his car at the time, and we'd just been to eat in Torreon. I'm not sure why he decided to stop on that sunny afternoon—maybe because he saw the kid's car or something—but I watched them try to open the trap door as Jesus shot them.

I'm not telling angel that.

Non-angel.

Evan.

I wipe my face and try to sound composed. "Just a lucky guess. Some houses in Mexico have those," I say.

"Is it abandoned?" he asks. He's doing something with his right hand and the bike's wheel bar, something tool-ish. Something maybe with a wrench? I don't know. I'm not mechanical. What I do know is that the left hand is still tucked into his pocket.

"It's empty, but we still shouldn't stay here," I murmur.

"I've almost got this straightened out."

I nod, not that he can see me, and wrap my arms around myself. I wonder if his story is a lie. Working for that bounty hunter company. I've never heard of anything like that, not that I for sure would have, but I might have.

"Is your hand hurt?" I ask as he lifts the bike, again, just with the right hand.

"Happened before this," he mutters. Once the bike is upright, he looks to me. "Could you gather those tools? I can't hold the bike up and do that, too. One hand and all." He mentions the hand too flippantly.

"Okay." I do as he asks, and as I tuck them back into his bag, I say, "Soooo...do you have a plan?"

"Once we make it to the border, we'll be fine. I've got a passport for you."

My stomach twists. "We'll never make it. They'll find us first."

Evan throws his leg over the bike and looks at me from underneath those long eyelashes. "I'm a good shot. Get on."

So I do.

I don't have a choice.

CHAPTER FIFTEEN

CROSS

IT'S HARDER TO drive the Mach with another person on the back. More weight to balance. More pressure on my shoulder.

I'm grateful that she didn't ask more questions back there at that house. My pride won't let me admit that I crashed a bike, and even though that's what most of America thinks—that I got ripped and forgot how to drive—I can't stand to say it out loud. It's just not true. I was pretty drunk, sure, but I wasn't drunk enough to crash. To do that I needed help.

It's weird remembering that with 'Missy King' behind me. Who thought I looked familiar. That had me sweating bullets. I wonder what she'd do if she knew who I really was. Not what she would do—what she *will* do. Because I can't hide myself from her forever.

I just hope she trusts me before that happens.

After we leave the farm house, she directs me to another road, one she says will take us through some rural land, and in the general direction of a city called Parral. After that, she says we should loop around Chihuahua and head for Ciudad Juarez, a border city where Merri says Cientos Cartel doesn't have a lot of sway.

We drive a dusty back road for a while, cutting through what must have, at some point, been cattle farms. I can chart the passage of time in the way the stars and moon cross the sky. It's late—or early, rather. I'm exhausted. I know she is, too.

The road ends and we're bumping over lumpy dirt. Meredith is wearing my helmet, so the sand gets into my eyes. My shoulder aches. My neck feels tight. Finally I swallow my pride and turn around to her.

"Where to?" I ask, like I'm not lost as lost.

She points at a grove of trees maybe two hundred yards ahead. "Don't stop there," she calls over the motor's noise. "Keep going. There's a river back here, I think."

I can tell she's pretty sure, which means she's been here with Jesus Cientos or his goons. I want to know what she went through. But I'm afraid to know, and could never ask, regardless.

Finally I see something sparkling, and we come up on the river, shaded by a cluster of those short, scruffy trees that seem to grow everywhere.

"Stop here," she calls, and I do.

She gets off first; I'm off two seconds later. I tuck my hand into my pocket and take my time unfastening my bike bag while she sits down on a rotten log and folds her arms across her chest.

"So you were really gonna go back to them?" I ask as I spread out a blanket.

"It was my only choice."

"That's pretty damn selfless."

She doesn't reply, just starts picking at her colorless fingernails.

"How long were you with Cientos?"

This time, she flicks her gaze at me, but she doesn't answer. Her green eyes say, *Do you really think I'll talk to you?*

"I'm on your side, you know that right? I chose to take this job, to come find you."

"Do you want a cookie?"

"White chocolate macadamia."

"You're from California."

"That's right." I answer smoothly, even though the comment throws me off. "How could you tell?"

"Your accent."

"Ah." But she's not saying I sound familiar, right? Because I'm now remembering every time I answered the land line when I was in high school and people thought I was my dad. Before she can put my familiar face and familiar voice together, I thrust forward the bag of girl stuff. "For you."

She sits the sack on the ground, beside the water, and takes three steps to the blanket. She lies on it and gazes up at the trees—or rather, the single one in this grove that's tall enough to block our view of the stars. "How do I know you don't work for Priscilla Heat?"

My stomach clenches tightly, but I don't let it show. Instead I frown, like this is preposterous. "Why would you think I work for a porn star?"

"Never mind." She tucks her hair behind her ear and looks down at the blanket, as if seeing it for the first time. "Are we sleeping on this together?"

"I couldn't bring two bags. If you like, I can sleep on the ground."

She shakes her head. "Just stay on your side."

I'm surprised she isn't more leery of me. I wonder if it's my hand, and try to push all the self-loathing away. She's tough. Been through a lot. She can probably tell a good guy from a bad one at this point.

I lie down beside her, looking up, like she is. I want to touch her, but I focus on the sky instead. Silence envelops us—silence and the sounds of water.

"I'm not sorry I killed him," I tell her.

She doesn't reply, and I feel my chest fill up with something warm and unnamable. Concern, I guess it is. Concern that's inappropriate, given who I am and who she is. Given what I knew and didn't do. And still I can't help but say, "I am sorry that this happened to you."

She rolls over, with her back to me. "We need to be up in two hours or so. We'll have to travel farm land until we're past Parral and Delicias, until we're very close to Chihuahua. Otherwise they'll find us. They probably have the police on their side."

"You're kidding."

"Not kidding," she says flatly.

Damn; I really didn't think this through. "You rest. I'll stay up." And figure out how the hell we're going to get out of this.

She never replies, but eventually I hear her breathing even out.

Merri

I KNOW I'M being a bitch. I even feel a little sorry for it. The problem is, I just can't help myself.

When he wakes me up about an hour before sunrise, after only one hour of sleep, I help him re-pack the bag and I try to find some equilibrium. I try to make myself feel human again. To feel sad for the loss of life yesterday, worried for the clinic, excited that I'm free. I try to care about this man who saved me, even if it's just one living creature to another.

But I can't.

Disliking him is easy, because it gives me a mission. It gives me someone else to blame, at least for a little while. Also, it helps me avoid temptation.

Evan is beautiful. Stunningly handsome, and cool under pressure. Reckless, charming, and considerate. He even bought me deodorant. Real deodorant. My favorite brand and second favorite scent, at that. I've basically been putting chalk under my arms for the last year and a half.

Since he likes *Battlestar Galactica*, I know he has good taste in TV, and before we take off on the bike, I find he has good taste in music, too. He's got a small iPod and it's fully charged. He hands me one ear-phone and takes the other for himself, and for the next hour or so, as we poke along at thirty miles an hour, through old, dried up fields, we're serenaded by Neil Young, the Grateful Dead, and Bon Iver.

Bon Iver is what really gets me. I had barely heard of them when I was living in Vegas, but the two or three songs I had heard, I adored.

After an hour or so on the road, I start feeling…weird. It's that particular light-chested feeling I remember from my high school days. From my kissy slut days. And I know what it means.

I'm hyper-aware of my arms around Evan;s hard, warm waist. Of the way his upper body tenses when we hit bumps. I can imagine that at this low speed, it's hard to keep us balanced, especially with that contraption he has for his left arm.

I shut my eyes and remind myself that I'm not sup-posed to worry about him. It's his fault we're in this mess. This was *not* my plan.

But aren't you grateful for it? a little voice inside me asks. *Aren't you glad you didn't have to go back to the car-tel?*

I wonder what it means for me that Jesus is dead It doesn't mean more safety right now, but it might eventual-ly. If Jesus was as humiliated as I think he was by my run-ning away, he might have kept coming after me, even if I made it to America. If he's dead, it all depends on Christi-na. Does she want to waste the resources?

She was one of the select few who knew he was gay. I think she hated me because she hated that he felt he had to hide behind a mistress.

Despite what happened before I ran off, I feel a sort of sadness that he's dead. For all he turned out to be a total sociopath, he wanted to be a school teacher when he was a kid. He was a monster, but in many ways he was good to me—at least for most of the time I was with him. I was one of the few people he could ask for advice about his boyfriends. I remember the last time he bought new cologne. "Which one makes me smell like salvation?"

It just seems impossible that he's dead.

But Evan is right; he shouldn't be sorry for killing Jesus. Jesus was one of the bad guys, and the main thing I feel about his death is relief.

I lay my cheek against Evan's back and shut my eyes, trying to gather my thoughts.

I don't want to go back to my old life in the States. Maybe that's part of why I'm feeling angry at him—Evan. I don't even know if I *can* go back. As long as Priscilla and Jim Gunn are around, I'll never be safe. And then there's Drake. The honorable governor from the state of California. Who thinks I wanted to blackmail him, to ruin him, and who, I assume, didn't mind one bit when Priscilla and Jim Gunn sold me as a sex slave. I have to assume he'd try to get rid of me again.

I tighten my grip a little on the man in front of me. Evan told me his company would protect me, but I have no reason to believe him. Jesus told me once that he would fly me back to America in one of his own helicopters if I stayed with him for five years. But I finally ran away because his actions said otherwise.

The bike hits a bump in the craggy farm road and I head-butt Evan. For half a second, as my butt flies off the warm, leather seat, my hands loosen their grip on his waist. When I grab him again, I realize one of my hands is on his crotch.

I scramble to move it, but not before a pleasant burst of warmth kindles in my stomach. I turn my head so I'm looking out at fields and not at Evan, and I inhale deeply a few times, reminding myself that I don't want a man again. Not really. I'm like one of the Sisters. The physical attraction is there, of course, when the guy is hot like this one is, but my heart isn't available.

Even so, I wonder, as we cut through a field at the edge of a trash dump site, what this man thinks of me.

Does he think that I'm a whore? That I had sex with the whole cartel? Does he think that I deserved what I got? He doesn't seem to know about the governor, so that's a point in my favor. I was a married man's mistress. Even though I was young and stupid and broke...it's not something I'm proud of. Not at all.

We're getting near the outskirts of Parral now. I know this area. The police in Parral could never be bought, and Jesus had some childish delight in travelling into their territory. Sometimes just to get an ice-cream cone.

If we can take little country roads around Parral and get to Camargo, we could stop for the night somewhere safe.

The sun is directly overhead now, meaning it's taken us at least an hour or two longer than normal to travel the distance that we've traveled. Between the music and my rambling thoughts, it doesn't feel like a long time, but I've gotten sunburned. I can feel it on my scalp and my forearms. Evan seems to be feeling the strain of our rough terrain and slow speed, too. His torso will twitch occasionally, the way muscles do when they're about to give out, and I can feel him breathing hard sometimes. When we reach a small grove at the edge of our current field, I rub his back and lean close to his ear.

"STOP HERE FOR A MINUTE!"

We each guzzle bottles of water from Evan's bag, and he offers me some beef jerky.

"Sorry I don't have any sunscreen." He's got his hand out near my face, like he wants to touch it, but he doesn't.

I just shrug.

Sometimes at the clinic we gave the poorer children tubes of sunscreen. I think about Sister Mary Carolina and my eyes sting.

In a matter of minutes, we're back on the road. I spend the next two hours crying on and off, thinking about how much I'm going to miss the Sisters and my kids. Wondering who I'll have to care about now. Praying they're okay, that the cartel didn't hurt them. I have to believe that they're okay.

Through a series of elaborate elbow tugs and shouts, I direct Evan to a tiny dirt road. It's been so long time since I've been here, I'm a little worried that my sense of direction is off, but then I see the little cemetery to my right and I know it won't be too much longer. Maybe a mile, tops.

My scalp stings, and I have to squint into the afternoon sun. I see two enormous cacti a few feet to the left of the road, and my heart trips. I tug Evan's right arm and lean my lips up near his ear. "We're stopping up here! Take a right beside those rocks over there and follow the path through the weeds."

Evan looks curious, and I nod at the rocks. "Trust me," I tell him.

He nods once and speeds up.

The house we're going to should be a total secret. It's partway built under a dirt mound, with only small parts of stucco showing, and they blend in with the dirt.

This was one of Jesus's love nests. I know about it only because, in the months I spent as his beard, he took me here a few times for a long weekend—a weekend he really spent with his lover, David.

David Perez. He was a short guy, buff with a shaved head and a half-moon tattoo on his left arm. I liked him okay until the last week I was with Jesus. After that, I hated him.

As we round the corner and get to the house, Evan gasses the bike and I hold on tighter. Even if this is the most we'll ever touch, it's nice to be close to a man this attractive for a little while.

I'm thinking lustful thoughts when we near the mound, and David steps out from behind a small tree and points a pistol at us.

CHAPTER SIXTEEN

CROSS

MEREDITH'S ARMS TIGHTEN around my waist, and she yells, "Go!" But it's too late.

We're going so slow that when I gas the bike, I can't maintain our balance and we fall to the right. I catch us with my leg and balance the weight of the bike and our bodies as I reach for the gun, then realize I can't hold the handlebar with my right hand *and* grab the gun.

Fuck!

"EVAN, GO!" she screams, and I want to go, I want to get her out of here so fucking bad, but I'm too late.

The bald dude with the gun is walking toward us as I try to push off with my leg and get us vertical enough that I can gas it without falling over. I try for half a second, which is as long as I need to know that I can't pull it off. I jerk my left hand out of its support system and yell, "Grab the handlebars!"

Meredith does, and I get my gun and fire a shot at homeboy's hip. It grazes him, and he shoots the bike's front tire.

"Shit!" Merri is off the bike, running, I assume until I

feel her grabbing my left arm. "Come on!" she shrieks, and our friend shoots again. The bullet clears my blue jeans, then the tank, missing skin and bone by no more than an inch. I fumble off the bike and throw it in the direction of our friend with the gun.

He lets out a howl, and it's only then I realize that he doesn't look quite sane. His bald head, gleaming in the sun, is scraped and scratched: fingernail marks. I made the same ones on my own skin when I tried to kick the Dilaudid. His face is streaked with tears. He howls again and shoots at Merri, to my left.

"Fuck!" I yank her forward and lead her around the dirt mound, tugging her behind me, "Are you okay?" She must be, because she's running and I don't see blood.

Our would-be killer screams as he fires more shots. They're wild, but I push Meredith in front of me just in case. We round the dirt mound, out of sight for a moment, but I can tell from his screams that he's getting close.

Jesus, I'm so out of shape. Fucking accident. I was stupid. Can't do this with one hand.

A close shot makes me jump; Meredith stumbles. She cries out as red blooms across her right shoulder. I rush her from behind, scooping her up with my right arm and throwing her over my shoulder, realizing belatedly that she's a sitting duck behind me, so I shift her to my front and hug her to me with my arm.

"Hold on," I yell into her ear. "I've got to shoot again!"

I find him in the narrow, jolting frame of vision over my shoulder. I aim for his throat but I'm running and firing backwards, so the shot goes wild. He somehow manages to shoot—

SHIT! I wait for pain that doesn't come, then look down and understand: It's my left hand. The fucker is spurting blood, but I can't feel it. Whatever.

He gets in one more shot, a crazy shot he fires with crazy eyes, and as he does I notice the handle of vodka sticking out of his pants pocket. I spot a bush and throw Merri behind it, and as I do, the bullet lodges in the sole of my shoe. I can tell because the bottom of my foot feels hot and I can feel a bump. I take one step toward him, aim, and fire two quick shots at his leg. The first misses. The second hits the bottle, shattering it. The man screams and falls to the ground, and I put two more shots in his head.

They're grizzly, disgusting shots, and the fallout is something I'll be seeing in nightmares. Merri shrieks, then comes zipping toward me like a beautiful, girl bullet. She throws her arms around me and says, "Oh my God, oh my God, oh my God oh my God he's dead! You killed David! That's Jesus's boyfriend. Oh my God."

Jesus's *boyfriend*?

"Evan, we need to move his body! Your gun is loud! Someone might have heard!"

"Yeah."

"OH MY GOD, YOUR HAND!"

Merri grabs my left arm, and I flinch, not because it hurts but because it's weird when people touch it. It makes me feel...uncomfortable. But she doesn't let go. She gets a death grip on my wrist and holds the hand up to inspect.

It's a bloody mess, but it looks like the bullet punched out that little flap of skin between my thumb and forefinger. I've studied the anatomy of the hand enough in the last six months to know it's bleeding heavily because the radial artery is nearby. I'm feeling dizzy, but it doesn't hurt. I use my right hand to steal my left one out of Merri's grasp and whirl her around so I can see the back of her right shoulder.

"He got you, too."

I want to rip her shirt away so I can really see the wound, but I can't do that one-handed...not unless I use my mouth to hold her collar steady.

"It was just a graze," she says, fingering the bloody spot. The circle of blood hasn't grown much larger than a teacup saucer, but.. "You've been shot before?"

"Of course," she mutters. She turns to face me with her hands on her hips again. The look on her face is somehow a mix of gentle, frustrated, and sad. "Can you help me move the body? I don't think there's anywhere good to hide him out here, but I'll open the back door and we can leave him in the laundry room."

"The back *door*?" I frown at the dirt mound, and that's when I realize... "That's a house!"

"Yeah." She winces as she moves her right arm. Then she shocks me by pulling off her shirt.

Holy Jesus H.

If I was dizzy before, I almost pass out when I see her creamy skin. My eyes jet to her huge tits, spilling out of a silky-looking sky blue bra, and travel down her soft, slim belly to the waist of her pants. Oh fucking hell, I want to kiss her there. She looks so soft.

She steps closer to me, sending my adrenaline boner into overdrive, and rips the shirt in half, using one half of it to wrap around my hand, right where the gunshot was.

"Will this hurt?" she asks, looking into my eyes before she ties it.

"I can't feel the hand."

"Well that's a good thing." She's breathing heavily as she ties it. I brush her hair off her forehead to check her eyes.

"I'm not in shock," she says. She touches my cheek. "Are you?"

"I don't think so. I don't need your help with David, either. I can drag him in if you open the door." I might need her help, but I won't take it. I can't stand the thought of this beautiful woman touching a corpse.

"Are you sure? 'Cause I don't mind."

I nod. "I'm sure."

"You need to keep that left hand elevated. When we get inside I'll sterilize and do a proper bandage."

I nod, because my head has started hurting and I'm feeling kind of off.

"The back door is right here." She points to what looks like regular dirt, then lifts a tiny, dirt-colored plastic flap and punches in a code. Some dirt falls away, revealing a plastic-ish, dirt-orange door. She opens it somehow—I can't see from where I'm standing—and I turn to get the body.

I try not to look at him as I grab one of his legs, using all my strength to drag him through the square doorway. I'm hoping Merri's gone further inside, but she's right there as soon as I stumble through the door. She presses something on the wall, the way you might with a garage door, and I can hear the door sliding shut as we maneuver the dead guy into the first room on the right.

It's a surprisingly normal looking laundry room with a stacked washer/dryer combo, a little brown rug, a shelf of laundry supplies, and a framed photo of two men embracing, holding martini glasses.

Merri and I settle the dead guy face-down on the rug, and my gaze returns to the framed photo. The bald guy at our feet is smiling in the arms of a well-worked-out Hispanic man with shoulder-length hair and a Hollywood-worthy smile.

"That's him," I mutter. The infamous Jesus Cientos.

Merri nods.

I glance down at the floor, where blood is pooling. "This shit is weird."

She nods and grabs a towel off a shelf.

"Let's go out into the hall now." She leads the way, lightly touching my back as I step by her. Then she stuffs the towel underneath the door.

CHAPTER SEVENTEEN

Merri

THE INSIDE OF this place looks just how I remember, which is not really a surprise. Jesus and I picked out most of the décor online. From Pottery Barn, of all places. It was shipped to an empty building in Camargo, the next town over, and Jesus and David loaded it into a truck and brought it here and set the place up themselves, one weekend when Jesus pretended to be away with me. I stayed in the basement suite all weekend, cross-stitching some pillows Jesus wanted for the guest room and feeling buried alive. The basement of an underground bungalow feels really, really underground.

When I snap out of my memories and look at Evan, I find him holding out one of Jesus's freshly laundered wife beaters. He's holding onto it with a dryer sheet because his hands are painted red. I wonder when he picked it up.

I slip the shirt on while he casts his eyes back at the door, and then I lead him into the half-bath behind the next door down. We wash our hands with pear-scented soap from Bath and Body Works.

Evan seems to be breathing hard. He looks kind of

wide-eyed and is moving slowly. I wonder what the odds are that he was wrong earlier, and he really is in shock, but then I brush the thought away. This is his job.

Still, when we walk back into the hallway, I look him up and down and ask, "Are you okay?"

This makes him laugh. I laugh a little too. "Stupid question I guess."

"Thanks for asking," he says.

I'm leading him down the hallway, past the wine cellar and into the mouth of the kitchen, where I'm slightly amused to see surprise transform his face.

His blue eyes are wide. "Am I hallucinating?"

"Nope." I pull out a chair at the weathered, white-washed breakfast table and move one of the blue and white breakfast mats so he doesn't get it dirty; old habits die hard. "Have a seat, I'll get the first aid stuff."

Jesus's love nest is half underground, and it's got central air. It feels good in here—probably seventy-three degrees, Jesus's preferred temperature—and the refrigerator is appropriately cold, so the antibiotic shots are still in good condition.

I find the first aid kit in one of the cabinets near the stainless steel refrigerator. There's an additional briefcase full of surgical supplies in the pantry. When I get back to the breakfast area, Evan has his right elbow on the table and his face propped in his hand.

Despite the shell I've tried to build around myself, I feel a bubble of concern form in my throat. Maybe it's the way he put himself between David's bullets and me. I was running so hard I almost didn't notice, but I glanced behind me and there he was, with both arms out. I don't care who you are or what your job is, that's pretty heroic.

He doesn't move as I approach the table, so I get the perfect chance to really look at him. His shoulders are so wide, it's almost a little ridiculous, like he might be wearing football pads—except of course he's not. Beneath his sweaty, blood-splattered black t-shirt, I can see every ripple of muscle, from the exaggerated roundness of his shoulders to that delicious indention that runs down his spine between smooth slabs of muscle. I'm checking out the bicep of his left arm, wondering how he keeps it so in shape if that hand can't move, when I notice a wicked-looking scar along his collar-line.

I've rehabbed enough kids to know that it's a surgical scar. Because I'm curious, I come up behind him and put my hands on his shoulders. This does freaky things to all my girly parts, and then he moans and I'm pretty much slayed right where I stand.

"I'm sorry," he says hoarsely. It's half-chuckled, like maybe he's embarrassed by his reaction.

"Don't be sorry." His back feels warm and hard through the soft, damp shirt, and his shoulders are super tense. I give them a squeeze, and I'm rewarded with another moan, this one deeper than the last. I swear, I can feel it vibrate way low down in my belly. He's practically lying on the table now, his head resting on his forearm so I can drink in all I want of his satiny dark brown hair and those strong shoulders, that lean, tough back. Just above the waist of his jeans, his shirt is stuck to his skin, so I get a peek of the top of his underwear. The skin they cover looks so soft and smooth... I can only see an inch of it—

Ridiculous.

I direct my wandering eyes back to his scar as I work his trapezius muscles. I see not just one scar, but several. One vertical along his cervical spine, just above where I think his C4-C6 ought to be, and another perpendicular to that, going from the middle of his spine at what I think is C5 level and heading around to the left side of his neck. The scars are thick. Still pink. This must be how he lost the use of his hand.

As I knead his shoulders and he makes delicious sounds, I wonder why on earth anyone would send him on a mission alone to rescue someone from a Mexican cartel. Sure, there are bad-ass seeming things about him, but twice we've crashed on the bike because he can't balance us with his left arm.

Don't get me wrong—I'm grateful. At this point, enough has happened that I'm grateful for Evan's help. I just don't really understand the situation.

I'm still hard at work on his shoulders when I notice the red pool under his left hand, which is lying on the table.

"Evan!" He shoots up so fast his head hits mine. "Ouch." I rub my sore nose.

He turns to face me. "What's wrong?"

Still covering my nose, I nod at his hand. "You're bleeding." I blush so furiously, I feel like there's a cloud of heat around my head. Sure, it's been a while since I've been around a guy, but this level of oblivion really is embarrassing. Unforgivable. What's wrong with me?

"Hold your arm up," I tell him.

He does, and I take a seat beside him with the first aid stuff in hand.

I grab his left elbow, which is propped against the table, causing him to lean a little closer toward me. I scoot closer to him, too. With my hand around his bicep, I look into his blue eyes.

"So you have no feeling in your hand?" He blinks, and I take that as affirmative. "What about your arm?"

"The bicep up," he says without expression.

"Okay, that's good, because you would feel some of this in your wrist and forearm I think."

I let go of him and clean my hands with alcohol towelettes, then untie my bloody shirt scrap and reveal his wound again. It looks darker red this time, which means some of the blood is finally clotting.

"I don't think it hit anything important."

The radial artery runs into the hand, and its location in the wrist is not too far from where Evan's wound is—but if he'd hit it, there would be even more blood. At least I think that's true.

I open then unfold two big gauze pads and gently guide his hand down onto them. Instead of spreading out, his fingers stay semi-curled. I study his hand for just a second, admiring the shape of it, before I notice him scowling.

I have the strangest desire to tell him, *You have nice hands*, but that would just be weird, so I swallow once and try to keep this as professional as I can.

"I'm going to spread your fingers out the way I want them, okay?"

He shrugs, trying to look unaffected. "Do whatever you want." His lips quirk up. "As long as I can get another back rub."

I smile a little as I work his fingers into the position

that I want them, with thumb and forefinger in an "L" shape.

Evan huffs his breath out as I let go of him and unwrap some Betadine swabs. I glance into his eyes, offering another little smile. "You ready?"

His face is hard. "Go for it."

I swab around the wound, glancing into his eyes a time or two to be sure it isn't hurting. He looks apathetic. I wonder if he feels the ghost of pain, but as I finish painting the entire wound with orange Betadine, I decide that maybe he's self-conscious.

I lie his hand down again, and when I'm looking into my lap, fiddling with the antibiotic syringe, I ask, "Are your injuries recent?"

After a small pause, he says, "Fairly."

So I'm right. He sounds detached, and when I look back up, I find him staring at the wall ahead of us.

I put my hand on his wrist. "I have to give you a shot in the wound, because I think you might have some bone fragments floating around in there. That means you have a greater chance of infection."

He shrugs again, his face caught somewhere between stoic and irritated. "Okay."

"When you get home, you might need a cast or something."

He snorts, as if to say, *Yeah right.*

I make quick work of the injection, and when I'm finished, I set the syringe to the side and start applying bandages. I'm starting with something that has some sticky to it, so while it's soft over the wound, it adheres to the skin around it, keeping out germs and water. It seems to take me forever to get that on. He can't help me by holding his fingers straight, and when I ease his arm up, with his elbow on the table, the hand flops forward. He stiffens again.

I'm not much for awkward moments, so I decide to be straightforward. "This makes you uncomfortable, huh?"

He screws his face up, looking at me like I'm slow. "I can't feel it."

I flit a glance at him. "That's not what I mean."

Out of the corner of my eye, I can see him working his jaw, and I wonder if I've crossed a line. Then I remember him saying, "I'm sorry that this happened to you," last night before I went to sleep. I didn't want his pity, and maybe he doesn't want my prodding either, but we're stuck together for at least another day, so tough titties.

"I'm saying you feel awkward about it. You don't like being injured."

"Would you?" His mouth draws tight.

"I wouldn't," I say. "I'm sure almost no one would." I wrap my way around the hand a few more times as I think about my own screwed up state. "No one wants to be anything less than strong and capable. Vulnerable means you have to trust other people. If you're anything like me, you don't like that one bit."

"Damn straight," he mutters, and I smile a little.

"May I ask what happened?"

"You can ask," he tells me. His mouth is pulled into a smirk, but it looks strained.

"And if I ask, will you tell?"

He mulls that over, then he says, "Maybe we can make a trade."

Oh, crap. I guess I walked right into this. I tie the

gauze off and keep my poker face on, hoping he'll forget I asked.

"Keep that elevated. I'll be back with some ice." I saunter off, remembering as I approach the refrigerator that I have my own wound to attend to. I guess he'll have to do that.

When I get back, he's getting to his feet, opening an alcohol towelette as he moves. "It's your turn."

While he cleans the small spot on my shoulder, I pick at the place mat and think about how weird it is to be here without Jesus and David. How weird it is that they're both dead. Then I think about the last week I spent with them, in Mazatlán, at Jesus's favorite costal mansion, and I feel nauseated.

It's really good that Evan breaks the silence. "Does anyone else know about this place?" he asks.

"I'm not sure. It's a big secret that Jesus was gay, and apparently he's been with David for quite a while. They'd been together about a year when I left, and since David was here today, I have to assume they were still together when you shot Jesus. This place was built the year before I met Jesus, and as far as I know, the only other people who know it's here are the three guys who built it."

"So we need to get moving," he sighs.

"No. Jesus killed them."

"Oh."

I heave my breath out. "Right. So Jesus brought me in to help him with some things, and of course David, but I d be surprised if anyone else knew."

"How sure are you about that?"

"I don't know." I freeze. "Why?"

"Just wondering." Something cold trails across the wound on my shoulder. I feel his breath on me, and I can tell he's not just wondering. There's a reason that he asked. I'm opening my mouth to ask him what that reason is, when abruptly he squeezes my shoulder. "All done." And that's the end of it.

CHAPTER EIGHTEEN

CROSS

I CAN'T DECIDE if my sixth sense, doom and gloom par-
anoia bullshit is a headache coming on, or something more.
I guess for the first time ever, I hope it's a headache. I take
a seat at the table and watch as Merri cleans up the first aid
stuff. I should be helping her, but my neck feels so tight, I
want to do whatever I can to try to relax.

I rub my eyes and tell her, "Thanks for patching me
up."

"Same to you." She smiles, and I find myself smiling
back.

"You know, we still need to make our trade."

"We need to find some food first," she says. "Aren't
you starving?"

I'm not, but I nod anyway. Ever since the accident, my
appetite hasn't been the same. I think the feeding tube
messed it up. My shrink at NVIR thought it was a nervous
reaction.

"Do you think there's food here?"

"I know there is," she says. "Food and wine. Ammo.
Jesus had this place well-stocked."

I frown down at the table. It's weird the way she talks about Jesus. So...neutrally. Like she's talking about her cousin or something. It makes more sense now that I know he never fucked her, but it's still weird. Dude committed horrible crimes, and she doesn't even sound like she dislikes him.

"You up for some wine?" she asks.

I haven't had any alcohol since the night I crashed. It used to conflict with the meds, and then I guess I just never had a reason. But right now I feel like I could really use a drink.

"You gonna pop the cork?" I ask her.

I lean over my shoulder to see what she's doing, and my neck zings a little.

She's got a loaf of homemade-looking bread out, and she's spreading something on it that looks like jelly.

"If I still remember how," she says. "I haven't had a drink in more than a year."

She looks so pretty right now, seems so normal, it's hard to imagine her with Jesus.

She finishes the bread and pulls out something else—beef jerky—which she sits on the table. Then she disappears, returning a moment later with a bottle of merlot and two jewel-encrusted wine glasses.

"The bread and jam are homemade. The merlot is local, too."

I snort. "What a hostess."

"Hey, I don't have to share." With some difficulty she pulls the cork, and my vision doubles as I watch her pour. She takes a small sip and sighs. "I'm just trying to be informative. It's my go-to, stressed-out mode, I guess."

"Is stressed all you're feeling?"

She laughs, but it's strained. "It's a good bit more than stressed. Honestly, it's too much for me to even begin deal with." She takes another sip of her wine. "So I feel pretty good at this moment. The wine...could be crap and it would still be good."

"Is that true for the company?" I joke, and she pretends to consider.

"It's not the worst thing about this situation," she says.

"Nice." I take a large drink of the wine. It's velvety, with a hint of molasses and a taste of plum, but like she said, it's been a while.

I rub my eyes, take the bread she hands me, and say, "I shot a lot of people you knew."

She purses her lips and just sits there, staring at her plate. I can tell she's fighting tears, and I think to myself, what the hell is wrong with me? Impulsively, I touch her arm. "I'm sorry. I shouldn't have asked. This whole thing is fucking weird—"

"Can you say frack please?"

"Huh?"

"Say frack." She wipes her eyes and speaks from behind the shield of her hand. "I really hate the F-word."

"Sorry," I say quickly. "My mom's Catholic, so I should know better."

She shakes her head. "It's not for anything like that. My aunt taught me it was tacky."

"*Taaaaaccky.*" I say it with what I think is a convincing drawl, and she shrugs.

"Ooooookay. You can make fuuun of myyyy aceeeeent all you wannnnt."

I swallow back some of my wine and watch her eat. I'm like a fracking cat. Curiosity is killing me. I need to know more about this woman—now.

"I was in a motorcycle accident." There. I said it. I shift in my seat, automatically searching for a position that will lessen the painful zinging of the damaged nerve endings in my neck. "Fallout was pretty bad and I was laid up for a while."

She considers me over the rim of her glass. I can feel her eyes urging me to go on. I take a long sip of my wine, hoping it will take the edge off my zings. "What do you want to know, Mer?"

"What happened to your neck?"

"I fu— fracked up the posterior joint, like pretty bad. Fractured C3, C5, and C6. Those are vertebrae near the top of the spine but you probably know that." She nods. "Couple of herniated discs around that area and a facet fracture."

Her eyes are wide, but to her credit, she doesn't bust out with something asinine or overly pitying. She bites her lip and says, "That sucks."

"I was in a coma for a little while after."

Again, her green eyes pop. "Really? But you look so...good."

That gets a laugh out of me. "Good genes."

"Good *luck*," she says, chewing some bread. "Really, though, it's a wonder you're alive."

I nod. "I had a stroke, too."

"What?!"

I scrub my hand over my eyes. Why the frack am I telling her all this?

She's looking at me with sadness, but it doesn't feel

like pity.

"I got moved from one place to another. Like a rehab place, to another rehab. When you're moving people who have head injuries, or I guess any kind of injury that's bad enough, sometimes their blood pressure goes up." I take a swig of wine and force myself to meet her eyes again. This is so personal, it's hard to get it all out, even though the facts are pretty straightforward. "If they get in too much during the transport...strokes can happen."

Her mouth twists. "That's awful."

I shrug, then feel like I'm bragging. Why am I telling her this? "I wasn't awake or anything like that, but sometimes I think I remember it. I just get this feeling... Kind of like dread or...I don't know, doom or something. I think maybe I can remember...almost dying."

She's chewing again, beef jerky this time, carrying on with her meal like she talks about these things every day. I heave a deep breath. I'm sweating. I feel awkward. Like I shared too much. Because I did share too much. I take another gulp of my wine and wish that I was Nightcrawler from *X-Men*. I could vanish in a poof.

I'm not looking at her, but I can see her out of the corner of my eye, and she looks calm and unperturbed. Just a girl eating. She says, "That must be weird. And awful. I bet no one can relate. That's an experience hardly anyone has had."

I nod, and it occurs to me that hers is too.

"I can't picture you as a sex slave." *Oh fuck.* Did I just say that? I squeeze my eyes shut. Drop my head into one hand. "Shit. I'm sorry."

"Uh-uh." She swallows some of her own wine. "Don't

be sorry. You just spilled your stuff, so I think we're being honest now. And while we're being honest, thank you. For today. I noticed that you got between David and me."

I shrug. "You waited for me to get off the bike before you ran. You grabbed my arm to help me off. Remember?"

She nods. "It was no big deal." She takes a bite of bread, then says, "And as far as the sex slave thing, I wasn't really a sex slave in the sense most people think. You know, since Jesus was gay. I was just a beard for him, most of the time." She says it so naturally, I almost miss the flare in her eyes when she says 'most of the time'.

I want to know everything that happened to her, and I want to know right now. But it's not my story to take. And I'm not drunk enough to go there.

"It was a lucky break," she says. "I guess. I mean, if there's something lucky about being sold, it would probably be being sold to someone who only wants you for appearances."

"Like my hand." I hold up my gun-shot palm and make a *bullshit* face. "When I think about this, I feel lucky."

She makes a *bullshit* face back at me, then sticks out her tongue. "I'm just trying to look at the bright side."

"Maybe sometimes there isn't one."

She looks down at her beef jerky. "Maybe."

I feel ashamed. I rub the back of my neck and try to move our conversation back on track. "So no one knew? About Jesus?"

She shook her head. "No. He screwed his way through most of the women in Mexico before he 'settled down' with me."

I close my eyes, because the zing is back. It shoots down my neck and through my bicep, down into my fingers. Damn.

"Are you okay?"

I flip my eyes open and try to lie. "Yeah. For sure. Just tired."

"We should go to sleep, I guess. Or try to."

I sit up straighter, ignoring the hell fire blazing down my arm. "Any ideas about when and how to leave without drawing attention from our friends?" I ask her. "I don't know if I can fix the bike this time."

She nods. "I have this fuzzy memory of Jesus having a garage somewhere in here. He should have a dirt bike. Possibly even a car. And there's a garage nearby where he keeps trucks. You know, like transfer trucks, for moving cargo." She scrunches up her face. "Drugs and guns."

"Okay. Well good to know."

"I wouldn't want to go to the garage because I bet they have that guarded, but if we're lucky, nobody knows about this place."

Jesus, there's that word again. Lucky.

Maybe if I'm *lucky*, I can dip into the wine cellar and dull some of my pain before the neuralgia takes my ass down to the ground. It's not something I'd ever do in normal life, but then back in California, it's okay to spend a day or two flat on my back.

"I hope we're lucky," I tell her.

Merri

THIS GUY IS a surprise.

When we met, I bought the whole bounty hunter thing hook-line-and-sinker. He seemed exactly as he presented himself. Chill. Secret agent or whatever.

But now— He's had a stroke. He's in his twenties, and he had a stroke. That's crazy. Crazy *bad*. And I feel drawn to the crazy. It makes me feel less like an oddity.

And then he said that thing about being lucky, and I have to admit, it kind of ripped my heart in half. He seemed so...bitter. Sad. But it wasn't like he was bitter at someone. It was more like he was bitter with himself. I could feel some serious self-loathing coming from him.

I show him to one of the two guest rooms—the one done in a nautical theme—and when I close the door and go to the one across the hall, I find myself wanting to talk to him more. Not just to find out more of his story, but because my own story feels so heavy tonight.

The room I've picked for myself was done in several shades of brown and beige and cream, with lots of textures: suede, leather, cotton, linen. The rugs are soft. The curtains on the fake-out windows dance gently in the air coming from the air vents. I turn a full circle, taking stock of every inch of the room. Not one thing has changed. I step into the en suite bathroom, and there's the old claw-footed tub. The bear-skin rug (the one that's really a bear's skin). The cabinet.

I take two slow steps forward, and open the cabinet with shaking fingers. And there it is. My old toothbrush, from the last time I was here. The one and only time I wasn't in the basement. It's pink and purple, with a tube of my favorite sensitive toothpaste on the shelf beside it.

I snatch the robe and gown out of the cabinet and dash back to the bed. I yank the covers down and climb beneath them and I think about my toothbrush in the bathroom and I start to cry. I cry because one time, I was almost happy here. In the basement, there's a box of books Jesus ordered me. Second-hand books from a used bookstore online, and when Jesus and I came here so he could meet David, I would lie in bed and read all weekend. And my life sucked so much then, I was able to fool myself into feeling almost happy.

I think about my sweet kids at the clinic and I really sob, because that truly did feel almost perfect but it was never meant to last. And now I'm gone! I'm not in Jesus's world and I'm not helping anyone and there's nowhere for me in America and I'm no one! I'm never anyone for long enough to figure out who I am and nothing stays the same, no one can ever make it right—it's just me. Like a fish living in a sand box or on a table. I don't know what my version of water is, but I know I'm never in it. I can never get myself straight. I'm not even a real person, and it hurts worse now that I don't have the children or the Sisters or even Jesus to buy me used books.

I'm pathetic.

I just want to go to sleep.

I cry and cry and cry and cry, until I feel like my insides have turned to liquid. I think of Sean and the tears slow down. I think of family back in Georgia and I can't feel much of anything. Soon I'm just lying there on my back, staring at the canopy, and I find myself thinking about Evan again.

The way his face looked when he said he felt lucky.

I don't feel lucky either. That's my secret.

I want to feel lucky, and I want to be grateful, and I want to be thankful for the breaks I've had, but instead I just feel lost.

I'm hugging my pillow when I hear moaning.

CHAPTER NINETEEN

Merri

I FOLLOW THE sound to Evan's door and when I get there, I'm not sure what to do. Is he having some kind of nightmare? I knock lightly, but the moaning doesn't stop. I try the door, and it's locked.

"Evan?"

I'm answered with a moaned word I can't understand.

I knock there times, hard and loud. "Evan, are you okay? It's Meredith."

I pause, weirded out that I gave him my real name. For a long time, I went by Missy and then I was Merri at the convent.

"Evan?"

My whole body tenses as I wait for him to answer. Finally he does: "'M okay. Jus' sleepin'." But I can hear him making some other kind of sound, the kind of sound weight-lifters make at the Olympics when they're trying to lift like two tons.

I open my mouth to say *No you're not sleeping*, but I remember there's no reason to be talking through the door. Evan's bedroom has another entrance. Because this is the room Jesus built for other pleasure slaves: the kind who, occasionally, would pass through here before being routed to another market—often European. Male slaves. So the en suite bathroom is a bridge between the guestroom and Jesus and David's quarters.

Just as I step back to turn and go the other way, I hear another awful moan, followed by the rustling of bedding.

"Evan? What's wrong?"

He doesn't answer, and that really bothers me.

I take off running toward Jesus's door before I realize I won't be able to get in. I don't have the code for that. Frack!

I run a few steps back toward Evan's room before I think to check—just see. Maybe David left the thing open. I run a few dozen yards down and SCORE. The door is cracked.

I've only seen the room once, and I don't bother to see if it still looks the same, or what is in it. I fly into the massive, kingly bathroom, unlatch the door to Evan's room, and burst inside like a marauder.

I don't know what I was expecting, but what I see isn't it. Evan is lying on the floor, curled over on his side, clawing his left hand with his right one and banging the back of his head into the three- or four-inch space between the floor and the bottom of the low-slung bed frame. His eyes are squeezed shut, his teeth are clenched, and he's breathing like someone who's in a lot of pain.

I close the space between us and drop down on my knees. I stare into his twisted face, realizing that the dark stuff on his lips isn't a wine stain; it's actual blood. He bites into the lip again, and I clamp my hand over my own mouth.

"Evan..." I whisper. "What happened?"

He doesn't make a move to open his eyes, only lifts his face just a little and draws his left arm up to his chest. The fingers of his right hand claw at his forearm; it's already lined with deep red scratches.

He moans again, and turns his head so the sweat on his forehead and face glistens in the low globe lights embedded in the ceiling. Another moan, one that sounds less human, followed by some more deep breathing. When he exhales, the sound seems like it's coming from the bottom of his lungs.

"Evan?"

"Sorry," he moans.

He curls over more tightly into himself and brings his right arm behind his head, pushing down against the back of his skull. He whimpers, and I'm pretty sure I'm going crazy watching this.

My hands are itching to touch him, itching to smooth his hair and find out where he's hurting, but I'm scared to hurt him more.

I shut my eyes as low, hoarse sounds of anguish come from his throat. He's tugging at his hair now, flexing the fingers of his left hand—the one he said he couldn't move. He lets out a bunch of little moans, like someone's hurting him and he just can't get away. Then he pants some more, and I get on my knees and move around him, looking for something to explain this.

"Evan, can you talk to me? I want to help you."

"Can't," he grits out.

"Was it the alcohol?"

He presses the palm of his right hand against his forehead, opening his mouth more so he can breathe more deeply. "It's the...wreck."

His eyes screw shut, and I'm astonished to see tears slip down his cheeks. He gathers his knees up near his chest and bites his lip again, and I'm positive I've never seen anything more painful-looking in my life.

I take my own deep breath, sitting up on my heels beside him. "You don't mean this wreck, do you? You mean the one before. The one where you hurt your neck."

He sucks back a half-sobbed breath. "It's the nerves."

He grits his teeth and his body trembles as both of his hands make fists. I shut my eyes and try to process what he's saying. I'm not a doctor or a nurse, but I know the spine is made of vertebrae, the bones; discs; joints; and nerves. When you damage bones and discs and joints, the nerves can get pinched and damaged.

"Does this happen a lot?"

His breathing is faster now, like he's building to something, and I wonder if he's going to hyperventilate.

"Can I get you pain meds? I think there are some here."

His eyes flip open. "No," he growls.

His words sound almost slurred, but his eyes hold onto mine until I nod. "Okay. I won't if you don't want it."

And it's like while he was speaking to me, the pain caught up with him, because he's covering his face and breathing really loudly again now.

"Evan, I want to help."

"You...can't." He's panting, and his face is so pale, I wonder if he might pass out.

"What do you do to help the pain?"

He swallows, and there's a faint shake of his head, followed by an awful moan.

"How long does this last?"

He claws at his face, then starts to pull his hair again. "Day...or so."

I almost fall over. A whole day. That...can't be real.

"Can I do anything for you? Help you to the bed? Do you want me to rub your back? I do massage sometimes. On children who've been injured. I've helped with pain management before..." and one of the key components is to do a few different stimulating things at once.

"Will it hurt you if I touch you?"

"No...worse," he pants. His eyes slide open just long enough to meet my own.

"I've got an idea," I say.

CROSS

I'M VAGUELY AWARE that I'm walking through a room and Merri is holding me around the waist. I'm shaking pretty bad and leaning heavily on her. We come into a bathroom and the black tile is cool on my feet. I'm leaning over, looking down my legs. My left hand burns like a billion needles from the gunshot wound. I spread my fingers wider because the pain of the gunshot is better than the agony coming from my neck.

Pretty soon I get a bolt of pain that makes my knees give out and I'm on the floor again, but she's urging me toward this big room. It's a shower. Big shower room. The tile is cold on my face. I think I like it. There's water. Don't like the water. Then her hands. Those hands on my neck. God, my back. Those hands know what the story is.

Cold water. Hot water.

"Jus' keep rubbing."

Merri

I WORK HIS back and alternate cold and hot water from different jets in Jesus's mega-shower. I sometimes whack him on the butt with a back-scratcher and other times I scratch the bottom of his feet. I learned this from Sister Mary Carolina. When someone's in severe pain, you can sometimes distract their brain from processing the pain signals by sending other signals. Signals for things that are only uncomfortable, like water that's a little too hot or icy cold, or long nails scratching the soles of someone's feet. I rub his back hard, like I'm trying to punish him. Most people get a lot of pleasure out of a borderline painful rub, but in Evan's case, that's not the point. I'm just trying to distract his brain from whatever's going on with his nerves.

I remember from the time I caught a bullet near my knee, that when my bed was super comfy and someone was stroking my hair, that's when my wound would hurt the most. I'd notice it less when a lot of things were going on. I would beg Jesus to take me out in his car with him, just to escape the pain.

I don't want Evan to be comfortable enough to feel his

pain. I want to throw a million things at him, at once.

I exhaust myself, changing his environment. Hot water, cold water, slapping him, kneading, scratching. At one point he moans, "Pull my hair," so I go to work on that. The harder I pull, the happier he seems. "That's good," he moans, and I think I understand why his mouth was bleeding.

I wonder why he won't take pills, and I ask him one more time before he rolls onto his side and says, "No more."

Don't ask him again, because it's too tempting. That's what he means, I think. I wonder why he won't take anything. Wonder if I should force something down his throat—but I decide to respect his wishes.

I'm straddling his bare back; I've taken to pulling on his hair with one hand and pressing on his upper back with the other. I haven't seen him be this still or quiet in what feels like hours.

Then I realize he's asleep.

No way in hell am I moving him. Lying on an uncomfortable surface is a great way to get through pain. I get a blanket, because he's soaked and I don't want him to get too cold. I get a pillow for myself, and I lie down beside him.

When he wakes an hour or two later, gripping my arm and weeping into the crook of his elbow, I start my no-pain show again. It goes all night. All day. I'm not even sure what time it is.

But nobody comes for us, and he gets through without quite as much moaning. No more screaming. A lot of the time while I work, he's just breathing.

CHAPTER TWENTY

CROSS

I OPEN MY eyes to find myself inside a massive, onyx and gold shower. Not just a shower. This place is like a bathhouse. I can count nine shower heads without moving my head.

I don't want to move my head, because it feels weird. Good weird. I close my eyes before I realize that's because someone is playing with my hair.

Awareness returns with a jolt, and I stop breathing. I'm in a super-sized shower with Missy King. Meredith Kinsey. I'm in a super-sized shower with Merri, and in the span of one second, a boatload of insane memories populate my brain.

Merri, stripping off my clothes. Merri, rubbing my back and neck. Merri, giving me water and playing with my feet.

"Anything to distract you."

God, I know her voice better than I know my own right now. I feel like she spent decades whispering in my ear. I feel like she spent eons lying beside me on the floor. That's what she did, I realize. She must have been in here with me the whole time. How long has it been?

I don't dare move or open my mouth to ask. Her fin-gers in my hair feel great. I know it's wrong—it's wrong for so many reasons—but I don't want her to stop.

But all of a sudden, the fingers in my hair go away and I can feel her getting up. When I think she's a few paces away, I slit my eyes and see that she's wearing a short, pale blue cotton nightgown. Since I'm on the floor, I have a nice view of her ass cheeks.

She turns to do something, and I shut my eyes as she sinks back down beside me.

"Can you drink some water for me, Evan?"

She thinks my name is Evan. *Right.*

I don't move, and I feel her small hand touch my shoulder, fingers tickling the skin before settling warmly on it. I think I'm naked under a towel.

"Evan..." I can feel her breath on me. Beneath the tow-el, I'm getting excited. I try to think about baseball, but I never did like that shit. Maybe I make a weird expression, because she cries, "Evan, are you awake?"

I open my eyes slowly, finding hers and giving her a small smile. "Guilty as charged." I start to cough because my mouth is dry, and she's right there with a glass. There's a pink straw in it. I raise my right hand to guide it to my mouth but I grab her hand instead.

"Sorry." A blush spreads across her cheeks. "I'm used to doing this part."

With her delicious little body half an inch away from mine I'm even thirstier. I gulp the water down. I finish, and she sits up straighter, giving me a great view of her amaz-ing rack. Waves of reddish hair obscure her face. She brushes it back, revealing a smile that looks shy. "This is weird, huh?"

"What, this?" I wave at myself. "Nah. I spend most of my time in showers with beautiful women, so this is just a normal day for me."

Her eyes widen, and I laugh. "Kidding." I push myself up on my right elbow, slightly embarrassed to find that, yeah, I'm naked and hiding a boner under a bunch of half-wet towels. "So I've been naked for how long?"

She blushes, and I'm surprised she still does that, after everything she's been through. "In a few hours, it will be twenty-four hours."

I give a low whistle. "That long."

She nods. "You had a rough time."

"So I hear."

"You don't remember after?"

"Bits and pieces." I never remember anything coherent. Just sensations. Most of them brain-killingly painful. I'm not gonna say that, though. Don't want to sound like a pussy.

She tilts her head to the side, then leans closer and smoothes my hair back with her palm. She smiles. "It dried standing straight up. Because I was rubbing your head."

I look into her face and try to picture that. My moaning, sleeping ass, attended to by someone who looks like the nurse you only get in a dirty movie. Someone who, even now, is looking at me with a double dose of concern.

Why does she care?

I like it.

I shouldn't like it. This is my father's former mistress. That's just fucking weird as hell. So why is it so hard to remember?

Moving stiffly, I scoot so my back's against the onyx tile wall, making space between us. I rub my right hand over the scruff on my face and look down at my bare legs, sticking out of the towels. I want to say thank you, but I don't know how. I've never had anyone around during of my neuralgia attacks. Other than the nurses at NVIR, and all they did was give me Dilaudid and let me ride it out.

I swallow hard and force myself to meet her eyes. "You were good to me. I remember that much. Thank you."

Her expression is understanding, as usual. Casual and warm. "I'm sure you would have done the same for me. You were in trouble, and I was here. You don't owe me anything."

But that's where she's wrong. I owe her a hell of a lot. More than I can ever, ever give her. So much more than I wish she had to know. I take a deep breath, noticing as I do that my neck and shoulders feel more relaxed than they have in probably years. Woman's good with her hands. I remember that much, too.

I look down at my chest. It's bare because the towels fell into my lap when I scooted back. It's bare and I can see the scars. For just that moment, I wish I could turn back time and be the old Cross Carlson. The one I was last year, before I found out about the woman my father sold as a sex slave. When I was wrapped up in my carefree world of bikes, women, and parties. I wonder what Merri would think about that guy.

I look up at her, and I really want to tell her who I am. It's not right to lie to her—not after everything she's done for me. But if I tell her now, she might not travel to the border with me. I *think* she would. No one in their right mind would stay here to face the cartel, but I don't actually *know*. What if she ran off or something?

Maybe I'll give it a little while longer—just another day—for her to get to know me more. To trust me more.

I'll tell her tomorrow, when we finally reach the border and I hand over her passport. Maybe even before.

Merri

EVAN IS LOOKING at me funny, and suddenly I feel self-conscious. I've been in this shower for the better part of a day, and I know I must look like dog poo on a stick. I bite my lip, remembering that I'm not even wearing a bra or panties. When I changed into this nightgown, it was only to get out of the disgusting clothes I'd been wearing since I left the clinic. Evan was in the shower, quiet between spells of pain, and I ran into my room and just stripped everything off. I don't even think I remembered to hang my underwear and bra so they'd be dry when I needed them next. Which would be now.

I put a hand up to my face and try to pretend I'm wearing something snazzy. Maybe a business suit, the kind I used to wear when I pitched stories in person.

Evan's eyes are stuck to me like glue, and it's weird to feel so embarrassed. We've been here in this shower together for a long time. I feel like I know him. For sure I care about him. And maybe it's just sad, because all the sweet, intimate things he said to me when he was half out of it...they made me feel good. Not just good as in useful, because I've been useful at the clinic. But good in another way. A way I really shouldn't want.

My eyes wander over the scars on his chest, and I want to ask about them. I want to ask how old he is and where he's from. Obviously we haven't had time to get to know each other...

I push away *that* urge and stand carefully, so he can't see under my gown. I hold up a finger—*be right back*—and go into the bathroom, where I grab two fluffy black robes and slide one of them on. I walk back into the shower, where I find Evan standing. One of the towels from the shower is wrapped around his waist. It's wet, so it hangs off his hips. I can see the little indention hot guys have in that area, the spot on their hips where I've always thought a woman's hands should grip. I can see how flat his belly is. Flat but rippled with muscle. Dusted with a soft trail of dark hair. I've seen his body before—all of it, in fact—but it was different when he was delirious with pain.

Now he's standing right in front of me, with his hair tousled and that five o'clock shadow thing going, I want to walk over and wrap my arms around his shoulders. My sleeping beau is awake, and I just want to hug him again, like I did when he was sleeping.

Geez, I don't even know this guy. I must be a lot lonelier than I thought.

I put on a smile and try not to let my eyes cling to his body. "You're up. How do you feel?"

CROSS

I FEEL LIKE I just got off a bender. I rub my palm over my hair—which is sticking up in every direction—and I avoid her eyes as I say, "Alright."

I can't seem to look at her at the moment, so I look at the robe she's holding. It matches the black one that drags the shiny floor. She blinks and holds it out. "For you."

Even leaning close to her to take the robe feels...like too much. I grab it and try to get my left arm into it quickly, without too much struggle. All I can think about as she watches me out of the corner of her eye, messing with her own robe and trying to look inconspicuous, is Suri, always offering to help me with everything. I don't want help. I don't want to *need* help.

I pull the robe roughly up my left shoulder, which still feels a little tender, and jab my right arm into its sleeve. Merri starts gathering damp towels off the floor, but before she can bring them to her chest to carry them, I take them from her.

"I got these."

As she looks up at me, her hair falls around her face and I feel like someone just lit a light bulb inside my chest.

I hold the towels closer and grab a few more off the floor. Then I walk into the bathroom, because I can't keep being in the shower with her. The space is too damn small.

She's on my heels; I can see her—all long, wavy red hair and enormous tits—in the opulent gold mirror that stretches across the wall. "Do you want to go find some food?" she asks.

"Yeah," I mutter, glancing at myself in the mirror. I look about as rough as I feel.

I lead the way through a cavernous bedroom with a larger-than-king-sized bed that has thick, wood posts and a brown canopy.

"I guess this is the love nest."

From behind me she says, "Yeah. Why don't you leave the towels by that fireplace? You know...so we don't have to go in the laundry room."

"Right." Where the dead dude is.

I dump them by the marble fireplace and give it a frown. "This thing work?"

"No, it's probably just for candles." And yeah, now that she says that I notice it's filled up with half-melted candles.

"Sexay."

I catch her eye for the first time in a while and her mouth is pulled into a pensive expression.

"Sorry," I say. "I like to make inappropriate jokes about the dead."

She smiles a little, leading us through the bedroom door, into the hall. "Once, when I was a little kid—like four, I think—I was in a beauty pageant. When it was time for me to go to the microphone and sing my solo, I got nervous and decided to lead with a joke. I said, 'How long did it take for the chicken to cross the road?' Everyone was either staring at me or laughing, and I loved it. I waited so long I couldn't remember what I was going to say, but I knew poop was funny, so I said, 'Three farts.'" She grins. "Needless to say, my aunt was not amused."

"Aunt?" I ask as I follow her back toward the kitchen.

"Yeah. I grew up with my aunt and uncle."

I shouldn't ask, but I can't seem to help myself. "Your parents...they, um, passed away?"

Her veil of reddish hair moves as she nods. "My mother died when I was born and so my Aunt Britta and my Uncle Walter raised me. They have a son, Landon, who's a year older than me." Glancing over her shoulder, she frowns. "But I guess you know that. Do you?"

"I don't know your history," I hedge. "I just came to find you and bring you back."

We make it to the kitchen and Meredith holds out a chair for me. "My legs are kind of crampy from sitting, so I figured I'll rustle up our food," she says. "Also, though, I have a question."

"Shoot."

"I was wondering," she says, going over to the freezer and opening it, "what's the incentive? For coming to find me, I mean."

CHAPTER TWENTY-ONE

CROSS

SHIT. I DON'T want to lie to her. I stretch my left arm out in front of me and pretend to examine the bandage for a second. "Um, there's not really anything in it for us other than a paycheck. The company just takes contracts from government agencies or private individuals on people who are missing." I force myself to meet her eyes. "Also it's the kind of job you can feel good about doing."

She presses her lips together, poking and prodding several frozen Ziplock bags on a small granite island. "Can I ask you something else?"

I nod, even though it's the last thing I want.

"Who contacted you about me?"

I shrug. "I think I heard from your co-workers that it was your aunt, but that's not really part of my job."

"It's okay. It doesn't matter I guess."

But she looks disappointed, so it does matter. "I'm sure lots of people missed you. Your aunt filed a missing persons report a while back. And I remember some women in Vegas reported you missing, too. My co-worker mentioned it to me, that there were several of them."

She smiles a little. "I made a few friends there." She holds up a bag. "Sausage okay with you?"

"Yeah. While you cook it I was thinking of going outside and checking out the bike. See if I can fix it."

Her mouth pulls into a frown. "He shot the tire, so I bet you probably can't."

"I don't know, I'm pretty handy with bikes."

"I guess you would need to be." She sits a pan on one of the stove's many eyes. "They must trust you a lot to send you out here with your hand the way it is."

I bite the edges of my tongue, not sure how to take that. Is it a compliment? An insult? It isn't pity. That, I like. I don't want to talk about my non-existent company anymore, so I just shrug and say, "Guess so."

We're quiet for a while. The kitchen fills with the smell of sausage.

She's pushing it around in a skillet when she turns back to look at me. "Don't go outside."

"Why not?" I raise my brows. "Did something happen while I was out?"

"No, nothing happened. I just...I don't want to take any risks right now, when you just woke up. I mean...I feel like I just got you back." Color stains her cheeks. "I'll be up poop creek if something like that happens again."

"Poop creek?" I raise my eyebrows in a skeptical way. She crosses her arms under her chest and I beat her to the punch. "Or maybe it's that you...missed me?" I'm teasing, mostly because I don't know what else to say.

"I did." She gives me that smile again. "You're not such bad company."

I look down at my hand. "Even with my howling,

moaning alter ego?"

She bites her lip. "That was pretty awful. Does it happen a lot?"

"It happens about once a month. Sometimes twice. It just depends."

She pushes the sausage around, adding a dollop of butter to the pan. "What triggers it?"

"Stress. Fatigue. Maybe just the wind blows wrong. My neck's pretty fucked up—fracked up," I say as her eyebrows arch. "So it's kind of unpredictable."

"I could tell it was your neck. Sometimes I'd rub it just right, and you'd seem to feel better.

"Really?" That s surprising. "Who would have thought?"

"A masseuse, probably. Have you ever been to one?"

"Other than you?" I look her over. "Three. None of them helped."

"That's surprising," she says.

"Maybe you're just better. Are you licensed and shit?"

"I'm not certified in America or anything, but I trained. At the clinic."

It hits me. "The Sister, the one I met, she trained you."

"Yes."

"She rubbed my neck. The security sensors went off because there's metal caging in there, so she poked around."

She cooks some more in silence. After a spell, she looks up again. "Can I ask another question?"

"Shoot."

"How long has it been? Since your wreck?"

"Six months-ish."

She chews her lip again, now adding some pepper. Then she looks at me. "How are you doing, if you don't mind me asking. I mean...how do you deal with that?"

"Without wanting to blow my head off?" I give her a pointed look. "Is that the question?"

She nods. "It looks so horrible. I can't imagine how you bear it."

"What would you do?" I ask her.

"I think I'd take the drugs. A lot of them."

The unspoken question is obvious, so I decide to tell her why I don't do drugs. One, she'll probably trust me more when she hears my pathetic story. Two, I want to tell someone.

Normally, it'd be hard to talk about. But with Merri, the woman I left to die in Mexico, who thinks my name is Evan...there's no danger. She's going to leave my life soon anyway.

I watch as she pushes a few pieces of sausage from the pan onto a plate. She carries it to me, along with a napkin, then returns to chop the link into more pieces. Her back is to me, and she seems casual. It's like she can sense that I'm about to spill.

I enjoy a mouthful of the sausage before I ask, "Have you ever taken any narcotics? You know, Morphine or codeine? Oxycodone? Dilaudid? Stuff like that?"

She nods. "A time or two, for serious pain, like when I had my wisdom teeth cut out."

"But not for longer than a week or so?"

"No. I've never been a drug addict, if that's what you're asking. And I haven't been in much pain either, so I guess I'm lucky in that way."

I smirk. "Yeah." This girl is exactly who I picture when I picture 'lucky'. "Well I was on something from the moment I had the wreck, back in November, until I woke up from my coma a couple months later."

Her eyes bulge. "Months? When you said coma, I thought you meant like a week or two."

I shake my head. "It was a long stretch, but I had a lot going on. I guess I was smart not to come out any sooner. If I had come back during the spinal surgeries..." I rub my neck and make a face. "By the time I got moved from one facility to another, I was like a level three on the GCS, the scale they use for people in comas."

"So you could be roused if they, like, hurt you, but not for anything else?"

"Something like that."

She nods and takes another bite, still standing over at the island.

"When I did come out of it, I was able to get by without too many painkillers. They had me on all kinds of other shit, but the pain was kind of manageable. And then they noticed that I couldn't use my hand." I look down at it, at the wet bandage and the semi-curled fingers. "One of my doctors—this well-known surgeon—wanted to go into my neck again. He thought that he could fix my neck and hand."

Her face draws up, and I kind of want to quit talking. I'm not sure if I can handle her pity. I chew another piece of sausage, and it seems like her whole body goes still as she watches me.

"I went under on a Tuesday in March. But, I guess since I had had so much anesthesia and so many drugs, somehow something was off with me. They didn't get me all the way under, and I remember the first part of the surgery."

Her hand goes to her mouth and her green eyes widen, but she doesn't interrupt.

"The last thing I remember is when they noticed. They told me it was an hour and seventeen minutes in. They upped the juice, and I finally went out. When I woke up, my neck was in a brace and the pain..." I swallow, almost convulsively. "It was terrible. Whatever he had done had irritated things more. I'm not sure what. Nobody knows what, because there's so much back there that's messed up." I chew on my lip, then stop because I notice it's already scabbed. I inhale. Exhale. Keep on going. I've never had to tell this to anybody. Lizzy and Suri were both there.

"I couldn't take that kind of pain, not all the time like that. So they went in again. My doctor and another dude from New York. They did a better job, and when I woke up, I was able to back down on the Dilaudid a little bit. It wasn't constant—the pain, I mean. It would get really irritated like once a week. The other times, the arm would tingle but it wouldn't hurt.

"Well I was still inpatient, in a rehab facility. And when you're inpatient, it takes a long time for doctors and nurses to make decisions for you. So if I had a flare-up on a Thursday, they'd keep me on the heavy dose of Dilaudid until maybe Tuesday—long enough so everyone signing off on things felt sure. Maybe Wednesday and Thursday would be taper-down days. And then maybe I'd have another attack on Friday."

Her eyebrows arch. "So you were on something all the

time."

I nod. "Yeah. I never had a week without a pain attack, so I was always on the Dilaudid. I was never really conscious. I just..." I rub my face. "I couldn't remember anything. On the days I got the most, I would just...float. And it reminded me of being in a coma again."

I glance at Meredith. Her face is a mask of sympathy.

"Eventually they backed it down, and I went through withdrawal. I wanted to go off it, but I couldn't stand the pain without it. When I would do PT for my hand and hip—I hurt my hip, too—they would have to give me some more in my IV before they even wheeled me down to the PT room. It just hurt too fu— fracking much. I went home with an oral prescription for it, and I thought I could do it different than they did in rehab. I would try not to take it unless I knew it was going to have a pain attack. So I went home and I didn't take it." I laugh. "When I wouldn't take it, I'd flip my shit. Start seeing things and hearing things. I'd get all achy like I had the flu and I'd get really sick to my stomach.

"So after a while of that, I went back to taking it. I just took it like they told me to. Every day. I couldn't drive, and I couldn't ride a bike. I didn't even have the energy to do PT. Sometimes between doses I would get edgy and my mind would do weird shit. Other times I would forget to get it refilled.

"That's what happened. I had two different strengths of Dilaudid—one was kind of a top-off dose for when my usual dose didn't deal with the pain, to help me avoid having to go to the ER for IV meds. One night I got a bad headache and I had forgotten to re-fill my regular dose. I had one more of those weaker pills left, so I took it and of course it didn't work. I should have had a few more of them to take before I took the stronger dose. I should only have taken one of the stronger dose, and I did that, but it wasn't enough since I hadn't had enough of my regular dose. So I took another one of the strong pills. And I guess this was a really bad headache, or maybe I had just built up a tolerance to the Dilaudid...because that didn't work either. I think the problem was that I had no idea how to deal with pain. I had never had any pain management, so I couldn't take it."

I suck on the inside of my cheeks, staring at the table because I don't want to look at her.

"I called my pain doc but I didn't get a callback right away and it was three in the morning. I got into the shower with the water on scalding and it helped for a second, but pretty soon the pain was back. I tried cutting the underside of my bicep with a razor blade just as a distraction. It didn't work, so I called the doctor again and when I didn't get him, or one of my friends, I took another Dilaudid. Which didn't work...so then I took another one. Remember this was the top-off dose. One for an emergency, in case the regular dose wasn't working. So I took...three or four. I guess I passed out. I don't know. But the friend I had called couldn't get me when she tried to call me back, so she called my doctors, and when no one could get me a few of them came over."

The friend was Lizzy, and she still won't talk about that night. I look down, remembering how upset she was, and when I look up Merri is a few steps closer. Her eyes are wide, concerned, like it's not the past but happening right now. "What happened?" she murmurs.

I look her in the eye. "I almost died." A morose laugh escapes my lips. "Again.

"After that I said no more Dilaudid. I had to find a way to tolerate it without. Something that wouldn't fuck me up every day and make it impossible to live." I shrug. "So I tried a bunch of different shit, and in the end, I learned to meditate."

Merri is frowning, shaking her head like she's protesting something unfair. "But that didn't work."

I frown back. "What do you mean it didn't work?"

"The other day. Yesterday. You were still in so much pain."

I shrug. "Well, yeah. But you don't see me trying to jump out any windows or light my hair on fire."

Her lips pull together and her eyes shimmer with tears. "No, Evan," she says thickly, "but is that the only goal?"

I blink at her. I'm so shocked by her reaction that I don't know what to say. "It only happens every few weeks."

Her eyes widen, spilling a tear down her cheek. "And that's it? There's nothing they can do for you?"

"It might get better over time."

"Could you try another surgery?"

"I don't think so. I don't know of a doctor who could do things differently than mine did."

"Have you looked?"

I stand up, drumming my fingers on the table as my left arm hangs beside me: Illustration A. "No. I mean, what does it matter? It's pain, not cancer."

"It's your quality of life. Evan, that's everything."

My name's not Evan. I have to press my lips tightly shut to keep from saying it. With her eyes wet and her face all pinched up, it's like it's her pain and not mine. I've never felt like such a fucking fraud.

Just then, she strides to me and throws her arms around my neck.

CHAPTER TWENTY-TWO

Merri

I PULL AWAY from him, and I can feel myself blushing. There should be another word for this. One that more resembles *burning*.

With my hands dangling at my sides where they belong, I glance up at him, feeling like the old-school, mid-twentieth century definition of the histrionic woman.

I mean, it's not like we're good friends or anything. What logical reason do I have to be this worked up over Evan's quality of life?

I get the nerve to peek at him, and I confirm I'm right: He looks edgy. Uncomfortable. Like I've crossed a line.

He shifts his feet, like he wants to step away, but instead of doing that, he looks into my eyes for a few long seconds. The depth of his stare actually makes me shiver; I get the feeling he's trying to find something there. I'm doing the same thing, but whatever I see in the depths of his blue eyes feels nameless.

A second later, he thumbs a tear off my cheek, his perfect lips pressing together in a sad, resigned kind of look. "Don't cry for me, Meredith. I'm doing fine."

I nod, feeling a glow all over my body because I'm standing so close to him.

I want to touch him. For this reason, I make myself take a small step back, tilting my head up more to meet his eyes. "I'm sorry for going all emo on you."

The grave look on his face slips, and for a second I see something else—something vulnerable in his beautiful features. It's gone the next second, replaced by something stoic and untouchable.

I back away a little more and he lifts his hand, like *he* wants to touch *me*. Instead he just holds it there, palm out: the classic symbol meaning 'stop'.

That's what you should do, dummy. Just stop this. You're living in a fantasy.

Evan seems to be searching for something to say. His eyes, on me, burn. I swallow and he tilts his head a little, looking unhappily perplexed. "I didn't deserve what you did for me, but I appreciate it." He looks me over, head to toe. "You're a good person, Meredith Kinsey."

Before I can respond, he lowers his hand and turns to go back to the table. He glances at me over his shoulder as he moves, and when he sits down, he bites into a piece of sausage. I move back behind the island and force myself to be calm, the way I would be if one of my children got hurt and I didn't want to alarm them. I force myself to behave calmly as I eat my own breakfast, but internally, I'm going a million miles an hour.

I feel mortified. Desperate. Hungry. The feeling is familiar, and from long ago: It reminds me of the way I felt about Sam, the assistant band director. My first full-on crush.

I pour myself a glass of water and sigh, because how typical is that? Will I always be the blushing girl with the inappropriate crush?

Well, I guess I'm not blushing anymore, that's for sure, but this guy is still very much off limits. Not because of all the many obvious things, but because of my secret. The one he doesn't know—and I won't tell him. The one that's the likeliest of all my baggage to reach across time and distance to end me.

What I should tell him is that I'm not the kind of person he thinks. I probably never was, but I'm definitely not now. "That's not even my name," I murmur.

His eyebrows shoot up. "What's your name?"

I shake my head. "Kinsey wasn't ever really mine. It was the name I took on when I was adopted."

Silence spreads its roots between us and I think about everything Evan doesn't know about me. I wonder if he'll find out when I get into the States. If his colleagues already know the most sordid part of my story. What Evan would think if he knew, too.

He doesn't seem to care about my past, but that's probably because he only knows me as a victim.

"When do you want to get on the road?" he asks. The low rumble of his voice makes me jump.

I push my hair out of my face and try to look less spazzy. I shrug. "Tomorrow maybe? Like really early in the morning. They tend not to be out then."

"Sure." He stands up. All traces of his earlier moodiness are gone, and I get a pleasant vibe again—the kind of vibe that says we might be friends. "And you're sure no one knows about this place?"

I shook my head. "Jesus was really good at tech stuff. This place is completely self-sufficient and off the grid."

He nods. "I guess tonight we'll just hang out? We could watch some TV...well, I guess no cable—"

"Jesus set up satellite somehow. It's illegal," I shrug, "but apparently no one can tell."

"Satellite it is." He smiles, a smile that looks real and gentle and handsome enough to bruise my heart. "I could use a night of relaxing and I have a feeling you could, too."

He doesn't know how right he is.

I SPEND THE next two hours soaking in my room's tub, drying my hair, trying to assemble an outfit from the clothes I find in my drawers, and pacing around the room trying to remind myself that Evan No Last Name is no one to me. We're not friends. We're not even acquaintances. The pull I feel is because I spent the last day and a half taking care of him. And...okay, also because he's extremely attractive. And nice.

And I'm lonely. I'll admit it. I'm lonely and pathetic. I feel like a spinster and I'm still not even through my 20s. I know I won't ever walk down the aisle or shop for a new house with double vanities and his and hers closets. I won't have a family or kids. At this point, I'll be lucky if I can get into the witness protection program and befriend my neighbors without worrying that one of them will kill me on behalf of the Cientos Cartel.

I took a nice life and screwed it up because I was foolish. I messed around with a married man for money.

I remind myself that even if I allowed myself to have feelings for a man again, it wouldn't be fair to him. I would always have to end things before they went too far.

I end up wearing men's purple work-out shorts and a V-neck white undershirt. I find some of my old mascara in the bathroom and can't resist putting it on, if only to feel a little human. It's been a long time since I wore makeup, and I'm surprised by how long my eyelashes look.

As I study my reflection, from my mother's striking green eyes to my Maw-Maw's rose-cheeked, heart-shaped face, to my father's strawberry hair, I think about my aunt and uncle. I feel a crushing wave of remorse for what I know I put them through. Granted, I didn't plan to run away from Atlanta, but I still *did*. My intentions don't change the sleepless nights I know my aunt endured and probably still does. My uncle and my cousin...surely their lives were changed knowing that someone raised in their house just vanished like I did.

I was selfish. Maybe I've changed—I like to think I have—but it doesn't matter really. My bad deeds are going to follow me forever.

This is my mood when I step out into the hallway and start to look for Evan.

I find him in the kitchen, and my first glimpse of his outfit has me snickering.

He's wearing a pair of Jesus's jeans, which he's cut off at the knee, probably because he's a good five inches taller than Jesus. There's no fixing the crotch area, though, which is T.I.G.H.T. My eyes run over him, and I know my face is red, because you can see a lot of...well, him. *Look up, look up,* I tell my pervy self. His shirt is a light blue and white button-up which he has rolled up to the sleeves. It makes his blue eyes glow, and I laugh a little because I'm pretty sure if he moves the wrong way, he'll make the buttons pop.

"I didn't know you were dressing up." I grin, and Evan flips me off.

"This is the best I could do." He grimaces, and I giggle.

"Look at you, Mia Hamm." He nods at me, and I swing my foot, like I'm kicking a soccer ball.

He snickers, and I flip him off. "Whatever, George Michael."

Evan winces, and I saunter past him and start searching the cabinets for something to eat. I find a bag of popcorn. It's a brand you don't see so much in the States, and Evan takes it from me, reading the Spanish popping information under his breath.

"You speak good Spanish," I tell him. "Did you learn it in school?"

He nods. He looks like he might say something else, but then he steps over to the microwave and starts the popping. As I lean against the counter watching him, I feel weird being here. Like Jesus and David never existed and this is our hotel or something. It's...inappropriate.

I've been struggling for a day or so now with the feeling that I should be mourning their deaths, but there's no way I can. Living with Jesus was like living with a performing tiger. I survived okay for a while, but eventually he bit me. Not for any reason other than *he's a tiger*, and that's what tigers do.

I look down at my fingernails, wondering what would

have happened if Jesus had gotten me back. It's hard to say. But I think I can safely guess that I wouldn't have liked it. I'm lucky Evan came for me.

"What do you want to watch?" I look up at him, leaning against the counter top across from me. The way he's leaning puts particular emphasis on his... Um, yeah. I cast my eyes to his face, which is serious almost to the point of sullen, and that helps me laugh, because he looks ridiculous. He grins, and his grin reminds me of a lazy dog. Just chillin'.

"Stop laughing at me." He lunges to punch me lightly in the arm, then turns his body so his shoulder bumps into mine. "What do you want to watch?" he asks me.

His handsome face is so close to mine that I can hardly breathe, much less answer.

He bumps me again, and I swallow back my nerves. "What about old *Southpark* re-runs?" Evan narrows his eyes at me. "Are you sure?"

I nod. "I like *Southpark*, except the few where they make fun of religious stuff."

He laughs. "Of course you don't."

"Why of course?" I scrunch my eyebrows. "Because you have a hard time believing I'm religious?"

"It's just..." He frowns. "You're not lying to me, are you? You, right now, are the real Meredith?" He shakes his head. "I guess that sounds crazy..."

I think I get it... "You're wondering if I had to be someone else when I worked at a brothel in Vegas, or when I was some drug lord's beard. Or if I'm being someone else now, so you won't know how messed up I really am." I press my lips together. "It's an understandable question, but yeah, I'm me. The brothel work was furthest from my norm, but I had a specific role I needed to play for my primary client. It probably wasn't anything like what you'd think."

He doesn't say anything, and I wonder if it bothers him, that I used to mess around for money. He reads my mind, drumming on the counter as he says, "I just can't picture it."

The microwave dings, and I slide a glance his way as I step past him to get it. "Dare I ask what part?"

He grabs some paper towels and I get two Cokes from the refrigerator, and we head into the living area. "The you as someone's call girl part. Whether it's a pimp or a client or a kingpin, you just don't seem like that to me. You have your college degree, right?"

"Yes."

"You used to write for newspapers."

Yes. Damnit. Before now, I hadn't been sure exactly what he knew about me, but… "Did you read my columns?" My cheeks are hot again.

"Yeah. Pageant participants as cattle." He smiles as my discomfort. "So tell me what happened." He crooks an eyebrow, giving me a look that's surprisingly intimate.

I plop down on the couch and hold the popcorn bowl tightly in between my palms. "Sometimes things don't turn out the way you plan. Or is your life exactly the way you meant it to be?"

CHAPTER TWENTY-THREE

CROSS

I WANT THIS to be a fun night for her. It's pretty ridiculous; as if a fun night with her former John's son will make up for being sold into slavery.

But still, I'm wanting to kick myself for going down this road. I don't need to talk about this shit with her, and I already know that. Some things should stay unsaid, and her involvement with my father is definitely one of them.

I flip channels, watching the images flicker on the massive flat screen as I wrestle with myself—but I already know the outcome. Now that I've peeled back the skin on this, I'm going to dig right in. I can't help myself. "I told you my sob story." I say it like a challenge. "Let's hear yours."

She rearranges herself on the huge leather couch, sitting the popcorn bowl between us and drawing a pillow into her lap. She balances her Coke on the pillow and frames it with her hands. Her long, pale red hair has fallen like a veil between us, but as she taps a frenzied rhythm on the Coke can, I can see her face. I can see the struggle on it.

She sighs and takes a long gulp. Then she tucks her

hair behind her ear and looks at me. Her mouth is set into a grim line. Her beautiful green eyes are flat. "Just after college, I dated this guy who put me in a really bad situation, and I had to leave Atlanta, where I was living. At the time I was researching for a freelance article on escorts in Vegas. So I went to Vegas." She huffs her breath out, causing the wisps of hair around her face to dance. "I guess I kind of ran away to Vegas."

My mind is reeling, wondering what could have happened to make her run away; wondering why the police wanted to question her. I remember something I read online back in Napa, at the library: about how the police in Atlanta wanted to question her in relation to some guy; I think his name was Sean something. I must be making some kind of pissed off face, because Meredith shrinks away a little, pulling the pillow closer to her chest. She traces the rim of the Coke can with her fingertip, and I want to tell her not to. She might cut her finger.

"When I got there, out to Vegas, I ended up getting to know the manager and owner of this brothel on the Strip. I was working on my story, but I ran out of money, so I ended up crashing there. I wasn't sure what I'd do..." She bites her lip, glancing at me and then down at the floor. "Because of the...circumstances, I couldn't go back home. I was going to get a job waitressing or something. I'd even put in some applications. And then one day, I was on my way to the gym when a client saw me, I think, and it wasn't long after that the owner told me that this guy felt I fit the bill for what he wanted." Her eyes, on her Coke can, flick to mine. She watches me carefully, waiting for my judgment.

I'm gritting my teeth, so I try to relax my jaw and calm

my mind. Do I hope this client was my father, or someone else? The possibilities seem equally awful.

"In what way?" I choke out. I swallow so what I say next doesn't sound so fucking ragged. "How'd you fit the bill?"

She shrugs, like we're talking about the rain. "The client wanted someone young who wasn't seeing many or any other clients. And he wanted a Vegas girl, so I became his Vegas girl."

And there it is. It's all out on the table. Meredith was my father's Vegas girl.

I nod, keeping a lid on my feelings, and then without meaning to, I'm up, striding into the kitchen. My heart is pounding and my mouth feels dry. I turn a quick circle, careful not to look at Merri. But from where she's sitting, she might be able to see my face. And if she sees my face, she'll know. I wheel around again and jerk open the refrigerator. I grab the first thing I see—a bottle of beer—and curse as I realize I can't twist the damn top off. Not with one hand.

I stand there, breathing hard and staring at it, and Merri's soft footsteps whisper across the stone floor. I don't want to see her but she stands in front of me. She has her arms folded over her stomach and her pretty little bow of a mouth is pinched into a sour face.

"You know, you asked."

"I nod." I do know that. I just didn't plan to feel so fracking jealous. I pop my jaw, and Meredith's eyes widen. She takes the beer from me and twists the top off. She takes a long swig and hands it back to me.

Her eyes, when she looks at me, are hard. She bites her

lip, and her face softens. Her words are soft, too. "I didn't think that you would act this way."

What? Jealous? I frown. "What way?"

"So...disgusted."

My eyes widen. "Is that what you think I am?"

"Isn't it?"

I tighten my grip on the beer bottle, tilting my head back to get a swallow—and break eye contact. The liquid burns my throat and pretty soon I have no choice but to look at her again. This time, her eyes and face are sad. Because I made her feel judged. Which is really unforgivable.

"Hey...I'd never judge you. And I'm not disgusted." I bump her shoulder awkwardly with mine, and she steps quickly away. She leans against the counter, putting some space between us, then turns sideways so she's facing me.

"It's not something that I'm proud of. The man was married, and what I did was wrong. I could tell you that I did it for money, because I did, but that wouldn't make it right. The affair didn't last long, and the two of us were never emotionally involved. He didn't want to get to know me on more than just a superficial level.

"If I could go back, I would find another way to make money. Even prostitution would have been morally better than that. At least I think so."

I nod, trying my damndest to act casual, but my throat is so tight I can't speak.

"I'm sorry." Her lips twist into a frown as she notices my clam up. "Does this make you uncomfortable?"

I take another swig of the beer and lie my ass off. "Hell no. Sex?"

"Well, it wasn't actually sex."

"Even if it was. I'm fine with it." I shrug, and she gives me a doubting look.

"You don't have to worry about my feelings."

"My feelings are that you were young and desperate. Isn't that what you said?"

"I had no money, and the job is what got me through, but it's also what got me here."

"How?"

She shakes her head and walks back to the couch. I follow, moving the popcorn onto a table so there's nothing in between us. Merri's got her arms around herself. I put my hand on her forearm, and her eyebrows scrunch low in confusion. It looks like she thinks I've lost my mind, except I can see her cheeks getting pinker. I can see the way her eyes fill up with tears. So I take her hand.

"Look, Merri...I swear I wasn't judging you. You want the truth? It makes me fu— it pisses me off."

She shakes her head. "But...I don't get it. Are your reasons like, religious? Or moral? It just pisses you off that people do what I did at all?"

I squeeze her hand and look down at it, so I don't have to look into her eyes.

"That's not it." Against my will, my gaze finds hers. The words get hung up in my throat. I swallow. "I just don't think he was worthy of you."

Merri

I'M NOT SURE I heard him right. "Worthy of me?"

"Yeah." His voice sounds low. "When married men take advantage of young girls in compromised circumstances, that makes them sick fucks."

I flinch a little at the term, and he frowns. "Sorry. Fracks." He lets go of my hand and stands up, wiping his right palm on his ridiculous cut-off shorts. "Sex or not," he says, "it's wrong. Wrong of him. And then what happened next. How the fu— How did that happen, Merri? I want to know."

I stand up, too. If I'm going to tell him—and I'm not sure that I am—I'll need to put some distance between us. With a sideways glance at him, I walk to the refrigerator and grab another beer, downing half of it before I turn back toward Evan. He's still standing in front of the couch. He looks intense. Upset.

Why does he care so much? "How do you know he wasn't worthy of me?" The words are soft, pulled from my throat. His blue eyes are on me and I want to run and hide. Instead I step a little closer to the living area. "It's true that I was innocent, but what if at some point I wasn't anymore? You don't *know* I wasn't."

My ears are ringing. I can't take my eyes off his face. I watch as his expression goes from staunch to passionate.

"Yes I do." He says it so vehemently.

I shake my head. I'm surprised to feel my eyes fill up with tears. "You don't know anything about me, Evan."

I stand there, shaking slightly, thinking of the things

I'll never tell him, as Evan walks slowly to me. With his eyes on mine, he gently takes my hands and clasps his right one over both of them.

"Listen to me, Merri. I know we haven't known each other long, but it doesn't take long to see that you're a good person. A person who takes care of other people and tries her best to make things right."

For the longest time, his eyes pierce mine. I feel like he is looking down into my soul. It's all I can do not to shrink away. And then, in the span of one of my racing heartbeats, his lips are on my lips. The sensation of his mouth fluttering over mine sets a fire inside my chest. My stomach clenches in a knot as he gently touches his tongue to the corner of my mouth, like he wants to come inside but doesn't dare; I feel the warmth of his breath on my throat as he moves his mouth off mine. A squeeze of his hand around my shoulder, then he pulls away.

My heart is beating so fast I think I might be sick.

Evan is standing there wide-eyed, like something catastrophic has just happened.

"Meredith." It's whispered. He whirls around and I hear him mutter a curse word.

I shut my eyes. I don't want to see regret on his face if he turns back around. I don't want to know what happens next.

My eyes are still shut when his hand clasps mine again, and when I open them, his face is serious. Contrite.

"Come with me." He gently tugs me toward the couch. I follow his lead, sinking down into the leather though it feels like I am floating halfway to the ceiling. I'm feeling too exposed to look at him, so I train my eyes on a spot on the wall.

He lets go of my hand, and I look over at him just in time to see the caution on his face as his right hand reaches for my knee. His fingers touch down on my skin and the sensation is delicious. I get hot all over; hotter, still, when he brushes his thumb over my knee.

"We haven't known each other long, but we've been through some shit, and I can see you, okay? I've known a lot of women, and I know how to spot an asshole when I see one."

I shake my head. Clearly he doesn't. Only an asshole leaves her family without a word and goes and messes around with some other woman's husband. Tears blur my view of the room, and I look at the floor. "I think the female version of asshole is bitch."

"Who told you you're a bitch?"

I scoot a tiny bit away from him, forcing his hand off my leg, because I just can't stand it there right now. "Nobody did. Nobody had to. I'm not saying that it's all my fault, but I made some bad decisions. Now they're mine to bear. I can't blame anybody else for that."

Out of the corner of my eyes, I see him lean over, resting his elbows on his knees. "So tell me what happened. What kind of bad decision is punishable by what happened to you?"

It's weird when he says it that way. It almost makes me feel like he's right—like I *am* a victim. I swallow hard, chasing the feeling away, and feel my guilt wrap its fingers around me again. "I'll tell you. Just please don't expect to have the same opinion of me when I'm done."

He's leaning over his knees more now, and I'm glad of

that, because I don't think I could tell this story if his eyes were on me. As it is, I'll leave a big part of it out: what happened right before I left Jesus. I put a pillow in my lap and angle it between us, giving myself the barest semblance of privacy. Then I turn my gaze to the muted TV, where a Mexican soap opera is playing.

How very fitting.

"I'll never forget that night." I pick a spot on the wall to stare at and try to forget that Evan is beside me.

"I'd been seeing my client for a couple of months. Most of Vegas knew I was his mistress. He wasn't in the city all the time, just sometimes for business, or I guess when he wanted to have fun. He was kind of a guy's guy. He liked to gamble and go to pool halls with his man friends, and maybe they would see some strippers there. He didn't always have to be with me. I liked that," I confess. "It gave me more freedom.

"I was getting by because he paid me by the month. He paid me the same thing every month so I would have stability. And he paid for my room at the brothel." I sigh at the memories, which are so sad now. "It was kind of like living in a hotel...or a dorm. Lots of other women. It was fun I guess. The sorority I never had." I snicker humorlessly. "And just like sorority bitches, there were lots of jealous women. People who wanted this man." I pause, linking my fingers together, as I try to remember the way Drake Carlson looked. The way he smelled. The way he held me. "He was a nice enough man. He looked nice. But there was never any chemistry, at least on my end. Maybe it's because he paid me. That has a way of taking chemistry away. But I think it was because of his age."

"He was older?" Evan rasps.

I turn my eyes to him and find him clenching his right fist atop his knee.

"Yes, he was an older man. Old enough to be my dad, I guess." That thought is creepy. "Women of different ages wanted him. He was kind of...well-known, I guess you would say. One of the women who wanted him was a porn star."

I get a funny feeling in my stomach so I look over at Evan. Suddenly I wish that he would take my hand. I've never told this story to anyone before, and now that I'm upon it, I feel...damaged. Like something inside of me is bleeding.

I link my hands together tightly and look out at a vase beside the massive, mahogany entertainment center, but I can't find the words I need. I look back at Evan. He's got his elbows on his knees, but he's shifted back a little, so his back is against the couch and I can see his face; I can see he looks like he's awaiting his own death sentence.

"Evan...are you sure you want to hear this? I don't have to share it."

He nods once. "Yes, I'm sure. Go on." His body looks stiff enough that I could break him with a tap.

I swallow hard, wishing I'd never started down this path.

"There was a porn star who I had heard had a big thing for my client. She didn't understand why he was paying me to be his escort and his mistress when he could have her. She was older." I exhale, seeing Priscilla's made-up face inside my mind. She had veneers and they always kind of scared me. They were too white. Almost like a vampire's teeth. I rub my eyes, feeling a lot older than my years. "She was pretty in that porn-star way and lots of men in Vegas wanted her. I guess lots of men everywhere wanted her." I shrug. "My client had met her once before, but he didn't hit it off with her. He thought she came on too strong, and she made a derogatory comment about his wife. That had made him mad."

I hear Evan swallow and I look over to find him looking slightly gray. "Are you okay?" I ask. "Should I stop?"

I don't really understand why he's acting this way, and maybe it's not my business anyway. Then suddenly I think get it: It's the wife thing. He's probably appalled to hear the details of my 'affair'. I bite my lip. I can't really blame him.

I take a deep breath and I can feel his eyes on me.

"Go on."

I need a minute to collect myself, so I ask him, "Do you know of Jim Gunn? He's done this more than once. Sold women, I mean." There was another one: Ginny something, I think. She was a little while before me, and one time Guapo told me she was sold in France. I'm sure there might have been more before her, and some after me as well.

I glance at Evan, and he looks distracted—or maybe upset. I just want to bring things back to Earth a little before I drop anymore sordid details on him, so I ask, "What about Priscilla Heat? Have you ever seen her movies?"

Evan's brows knit together and his mouth twists, like he's confused. "Do I know of her?" He shakes his head almost violently, like he's trying to get a bee out of his hair. Without really looking at me, he rubs a hand over his face.

"No, I haven't seen her movies."

"Oh. I guess I thought..." I shake my head. "She's kind of big time."

He clenches his jaw and moves his head just a little, like he wants to shake it but his neck hurts.

When he says nothing more, I continue hesitantly. "My client didn't like her, and she didn't like me. She knew I wasn't really...in the industry. I think that made her mad. Some women reacted that way when they heard about me. I was a kept girl at a brothel, but I'd never prostituted myself. People used to joke about how I couldn't satisfy my client. How could I when I didn't have any experience?"

"How could you?" Evan growls. He looks infuriated, and seeing his face like this makes my throat close off. I swallow hard, feeling stripped. Feeling ugly.

"I-I don't know how I could." I shrug, unsure what is making him so mad but taking his anger upon me nonetheless. "I just tried to do the best I could." A tear spills down my face, and before I know it, I'm up and on my feet, dashing down the hallway to my room. I slam the door and fling my body onto the bed. I feel...humiliated.

I remember a line from *The Only Alien on the Planet*, one of my favorite books in honors eighth grade English. The main character is lamenting a part of his life that was lost because of some really awful crap he went through. His friend is telling him that he'll get over what happened, and he says, *"Whatever I become. Wherever I go. There will always be—this."*

His friend asks if he can just move past it.

He says, *"No."*

I feel that sentiment so strongly right now. I just want

to live in a world where I was never Missy King. Unless I can erase my past, I'll never be happy. I'll never be free.

All the misery and shame that I've been ignoring while I worked at the clinic bubbles up, and I am sobbing in my pillow. Sobbing for my pretty, framed college diploma that I left in my old place in Atlanta. Sobbing for the way my byline looked in the pretty, sleek newspaper fonts: MEREDITH KINSEY, STAFF WRITER. God, I want to see that again. I cry for my aunt and uncle, for my buddies at *The Red & Black*. Every year there's a reunion and I've never even been. I should have gone. I should have a job, a boyfriend. I should be down here writing about this stuff. I should never be living it. And then I sob harder because somewhere in my heart, I know it's not my fault. It's Priscilla's fault and it's Jim Gunn's fault. It's Guapo's fault and Jesus's fault. It's not my fault. And that makes me a victim.

CHAPTER TWENTY-FOUR

CROSS

I WATCH MERRI disappear, then I step into the hallway leading to the laundry room and smash my fist into the stony wall. It's a stupid idea, but it makes my heart stop pounding so hard, and with the pain buzzing through my head, I'm not seeing red anymore. I walk back to the kitchen sink and run my bleeding, bruised knuckles under cold water while I try to get myself together.

I'm going to go after her, of course. We're in this together—even if she doesn't know it yet. And after we get back to the States, I'm going to beat my bastard father to a bloody pulp. I should have done it the last time I saw him, and I hate myself because I didn't. I guess I was reserving final judgment for when I found 'Missy'. And the only reason for someone to do that is if they think that maybe—just maybe—it's the victim's fault.

I lower my hand to my side, glad to feel it pounding. I deserve it.

I draw the hand back up to my chest and work the fingers. The stinging, aching pain is nothing to the pain I've felt before, so it doesn't bother me that much. I don't think anything is broken.

I hold out both hands, the battered right one and the useless left one, which hangs limp from my wrist. I look at my hands, and at the opulence of the room around me. I think about the dead man in the laundry room and the dead back at the convent clinic. I think about Merri racing down that hall because she couldn't stand to face me anymore, and my eyes sting.

I take my time walking down the hall to Merri's room. I practice some of my meditative breathing and try to send my emotions away for now. This is not about me.

I knock twice with my elbow and when she doesn't answer, I press my ear to the door. I can hear her sobbing.

Fuck.

I feel like a predator slipping into her dark room, but there's no way I'm going to stand out in the hall. I see the bump of her form on the bed, a curled-up ball that melds into the shadowed shapes of the pillows. More than anything, I want to lie beside her, but I'm not sure if I should.

"Merri?"

When her sobbing continues, I climb up on the bed and lie on my side, leaving a few inches of space between our bodies. I'm getting near wall-punching frustration levels again when I decide to take the small liberty of putting my hand on her back.

Within seconds, she rocks against me and I have my arm around her.

"That's right. Here." I shift her closer to me, so her back's against my chest. My left arm is wrapped around her mid-section; her soft t-shirt tickling the upper part of my arm, where I still have feeling. Her sobbing doesn't sound as violent as it did a few moments ago, but she's still pretty upset.

Moving gently, slowly, I lower my face to the back of her head, nuzzling her hair. When her crying quiets a little, I brush my lips against her head and whisper in her ear. "It's okay, Merri. It's okay."

I can feel her shake her head. I press my face against her hair and wish like hell that I could clasp my left hand around her. Really hold her. Half a heartbeat later, her hand comes up and clasps my arm. She folds me more tightly around her—effectively doing exactly what I'd wanted.

The room is quiet except for her gasping breaths. I can feel her frantic heartbeat underneath my arm, can feel her ribcage furiously pumping in and out. I continue whispering, a mantra of *it's okay*s and *shhhh, Merri*s.

I lie against her a little more and murmur, "It wasn't your fault. No matter what you did, you didn't deserve this." Re-balancing my weight, I take my right hand from under my cheek, where it was propping me up, and use it to play with a strand of her hair. "Sometimes good people make mistakes. You know how you can tell if you're one of the good ones?"

"No," she whispers, tiny in the dark.

"Because good people feel guilty afterward."

For the longest time, I play with her sweet-scented hair. When I shut my eyes and allow myself to focus on the soft warmth of her against me, my cock gets the wrong idea, so I shift my legs where Merri can't feel it up against her back and try to focus on her hair.

"You're good at that," she whispers hoarsely.

"This?" I twirl her hair around my finger and nuzzle

the back of her head again. I'm not trying to come onto her, though I would like to; I can simply tell she needs to be touched. She needs to be held and cared for, and I'm happy to do it. She did the same for me.

"Yeah," she murmurs. "You must have sisters."

Mention of my family pierces me, but I try not to let her feel the tension in my body. "No sisters. Just me."

She waits a moment, and even though I don't have feeling in my hand, I can tell she's stroking my wrist and the tops of my fingers, on the side of my pinkie, where it's free of bandages.

"Is that uncomfortable?" she whispers.

"No."

Some of the tension leaves her body. I can feel her sink into the mattress. I wonder how tired she is. Whether she was always afraid, back at the clinic. I wonder what her life was like with Jesus. But Merri's not offering any stories. Just whispered questions.

"Where will I go when we get to the States?"

I don't even think before I answer. "With me."

"Really? You won't leave me when we get there?"

"No." I wait a breath or two. My pulse sounds like a drum inside my ears. "I still want to know what happened," I say. "It doesn't have to be right now. You can wait and get a notepad or a computer and write it for me if you don't feel like saying it. But I need to know. I won't let these people get away with what they did to you."

A hoarse sound vibrates in her throat. "I'll tell you," she whispers. "But Evan?"

"Uh-huh."

"Don't stop holding me."

Merri

IT WAS A Monday, and I thought Drake had gone back to California. Jim Gunn called and told me different, so I rushed around my little room, getting ready. I wore a pretty, knee-length brown dress that I thought made me look classy. Like a college girl going out to a piano bar. I'd gotten some emerald earrings as a gift from Drake a week or two before, and I remember tilting my head to make them sparkle in the mirror.

Missy King, he called me. *"You're not my mistress,"* he said. *"Mistresses are old. You're my Missy."*

"And King?" I asked him.

"It sounds regal. Only the best for my girl."

I accepted the name because I didn't have another one.

"I was going out with him that night," I whisper. "I thought he had already gone home—that he wasn't in town—but Jim Gunn, one of his Vegas body guards, called and told me he wanted to see me. So I got ready for him."

I exhale, and Evan's body tightens around me.

"Well Jim Gunn pulls up to get me, and he isn't in the Bentley like he usually is. He's in a SUV. I don't know what kind. Maybe it was a Suburban. It was big and black. And Jim is driving like he usually is, but this time I'm not alone in the back seat. Priscilla Heat is there, and...I'm sorry if this is graphic or gross, but it smelled like sex." Tears fill my eyes, because I hate what I have to tell him next. Evan's hand smooths some hair back from my face, and I squeeze my eyes shut, letting the tears fall down my cheek.

It's just like confessing. Just get it out.

"As soon as I'm in the car, she smashes something into my face, and I guess it made me pass out. When I woke up, I was in the very back of the car, like where you put luggage, Priscilla was dressed differently. More casual, almost in a workout suit." I remember it had those tacky fake jewels on it. I remember her lipstick was blood red. I remember how she held me down with her hand on my throat. It makes me shudder. Evan holds me closer.

"She told me she had found out who I was and that they wanted to find me back in Georgia." I pause, remembering that Evan doesn't know what I'm talking about. "The trouble with my boyfriend there is he was dealing marijuana and when they caught him, I was with him. I had always worried he might have blamed it on me or something." I exhale slowly. "Sean was that kind of guy. And when Priscilla said that, I really thought he had."

Evan's arm around me tightens, and I feel him nod. I shut my eyes again.

"She had a phone, and she showed me the Georgia number for reporting someone like me. She said that she would keep me tied up until they came to get me if I wanted, or I could go along with something she was planning."

I chew my lip until I taste a coppery tang. Evan's fingers are stroking my hair. It makes me feel strong enough to keep going.

"I don't know why, but I decided I didn't believe her, so I told her 'no'. She said Jim Gunn had gone to tell the— my client that I had made a play for Jim Gunn. That I'd been having sex with him. She said she was going to tell my client that she had heard I was a journalist from Georgia, and tell him my real name so he could confirm, and tell him I was trying to blackmail him. Either I would give over this footage I supposedly had of he and I to someone in the media, or he would need to pay me several million dollars." Another big, deep breath. My voice cracks. "That just makes me so mad, still."

He strokes my neck, and I can hear the echo of him saying, *It's okay.*

"I told her she could kiss off, but...she had this Taser." When I say that, Evan's body stiffens so much I wish I hadn't. I put my hand on his arm again and stroke his warm skin. "She had the Taser, and she used it on me a few times." Tears drip down my face. I lick the salt off my lips. "I wasn't strong like you. It didn't take that long for me to cave. I let her call him and I told him what he'd heard was true."

Evan nudges me, and I realize he's wanting me to turn around and face him. I want to. I want to be held so badly my stomach churns—but I just can't. I rock back against him and bury my head in my elbow, and he folds himself around me. Silence swims around us, and there's no pressure in it. Evan is just here, and I think that's why I'm able to keep talking.

"She was supposed to let me go after that. I would never tell anyone what had happened. That's what she said. But instead, when she got off the phone she knocked me out again with...I guess it was ether or something. And when I woke up, she and Jim Gunn were in the front seat and I was in the back of the SUV, and they told me we were going to Mexico."

I stop speaking and focus on my breathing. I don't want to tell him anymore, but my mouth seems to move on its own accord. My voice is husky, words too fast.

"I remember I could see the stars through the windows. I've always loved the stars. They always seemed like so many possibilities. And I remember how it felt to know that none of that mattered anymore. My life—" my voice cracks, so I swallow and breathe deeply. "It was over."

My throat seizes up, as if my body is trying to force me to stop talking. Everything that follows is too painful to remember in such detail, but I know I can't stop the story here. Evan will ask me more questions.

"Guapo bought me in a crappy little house just outside Guadalupe Victoria. I think he paid them a few hundred thousand dollars. He took me to Jesus's penthouse apartment in Chihuahua and Jesus made me his beard."

I inhale again, surprised that I'm not crying. The inside of my cheek is bleeding from where my molars have sunken into it, but I'm not crying. Not anymore.

I'm not crying until Evan presses his cheek against mine and kisses my salty skin. "You were the victim. I promise."

I bury my head in my hands, because he sounds so sure. It makes me want to cry. I wanted to be a good person. I wanted to do things right.

He's rubbing my shoulder now, stroking my back. His fingers are a benediction, cleansing me. Soothing me. I can feel him breathing behind me. His chest is so much bigger than mine. So much harder. All of a sudden, I have an absurd desire to turn around and kiss his throat.

I arch my back against his soothing strokes and it's like he heard my thoughts. He turns me around to face him, and suddenly I can smell him: a potent blend of heat and skin and male. I don't dare kiss him, but I can't stop myself from nuzzling his throat. God, the way he feels. Those blue eyes. I'm looking up at him and I can see them glowing in the darkness. I can see his mouth. I want to kiss those perfect lips, to tell him how much he means to me. How much this means.

The thought is like a directive. I arch my back, wriggling closer to him, so my breasts are pressed against his chest, and I see his eyes widen. Then my lips touch down on his, and Evan jerks.

I'm worried he will pull away, but then he groans—and that's a sound I remember. My head spins wildly as his mouth responds to mine. God, he's hungry. I wrap my arm around his back and hip, trying to squeeze him to me as our mouths dance. I slide my tongue inside his mouth and tug him closer and he throws his head back, shuddering as he breaks contact.

"Careful, baby."

I run my hand over his neck, tickling his hairline with my fingers, but I can't be careful. I can't do anything but pull him closer to me. The way he's breathing—fast and hard—lets me know he doesn't mind. I find his mouth again and this time, he is rougher. Hungry.

"God you taste so sweet."

I am gasping. "*You* do."

I'm lost in the sweetness of him. Unexpected. I never thought a man could be like this. So gentle and rough and soft and hard at once. I want him so much—and Evan wants me, too.

He eases me back against the pillows and he climbs on top of me. I can feel the weight of his body between my legs. I grab his butt and press him into me. I can feel his hardness where I want it most. The world spins.

"Merri. *Merri*." He groans again and starts to sit up. I grab his biceps, pulling him back down.

CHAPTER TWENTY-FIVE

CROSS

"DAMNIT, MERRI." THIS, as I sink down on her small, soft body. My right hand tunnels into her hair, caressing her forehead. I press my mouth to hers and Merri tastes delicious. Like a peach. Her lips are warm and velvet soft. Mine glide against them, and as she works her way into my veins, I feel my body trembling. Her hands are wrapped around my biceps. Her hair is everywhere. Her eyes are shining in the dark.

I kiss her once more, then pull away. I need to go. Now.

She takes my face between her soft palms. "Don't, Evan."

"I can't stay."

But her mouth won't let me go. She kisses my throat, and I press myself against the heat between her legs and it feels incredible.

She's got her arm around my back, keeping me locked in place, and it's all that I can do to keep my fingers from trailing in between those curvy legs and finding her damp heat.

She glides her hands down my sides and I moan her name. Oh, fuck. How long has it been? I can barely get my fucking breath.

"Evan." She tugs my hair, bringing my mouth down over hers, and I don't hold back this time. My tongue plunges inside her, tasting and teasing, and I squeeze her breast, stroking until her nipple hardens under my hungry palm.

She shudders, and I swear to God I see stars. I'm slipping beyond my stopping point when, with a ragged breath, I wrench my mouth off hers. It takes every ounce of willpower I have, but I pull myself away.

"Be careful what you ask for, angel." It comes out almost a growl.

Her fingers skate over my mouth. "I needed that," she gasps. "I'm sorry."

"There's nothing to be sorry for." Unraveling her hair from around my hand, I back away from her, rising up on my knees and pressing my palm hard against my cock in a futile effort to calm myself down. "Be careful. You're almost too much for me to resist."

"What if I feel the same way?" Her voice is wobbly, like she hasn't spoken in a long time.

"You don't. You don't have a damn clue what you're getting yourself into." I sigh loudly, pressing my hand against my forehead.

Merri sits up, her gentle fingers curling around my elbow. I inhale the sweet scent of her shampoo and feel the heat of her body and see the confusion on her face, and I can't do it. I just can't be this damn close to her.

I'm off the bed and to the door before any more mistakes are made.

I STAND OUTSIDE her door for a few minutes with my back against the wall, breathing heavily and trying to will my erection away. I think about Merri on the other side of the wall, and the soft skin of the inside of her thighs, and all that long, red hair, and I know if I don't leave the hallway, I'll end up back in bed with her.

Walking makes everything worse, so I end up back in my room, yanking my shorts off and palming my stiff cock. One stroke and I can feel my balls draw up. My legs fall apart and all I can see is Merri's face, her breasts, her hair. I can feel her mouth on my neck and I picture it moving lower, down my chest and down my abs. I can feel her kitten-pink tongue lapping up and down my dick. I imagine the feel of my head in the back of her soft, hot throat.

I come, furious spurts that shoot all over my belly. It's the first time I've gotten myself off in months. It's the first time that I haven't felt alone.

Merri

I OPEN MY eyes, and I know right away something is different. The pale brown fabric canopy stretched above me lets me know I'm at Jesus's underground getaway, but that doesn't explain why my body feels so soft and languid.

Why I feel so…

Evan.

Holy crap, last night with Evan.

That's what's different!

I flip over on my side, desperate to see him there beside me in the bed, and I hear a whistle from the other side of the room.

"This way, sleeping beauty." He's sitting in a chair with his forearms on his knees. There's a leather bag at his feet—one I recognize from the bike. He must have gone outside to get it. My eyes slide up his body and I find him dressed in a deep blue t-shirt, ragged-out khaki pants, and scuffed-up boots. His dark brown hair looks shiny and clean, and his left hand sports a fresh bandage.

I sit up, pulling the sheets over myself, and I notice Evan's eyes comb over me. There's a weird expression on his face, like he's intensely interested…but unhappy about it.

"You sleep okay?" he asks.

"I guess so." I glance over him again, wondering where he slept. Wondering, as I did last night for hours as I tossed and turned, what he meant when I said I didn't know what I was getting myself into.

Looking over him again, I feel a misplaced sense of possession. A sense of excitement and concern. I want this man. My heart beats hard and fast, and I try to water down my feelings with mundane small talk. "Where did you sleep?"

"I was in here with you," he says. "You were quiet."

Meaning I didn't freak out or cry in my sleep. "That's good." I push my palm through my mess of hair. I probably look like crap, and Evan is all clean and showered. I grip the sheet pulled over me, feeling self-conscious and confused. He must notice it on my face, because he frowns. My awkward-o-meter starts buzzing and I know I don't want to talk about last night. Not yet. So I ask about his wound.

"How's your hand?"

He shrugs. "Not bad I guess. No gangrene yet."

"Good." I nod. "That's awesome." I look around the room for windows, but it's just a habit from when I was at the clinic. I know there are none here. I look at him again, getting hung up on those blue eyes. Not just his eyes...but everything about him. I like the way he moves, the way he speaks, the way he smells. I remember how much I liked his lips on mine and have to look back at the blankets.

I can't believe that happened last night. I can't believe how much I want him now. I feel so...drawn to him. Like we're magnetized. I fold my hands together and hope that he can't see it on my face. Seconds tick by. I can feel the tension coming off of Evan, too. He doesn't like what happened last night. That's the impression that I get. It brings me back to Earth.

When I think it's been a full minute of silence, I turn toward him and do my best to put on a neutral face. "What time is it?" I ask.

Without looking anywhere but my face, he says, "It's a few minutes after six."

"Oh, okay. That's good. We should leave here soon."

Evan nods. "I fixed the bike."

My eyes bulge. "Yours, with the flat tire? Are you kidding me?"

He shakes his head. "I got up early."

How early would he have had to have gotten up to do the things he's done so far today? I arch a brow at him. "Did you sleep?"

His mouth tugs up on one side. "Quit worrying, woman. I slept some."

"Is your head feeling okay?" I'm reluctant to pry, but I can't help wondering.

He shrugs. "Pretty good."

His eyes hang onto mine as the half-smile on his lips falls away, and again, no one speaks. This is incredibly awkward. I guess I've forgotten just how awkward things can be in these sorts of situations.

Something passes over his face—some emotion that is there, then gone—and I hold my tongue another beat because I think he's going to say something. *Last night was inappropriate*; *you mean nothing to me except in a business sense*: something like that. When he doesn't, I take a big, deep breath and force myself to act like things are normal between the two of us.

"So, are you ready to leave? I can just get some clothes on and then I say we just...go."

He nods, just as stiff and forced as I am. "I don't think we have the time to focus on...the laundry room."

Right. He means the body.

"We don't." It's horrible, but it is what it is. We need to get out of here and try to make it to the border.

Evan stands up, steps over to the bed, and hands me the bag from his bike. "Here are those things I bought you, if you want to use some of them now."

I frown, trying to remember what's in there, other than deodorant. I swear, my body temperature just climbed two degrees in the second he's been standing near me.

"Just the toiletries I showed you the other day, plus some clothes," he says.

"Clothes...?" I wiggle my eyebrows, praying he doesn't say 'panties'.

"Some shorts, some pants, a jacket. I should have given them to you sooner but I wasn't thinking." He shrugs, as if it all means nothing to him.

"Okay, well thanks." I take the bag. "Did you buy it yourself? That's really thoughtful."

He looks embarrassed. I think I actually see some color in his cheeks. Without thought, I reach up and cup his cheek with my hand. His slight smile spreads into an irresistible grin.

"I'm a thoughtful dude."

"Dude." I grin, too. "A California dude."

The smile falls off his face so fast, I wonder what I said. He takes a swift step back and nods gravely. "I am."

I'm confused. "Is that a bad thing?"

He shrugs. "No. Guess not." Looking like someone killed his puppy, he nods my way and slips quickly through the door.

CHAPTER TWENTY-SIX

CROSS

"THANK YOU FOR the toiletries. I didn't use all of them yet, because I'm going to wait on my next shower, but the deodorant is wonderful, and I much prefer these clothes to what I was wearing last night."

Merri is standing before me in the kitchen, looking sexy in a long-sleeved brown t-shirt, black cotton yoga pants, and the green and purple sneakers she had back at the clinic. The way her wavy, strawberry hair hangs over her shoulders reminds me of a fairy tale princess. And I have something that will make her look even better.

"I also wanted to give you this." I hold out my black leather jacket to her and belatedly decide I need to explain. "It's overcast." *And I want to see my clothes on you. Because I'm an inappropriate freak.*

She takes it, pulling it up against her midriff. "But you ride in front…"

"And you're my passenger." I crack a small smile, thinking how hot she'll look on the back of my bike. Then I remember who the hell she is, and I quickly wipe it off my face. "Keep the jacket."

I turn around and open the refrigerator, unloading bottled water from the door into my arms. I've already packed a few bottles, plus some homemade bread and beef jerky, into the storage compartment of the Mach, but I needed an excuse to turn away. I can't even look at this woman without getting hard. I laugh a little under my breath, because this is so perfectly fucking Cross.

In lust with my father's former mistress.

That's not how I see her of course. Merri is radiant. Lovely. But untouchable for the very huge reason of her history with my father.

It makes me furious, because her past isn't good enough for her. And neither am I. I hate myself for letting her languish in Mexico for so long. She'll hate me when she finds out. I know she will.

That's why I need to keep my distance now.

Without turning around to look at Merri, I carry the water into the hall, outside the laundry room, where I've got the Mach all patched up and ready to go. It took me a little under an hour to cover the two holes in the rear tire with the stuff in the patch kit I keep inside my bag. It's not 100 percent trustworthy, but it should hold. I've got our passports tucked into the small, flat zip pouch I've got strapped under my shirt. Merri's carrying my bike bag, and I guess I'll have to turn around and grab that from her.

I ignore the stench coming under the door of the laundry room and turn around and point myself toward Merri. My legs close the distance between us with long, greedy strides, as my mind counts down our time together.

From where we are, just outside Camargo, we can probably make it to Ciudad Juarez in five hours, give or take, if I drive like lightning.

There, she will find out who I am. If she doesn't get a glance at my passport, she'll notice the name on hers: Meredith Carlson.

Maybe I shouldn't have used Carlson for her surname, but my father is the patron saint of drug control in California, and this means he's funded a lot of upgrades for border patrol and scheduled a bunch of campaign stumps along the border, which means most of them know his name. After my last Mexican adventure, a lot of people know me, too: Cross Carlson, black sheep. If we run into trouble, I'm going to juice my name for all it's worth.

Merri is leaning against the counter with my big, heavy bag slung over her shoulder. I've got a great view of her profile: small, straight nose; smooth lips that always look pink and are maybe a size too big for her face (I think this is one of the reasons I'm always wanting to kiss her); full, squeezable cheeks; slightly pointy chin; soft, elegant throat. My gaze races down her body and I jerk it up before her eyes notice mine.

She presses those pink lips into a tight smile. "Ready?"

"Yep." I take the bag from her and sling it over my back, walking in front of her so my wandering eyes don't get me into trouble.

From behind me, she says, "Evan."

"Yeah?" I look over my shoulder to find her frowning deeply.

"Do you know...if I'm wanted by anyone in Georgia? The stuff I said my ex, Sean, might have tried to blame on me?" She catches her lower lip between her flawless, white teeth, and I want to punch the bastard in the nose.

"No, you're not. You're not wanted for anything. I ran your name before I left."

She nods. "Okay. Cool." But her lighthearted tone of voice doesn't go with her body language. She looks weighed down. Nervous.

I wonder if she feels fucked with, because of what happened last night. I wish I'd had more self-control.

Or less...

Heat washes over me, just the thought of last night making me hard again. I look from the bike to her. "Let's get out of here."

She nods.

I strap the bag to the back of the bike and take the black and grey helmet off the seat. "Here. This is yours, remember?" She takes it from me and cradles it to her chest, giving me a sad look.

"What?"

"I just...kind of think you need it more than me."

Because of my neck. I shake my head. "It's yours."

"Thank you, Evan."

After strapping the thing onto her head, Merri pushes the visor up and presses her back to the wall, getting in front of me and the bike. She opens a little metal flap on the wall where the door is and says, "Did you notice this? The camera?"

"Nah, I just chanced it."

"Well, there's nobody out there that I can see." She pauses for a second while she takes in a few different views on the screen below the metal flap, then looks back at me. "I'm going to press this button and make the door open. You push the bike out and I'll press it again so it closes, then hurry out and get on behind you. I don't want to linger."

"Me either."

"After we get going, we're going to take back roads for a little while and then get on a main road. I forgot the name of it but I'll know it when I see it. Just pay attention when I tap you and we should be okay."

When she presses a button on the wall, I've got my left arm in its support and I'm pushing the Mach awkwardly, the way I always do now. I high-tail it outside, where the dusty ground is mud and the sky is a sheet of melancholy gray.

I start the bike up, then get on, nearly falling over as I do; with my arm already in its strap, I'm not very mobile. But I manage, somehow, and then Merri climbs on behind me. She calls over the hum of the motor which direction to veer in. I nod.

Her arms wrap around my waist, and my cock hardens as I gas the bike and we coast down the path the late David chased us down. We wheel around the house/dirt mound and I pray no one is waiting for us on the road.

They're not. Our path is a barren, cracked ribbon of asphalt, faded pale from the sun and lined with desert scrub.

I drive fast: ninety. Behind me, Merri feels like everything I didn't know I wanted, and I wonder what it will feel like to lose someone I never had.

I was right about the drive. Slightly more than five hours later, we're nearing the end of our sprint to safety, on the outskirts of sprawling, dirty, sophisticated, dangerous Ciudad Juarez. Up until about thirty minutes ago, we'd seen almost no one.

We make a quick stop at a gas station and after we study the map for a few minutes, I walk Merri to the ladies' room, counting down the seconds until we're back on the bike. Before I pull back onto the road, she squeezes my waist.

"We're almost there, Evan!"

I nod, glad she can't see that I'm not smiling.

I'm a selfish ass.

As we work our way through almost an hour of thick mid-city traffic, I'm tense with wanting to get her somewhere safe, but a part of me is also glad for every minute spent without her knowing who I really am.

You need to get over it. Forget about her. The sooner the better.

I know that's the logical thing to do, but logic means nothing to me. I can't think straight when I'm near Merri. That she's the one girl I can't have: that's a curse I fucking earned. I tell myself I'll have to tough it out, and when I feel the hollowness inside my chest, I just ignore that shit. Nothing else I can do, right?

There are a couple ports of entry into El Paso, and we're headed toward the one Meredith thinks will be the least busy. It's a tiny bridge near some farm land, and by the time we reach it, my heart's pounding hard enough to make me sweat despite my lack of bike helmet.

Merri's grip tightens on my waist, and she presses her cheek against my back. I inhale deeply, trying to save the moment onto my hard drive. I have the sinking feeling I might need it later. For the next five minutes as we wait on a transfer truck to pass, my neck aches and my arm feels strange, but I know it's just from stress. Nothing weird going on here. I've got the appropriate papers, plus our pass-ports. As soon as we get through the checkpoint, Merri will be home free.

I try to find happiness in that.

When the wooden bridge spits us out at a rickety ply-wood wall topped with barbed wire and outfitted with a rusted metal tower, my stomach clenches so hard I think I might be sick.

Merri's hands stroke my back. She's feeling grateful, I realize. She lets out a little whoop, and as a black van is waved through the gate, I'm washed in cold sweat, kind of like the feeling you have when you're in opiate withdrawal.

We roll closer—close enough so I can see two dark-haired border patrol guards with automatic rifles—and I tell myself again that I'm just being paranoid. Feeling nervous because I had to ditch my gun at the last bathroom stop be-fore the chekpoint. Anticipating what's going to come next, with Merri.

I swallow hard as we get close enough that I can see the tallest guard's eyes. They go right past me, seeking Merri's face behind the helmet. Sweat breaks out on my chest, and I have the overwhelming urge to gas it right past him.

I slow down, though. Automatic rifles make big holes in bare skin, and Merri is behind me.

I slow down, and both guards lunge at us. Before I can even stop the bike, the larger one's hand is locked around my left arm. The shorter one shoves his gun into my face.

Merri

MY ARMS AROUND Evan's waist go numb as the barrel of the semi-automatic is shoved into his face. Before I can scream or even flinch, the larger guard points his own gun right at my nose.

"Get off the motorcycle!" he screams in Spanish. He waves the gun, his torso bobbing up and down as his face twists furiously. "You are coming with us!"

I blink at him. Logically, I understand why this is happening, but some part of my mind—the innocent part, the part that still has dreams and wants—is stunned to stillness. This just can't be real.

"GET OFF THE BIKE!"

I shut my eyes as the cold, hard muzzle digs into my forehead.

I know I should go with these men. I should spare Evan. We're still in Mexico, and even in a big city like Ciudad Juarez, the Cientos Cartel has sway. Enough sway to install two cartel lieutenants at a rural border patrol post. But my fingers won't let go of Evan's shirt.

"This is the girl! I have seen her before!" The muzzle slides down my forehead, bruising my temple. "Come on, bitch! Or you'll have a hole in your head!"

Somewhere in the back of my mind, like crickets singing in the background of a Southern front porch conversation, I can hear Evan imploring the other guard to listen to him. He says that I'm his wife, and we're headed back to our house in California.

I want to cry, because I want it to be true. But my emotions have dried up. My mind is only capable of processing the simplest facts. The one that stands out is: Evan will fight them for me. He won't let them take me; he'll fight, and he'll get shot. This gives me the strength to hold my hand up, signaling my gunman to lower his gun, and swing shakily off the bike. Despite my determination to surrender, my legs are weak as jelly. I collapse into the guard, who scoops me up under his arm and starts to run.

I shut my eyes. This can't be real. This isn't real.

I picture Evan and me, back on the motorcycle, both wearing bullet-proof vests. In my re-creation of our fate, when the faux guards pull out their guns, Evan just jets past them, through the gate that would have swung down over us. They're lousy shots and all their bullets miss us. In real life, I'm panting, probably close to passing out from fear. I've surrendered fully, accepting my fate, but I want to stay awake. I combat my near-debilitating terror by remembering the feel of Evan's warm, hard abs underneath my hands.

From somewhere close, I hear screaming. The shrieking peel of rubber on asphalt. Gunfire. *Evan!*

Don't open your eyes.

I tell myself the sound of whirring tires was Evan, jetting past the border.

It's time to go. Time to go to God.

I open my eyes with a plan to fight my captor. That way, I'll get shot and die without the rape I know is coming.

CROSS

THE GUARD WHOSE gun was in my face is bleeding all over the ground, his forehead ripped open like a busted watermelon. The other still has Merri. She's tucked under his arm like a football. He is running toward another fence, behind which is a navy blue Range Rover with shiny rims. As I gas the Mach and fly toward Merri, thugs dressed in military gear pour out of the Range Rover and start to run toward her, too.

Fuck no they won't. She's mine!

I lean forward, pressing the weight of my body against the handles so I have better balance, and with my right hand, I raise the stolen semi and spray all of them with bullets.

It's a risky move. One, because I wobble on the bike and almost crash. Two because the ones that don't fall, fire back. I feel a searing pain in my right calf but I can't think about that now. One of the car's passengers—a woman with long, black and white striped hair and a bullet-proof vest—is almost to Merri. It takes everything I have to raise the gun again with only my right hand and aim at just her.

As I pull the trigger, I actually pray. *Please, God.*

I only have enough strength in my arm to pull the trigger once. Somehow, the woman falls.

The other thugs running toward Merri start to scream and wail, but my eyes are trained on Merri. Her long, red hair ripples in the hot wind. Her legs kick. Her hands claw her captor's arm. He yells something.

I try to follow her as I swerve to dodge bullets. One thing they're screaming makes it through my head:

"CHRISTINA..."

"Christina, Christina!"

"Christina! No! No!"

I remember the name Christina. That's Jesus's sister.

I feel another bite of fire, this time near my throat. Adrenaline sweeps through me, and I make a bold decision. I point the bike at Merri and her captor, and I surge forward, toward them. When I'm close enough, I aim at the bastard's head and slam on my brakes as Merri tumbles to the ground.

Merri

I OPEN MY eyes, and all I see is ground and sky, flipping like I'm rolling down a steep hill. Pain shoots through my body—stinging, tearing pain—and I realize that's because I'm rolling on asphalt.

"MERRI! COME ONE! GET ON THE BIKE!"

That's Evan's voice. Blearily, I note some of the cartel's remaining higher-ups running toward us. I feel heat shoot through my hair and smell the bullet as I whirl around to find Evan, wide eyed and urgent, on his bike.

"GET ON!"

He can't help me and balance the bike at the same time. He's holding the phony guard's light-weight semi-automatic rifle with his right hand in the most awkward position I've ever seen in my life. The second my butt touches his bike seat, we shoot off like we're on the back of a runaway horse. Bullets follow us, pinging against the bike's metal. Ripping, again, through the curtain of my hair. Hitting Evan's right shoulder.

He screams "fuck," the bike's rear tire slides a little, then we pick up speed, shooting through the gate. It takes me a moment to notice that the roaring noise behind us is Christina's blue Range Rover mowing down the barbed-wire fence. They're coming after us.

Then I notice Evan's bleeding really bad.

"Keep on going," I scream. Blood is pouring down his back, but we don't have another choice.

I can feel Evan panting underneath my arms as he fights against the pain. We swerve around a mechanical arm and through a crack in a second, half-opened gate, passing a few cars that must be sitting, waiting for this interior gate to let them through.

I hear the roar of the Range Rover behind us, then hear metal crush metal and turn around in time to see the blue SUV bash into a white Mercedes Benz. Horns start honking but I don't care right now.

We're through. They're not. And Evan's blood is dripping in my lap.

CHAPTER TWENTY-SEVEN

CROSS

THE PAIN BRINGS tears to my eyes as I call over my shoulder, "Take the gun!"

I would pass the damn thing to her but I know I'll lose my balance if I try. The shoulder hurts like a motherfucker, and I know that for once my history with pain makes me lucky, because if I weren't used it, I could never stay upright on this bumpy ass road.

As it is, I try to breathe through my teeth and tell myself that if I can't keep it together, terrible things will happen to Merri.

Her left arm tightens around my waist and her right one comes around to take the gun. It's easier to drive once she has it. I pick up speed, back up to ninety, but I quickly drop down to eighty, then seventy. My vision is blurring, every time I inhale, smearing the yellow lines in the middle of the road.

I feel like we're on fast-forward. The scrubby bushes that line the highway are trembling furiously. The clouds in the vast, blue sky are racing overhead. My pulse comes in uneven bursts. I know it's because of the bleeding, but there's nothing I can do about it until we get into El Paso.

As it is, I'm worried we'll get stopped by cops. Or maybe that would help, I think hazily—they might help get me to a hospital—but they also might ask to see our passports.

I feel Merri's helmet bump against the back of my head just as her breath warms my neck. "Do you want me to drive?"

I struggle to swallow so I can answer her, but I can't get my throat to work. I'm shaking so bad now. I don't want to do it, but I brake and pull over on the side of the road, where I barely stumble off the bike before I'm violently sick. Merri's arms are around my back, and I'm so fucking disgusted with myself.

Time to phone West for another rescue, says a little voice inside my head.

You'll bleed out by then, a morose voice answers.

I can't stop the groan that comes out of my mouth. It's muted by the thumping of a helicopter. I look up, feeling like I'm living in a nightmare. The blades are slow...so slow. The helicopter lowers in the parched field out in front of us, kicking up dust.

"Is it them?" I hear myself ask. I don't even know who 'them' is. I can't think straight anymore. All I can do is look at Merri.

Her eyes are so wide. Her words sound very slow; unreal. "It's the border patrol." Her grip on my left arm tightens, and I struggle to keep the black to the edges of my vision. Her lips move, and I try to pay attention. She frowns, and I try to shake my head. I feel her hand on the side of my face.

"Evan, do you have those passports?"

I nod—so slow. I feel like I'm underwater. I raise my right hand to my chest, where the pouch is still strapped below my shirt.

Got to stay awake. Got to stay awake until I show them our passports. I'm going to need to explain this to Merri.

"Evan." I feel her hand on my back. "Are you okay?"

"Never...better, honey." Before the black takes over everything, I reach under my shirt and get the passports out.

"Give them these," I hiss, "and tell them we're married."

Merri

I HOLD ONTO Evan's blood-soaked back and stroke his wild, dark hair. The passports are lying in the grass at my feet. Out in front of us, only twenty or thirty feet away, are two border patrol officers, each carrying an automatic rifle. I don't know who they are or what their agenda is, but there's nothing I can do except pray they'll help us.

Evan hasn't passed out yet. It takes a lot for him to pass out. Right now he's got his left arm wrapped around my right knee and his face is pressed against my side. Every so often he'll mumble something that sounds upset, but I can't understand him.

The skin of his arms is cold and clammy. There's an exit wound just below his collar bone—I'm able to see it because his shirt is ripped open there—and that's good I guess, but he's still losing a ton of blood.

The agents are running, and I steel myself for the possibility that they're in the cartel's pocket. They're close enough for me to see their faces. One is short and broad, with red hair and freckles, and the other one is slim, with buzz-cut blond hair. Both are frowning. Both lower their guns as they get closer. I scramble for our passports as I let emotion wash through me.

"Ma'am, I'm Agent Frank Burns with the United States Border Patrol," the blond says. "Identify yourself."

I open my mouth, but before I can say anything, I start crying. It's adrenaline crying, so the tears come easily and quickly overwhelm me. Sobs punch through me, and Evan groans as I jar him. The idea that I hurt him makes me cry harder.

When they're so close I can see sweat beads on their faces, I thrust our passports at Agent Burns and grab Evan closer. "You've got to help us! We were coming through the checkpoint and...oh my God, these people shot my husband! He's bleeding really bad, please! You've got to help us *now*!"

Agent Burns glances over Evan and I, then opens one of the passports and frowns at it. My heart rate does double-time and I get a dizzying head rush. As his bushy eyebrows draw together, he sticks the passport between his teeth and opens the other one, like we're at a traffic stop and we have all the time in the world. After a long look at the second passport, he shoves them both into his partner's hand. Behind them, the ragged hum of the helicopter's blades shifts its tone a little and I worry it will leave.

The redhead takes both passports and opens the top one. I sob harder, letting myself get lost in the fear that they won't help us.

I'm confused when the redhead cracks an ironic little smile. "Carlson?" His eyes search his partner's face as my heart thuds in my chest. *Carlson.* Why did he say that name! Do they work for him? Oh my God.

Agent Burns turns his brown eyes to me and wiggles one eyebrow. "Cross Carlson, huh?"

I blink at him, not having any idea what he means.

He nods at Evan. "He wouldn't by any chance be the son of California's Governor Carlson, would he?"

The governor of California? His son? My brain is moving in slow motion. Are they asking me if Evan is Drake Carlson's son?

I shake my head. Tears are pouring down my cheeks.

"Is he..." I shake my head again. I have my mouth open to say *of course he's not,* and then I picture Drake's face. It was harder and older and his eyes weren't blue, but Drake had such a pretty mouth. Like Evan's.

"Oh my...yes." I hiccup a sob before I can get another breath, and then I'm nodding frenziedly. "Yes, he is. He is, and that means you have to help us! You have to take us to a hospital! Right now!"

The redhead frowns, looking me up and down like I'm a bug he wants to squash. "And you're the wifey?"

"I'm his wife," I grit. The words feel like barbed wire in my throat. "Now will you help me get him to the heli-copter? We don't have time to wait!"

Agent Burns looks me right down to the bones. "If you weren't who you are, we'd bring you in for questioning, Mrs. Carlson. You look a hell of a lot like a woman who's wanted for murder in Guadalupe Victoria. Tied up with the

Cientos Cartel. I bet that's why they shot your husband."

I nod my head, playing on the confusion that's bursting in my chest. Confusion about Evan, but the guard takes it as confusion over what he's saying.

I flick my eyes to his again, and he shrugs. "Bring 'em in, Arnie." My knees are shaking with relief when he turns back toward the chopper. Evan moans, and the redhead, Arnie, comes around to Evan's other side. Evan is—

No, not Evan.

CROSS!

The man clinging to my leg is Cross Carlson, playboy, black sheep son of Governor Drake Carlson.

He moans as he's hoisted to his feet and draped over Arnie's broad back. The agent starts toward the helicopter, but I can't seem to get my feet to move.

Cross Carlson. My Evan is a Carlson.

I hold my head, feeling like I'm going to pass out. When I think about the governor sending someone to find me after two years—sending his own son—I almost want to give myself to the cartel.

It's NOT ENOUGH, I want to scream. It's not enough that Drake sent someone to save me now! That he finally realized the mistake he made with me. It's not enough! After what happened before I left Jesus...

"Damnit!" I sink down into the dirt, holding my chest and gasping as I struggle not to totally break down. *I want Evan*...but he's no one! "Cross Carlson..." I sob the name. I don't want him! I don't want a Carlson anywhere near me!

I put my hands over my eyes and stare down at the dirt as my body trembles and my stomach roils.

"Ma'am, you coming?"

For the longest time, I can't look up.

"Mrs. Carlson!"

Who am I?

Missy King.

I'm Missy King. Just leave me here!

Drake Carlson didn't give a damn. Sean didn't give a damn. My father didn't give a damn. Nobody ever has. Shame at who I was—at who I am—rolls through me like poison. Cross never cared. He only wanted to lure me to the States. To his father. "Oh God…"

"MA'AM!"

I'm sobbing again as I glance up and out across the field. The guard looks annoyed. The sight of Evan's body slung over his shoulder pierces me, because I care about him. I care about him and he's Cross Motherloving Carlson.

I'm really not sure that I can follow them.

CHAPTER TWENTY-EIGHT

Merri

SECONDS LATER, ARNIE drops to his knees and dumps Evan to the ground. Across the field, I can hear Cross— Evan—Cross— coughing violently. The sound makes my whole body go cold, but I still can't move.

Tears flow down my cheeks, dripping down my neck and soaking my shirt collar. As I watch the agent pushing back Cross's head and bending over him, I want to yell at him to be gentler. But I don't speak or move. I'm rooted to the ground by wrenching, soul-deep disappointment.

What did you think, Meredith? That 'Evan' loved you?

I start to sob again, fully aware, even as I do, that Cross is fighting to breathe and I'm a selfish bitch.

I *want* to go to him.

I can't.

I can't go with him. If I do, I'll just be Missy King again. It's true that I'm Missy King here, too, but at least in Mexico, I took control of things. I ran away from Jesus. I helped kids at the clinic. I learned massage therapy. If my only choices are being repossessed by Drake or dying here, I think I should just die here as Merri,

I turn and finally I have the momentum I need to move somewhere. I throw my legs out in front of me, sprinting toward the road and Cross's motorcycle. The thumping whirr of the helicopter blades is a roar now, and I imagine that behind me they're loading up. About to leave. I fist my hands and run harder, telling myself that this is my only choice. I can't be Missy King again. I can't go back to Drake Carlson. Not even for his son.

That's when I hear my name—my real name: "Meredith." It's like he knows I want to run.

But that's impossible.

I start to count aloud. I'm not turning around and I don't want to hear him—but there it is again.

"Meredith!"

His strangled, half-choked voice is barely audible, but I can hear it, and it sends a jolt through my whole body. I'm panting, half sobbing. *I can't be Missy King*, I remind myself. *I won't be Missy King again!*

I reach the bike and wonder if I remember how to start one of these things. I wrap my hand around the handle, and that's when I notice the blood all over the seat. I want to think of myself—of what I have to do—but all I can think about is how he clung to me in the shower, begging me not to leave him to face his pain alone.

I can't leave without making sure he's okay.

When I turn around, I see him, not on his way to the helicopter, but clinging to Arnie and limping toward me.

"Meredith?" I can't hear him now, but I can see my name on his pretty lips. And as I walk closer, I can see that there's blood on his lips, too. The guard is waving, looking at me like I've lost my mind.

Cross's face is pale as snow. His brilliant blue eyes look almost black against his bloodless skin.

Holy crap, he's bleeding out for me.

I rush toward him. If I tell him to leave, maybe he will. Maybe Arnie will make him go.

I get within a stone's throw and he moans my name again.

"I'm sorry," he rasps. His glazed eyes struggle to focus on my face as his words slur. "Don' leave me. Please Merri...don't leave me."

That's when he passes out.

I TRY TO convince the guards to take us out of El Paso, but they tell me Cross is losing blood too fast. Immediately afterward, I feel terrible for even asking, but I'm scared. We're way too close to Mexico for comfort, and I don't think it'll be hard for the cartel to figure out where we were taken.

During the brief flight to the hospital, I give them as much of Cross's medical history as I can, focusing mostly on what I know about his neck. If they have to put that breathing tube down his throat, they might need to know to be careful.

It's like being in the *Twilight Zone*, holding his hand as the chopper's de facto medical officer starts an IV, and reassuring her that all the scars on his hands and in the crook of his elbows don't mean he's a drug addict. He just had a bad motorcycle wreck a while back.

This helicopter isn't really equipped for landing at a

hospital, but because of Cross's last name, they make some special arrangements and I'm told we are landing on the roof in ten minutes.

I want to ask the agent who's acting as a nurse questions about what happened after we left—what happened with the cartel—but I don't dare.

The agent/nurse, named Lisa, reassures me that 'my husband' should be okay.

He wakes up only once, to insist no one give him any narcotics. I stroke his hair and tell him I've got it covered. With all the energy I have left, I'm trying to play the role of his wife. Now that I'm on the helicopter, I can't afford to have any of these people doubting our story. When his eyes flutter, I can tell he wants to talk to me. I'm glad he's too weak. For right now, I'm not allowing myself to think too much about the fact that he's a Carlson. I just need to get him to the hospital.

As soon as we start to descend over the roof, Cross's eyes flutter again. The nurse tells me it's because his blood pressure is pretty low, but Cross is looking at me, trying to tell me something. Finally he grits, "Marchant," followed by "Love...brothel."

During the months I lived in Vegas, I met a few great women who worked at Love Inc. I happen to know Marchant Radcliffe is the brothel's owner.

"You want me to call Marchant Radcliffe?" I ask, confused.

Cross coughs, and the nurse tells him to stop talking, but he's stubborn. His eyes hold mine for just long enough to croak, "My...friend."

It's weird to think of 'Evan' as a real person to begin

with, but it's even weirder to think of him as Cross Carlson, friend of high-rolling Marchant Radcliffe. Luckily, we're bumping down on the roof, so my thoughts are directed elsewhere.

As soon as Cross's cot is hauled out of the helicopter, we are whisked down in an elevator to what I can only assume is an operating room. When the army of doctors and nurses leaves me in a pale blue plastic chair just outside the stainless steel doors, I take a deep breath and go in search of a free phone.

I find one, as well as a computer accessible only if you pay it quarters. A kind-looking nurse slips me four of them as I sit down. I mutter, "thank you" and look up the brothel's phone number.

As I dial, I consider asking for an old friend, an escort named Geneese Loveless, but when the polite receptionist answers, I ask for Marchant and I tell her it's an emergency. That his friend Cross Carlson is in one of the ORs at the University Medical Center in El Paso with a gunshot wound.

I hang up before she has time to go find the pimp himself.

CHAPTER TWENTY-NINE

CROSS

I OPEN MY eyes to a blaze of white light, and within seconds I'm choked by panic. I can see arms, torsos, and faces moving over me and I know where I am. In a hospital. I thought I was out of the hospital...but maybe I'm not. Oh God. Oh fuck. What happened?

The voices around me get harsher, more urgent. I can feel someone holding my legs down. Someone else tries to hold my head still, and I can hear a soothing voice telling me I'm okay, but I know I'm not.

I'm not okay.

"Sir, you need to try to calm down. We're re-sewing your wound. You pulled the stitches out in recovery so we had to bring you back to the OR."

My heart trips over itself. I open my mouth, and it's hard to get words out. When I do, they sound thick and clumsy. "Did you give me...any sedatives?"

"We did," says the disembodied voice. "You had general anesthesia."

I attempt to shake my head, causing the hands on my temples to tighten. I shut my eyes and try to fight the tears

building behind them. After several deep breaths, I remember something—someone. I remember red hair, and the
memory makes me feel good.

Meredith.

I can feel myself trembling again. That's how much I
want her. With effort, I focus my eyes on the head above
me and manage to rasp a question: "Where is Merri?"

"Mr. Carlson, please calm down. We'll be finished
with this soon and you'll be settled in the ICU."

The ICU. I shake my head. I can't go to the ICU.

"I need Merri." Some part of me, some lucid part,
knows how pathetic it is that my voice is cracking, but most
of me just doesn't care. Using all my strength, I raise my
right arm and grip the first white sleeve I find.

"I need Merri!"

The only answer I get is a tsking sound, followed by
the sound of plastic crinkling.

"Get some rest," a male voice says. Black fuzz swallows everything.

Merri

I'M IN A closet near the OR recovery room. I know it's
crazy, but as soon as I hung up the phone, a couple of cops
walked past me, in the direction of the OR. Last time I
checked, Jesus owned a lot of cops in El Paso.

Coming here—turning back and getting in the helicopter with Cross Carlson—was a mistake. I don't know what

story he cooked up, so I'm not sure how to convincingly play the role of his wife, especially if the cops get suspicious and start really grilling me.

For the last year and a half, I've tried not to lie except when necessary to protect myself. And at the clinic, it was almost never necessary. So it bothers me that I'm sitting on a box in a closet full of paint and mops, contemplating how best to deceive the police.

Actually...everything about this situation bothers me.

I don't want to pretend to be Cross Carlson's wife, but in the last few hours, I've also decided that I don't want to leave without talking to him. I feel like I owe him that. I've remembered the shoot-out at the clinic, the one at Jesus's hideaway, and the one at the border checkpoint. I've remembered his kindness and humor.

I also remember what his mouth felt like on mine, and when my mind dredges that up, I have to direct my attention to the labels on the paint cans. I'm not strong enough to dwell on my feelings for 'Evan' right now. Not when I'm already feeling so directionless and alone.

I shut my eyes and listen to the intercom. If I strain my ears, I can hear what's going on, and I want to be around if I'm called to Cross's room.

Cross—my husband.

I wonder what the Carlsons really want with me. I think not knowing is what bothers me most. The governor and I didn't have a particularly deep or rewarding relationship. The guy was all about blow jobs and I was all about money. That was it. He was deceived by Priscilla and Jim Gunn about my motives, and I'd be surprised if he didn't still believe their tale. *My* tale. The one they made me tell him.

I prop my feet on an upside down mop bucket, entertaining the idea that Priscilla and Jim Gunn finally got caught. Down in Mexico, they have an expression that translates: 'you do it once, you do it always'—so in other words, once you get used to making big bucks selling people, you tend to do it again and again. Maybe they did it one too many times.

Maybe Drake Carlson realized that Priscilla and Jim Gunn used him as much as they used me. Maybe he started feeling guilty almost two years after the fact. But that doesn't explain why he would send his son—his injured son—to Mexico on a super risky mission to find me. The governor has enough money to hire someone else, so why didn't he?

Maybe he didn't want to risk anyone finding out.

I bite my lip. That could be it.

So the best case scenario is: guilt.

Only what if it *isn't* guilt? I remember trying to make a sexy joke once about Drake becoming 'Mr. President', and he raised his eyebrow like it was possible. What if Drake Carlson *is* running for president, and he's trying to tie up his loose ends? The problem with that theory is, I'm not a credible dis-creditor. Who would believe me, a former escort and former sex slave to the leader of a cartel?

But even a headline could be damaging.

And I did come from a "respectable" background. I went to college, unlike a lot of the people who get kidnapped. Cross knows I wrote for the student paper, so maybe they're worried I'm more resourceful than the average bear.

But if that's the case, why didn't Cross just kill me down in Mexico? Why risk bringing me across the border? In fact, that applies to all theories in which the Carlsons could want me dead.

I consider the idea that I'm some sort of revenge. Maybe Cross is using me to get back at his father for something. He doesn't seem like the sort, but he mentioned not letting people get away with what they did to me. And all the while, he knew it was his own father.

I don't understand, but the one thing I know for sure is I don't have all the details. I'd like to, and from the horse's mouth.

"Damnit!" I hear a pretty female voice on the other side of the door, and then it opens, and a topless girl walks in.

I'm momentarily stunned silent.

This girl looks like a model for Macy's. She's got chin-length, butcher-cut brown hair with sun-kissed highlights, and her hazel eyes shimmer with the kind of eye shadow job that only wealthy, fashion-conscious people can produce.

She's not actually topless. My eyes pass over her face and down her swan-like neck, drawn to her lacy bra, visible underneath a ripped white blouse. Small, pert boobs are on display—at least they are until her hands fly up to cover them. She has flawless nails, too. My gaze is roving her outfit, curious to see what this human Barbie wears, when her hands fly from her boobs to her face and she starts sobbing.

I take a step back and try to think of what to do, but it turns out it doesn't matter. As soon as the first sob pops out, the girl sinks down to the wax-shiny floor, tucks her legs up around her, and buries her head between her thin, tone arms.

A moment passes, and I notice her scent. It's all sweetness and vanilla. Not perfume. It must be lotion.

C'mon, Meredith, get with it.

The girl is sobbing like the world just ended and here I am, staring at her with my jaw on the floor.

I need to say something. I'm just not sure what. It's been so long since I've seen someone like her... Compared to this flawless creature, I don't even feel female. I'm like...desert scuz. With blood all over my yoga pants and long-sleeved t-shirt, I've considered putting Cross's leather jacket back on a few times, but instead it's sitting folded on a shelf above me; I want to put it on now, but that would just draw attention to what I'm trying to hide.

I'm in the middle of a mental tug-o-war, fighting my urge to see Cross with my fear of being found by dirty cops or the cartel, and trying to decide what to do about the girl, when she starts talking through her tears:

"What's wrong with me? What's wrong with ME?!" Her eyes fly up to mine, and I blink.

The girl hops to her feet and spins in a circle like a cornered humming bird. Then she throws up her hands. "I don't understand what's wrong with me!"

I don't either. I look the crying girl over, holding her desperate gaze with my calming one. I ask, "What happened to your shirt?"

She covers her face and starts to cry again. Just when I'm wondering how horrible it would be to bolt, she peeks at me from between her skinny fingers and heaves a teary sigh. "I tore it."

I frown—that much is already obvious—and she shakes her head. "No, I'm saying *I* tore it. I got pissed off, and I tore it! Like a wrestler!"

I laugh a little, then cover my mouth, feeling terrible, but the girl starts cackling, too.

"It's okay. I'm insane. I know."

I shake my head, because even though I have no idea what's going on with her, I definitely understand the senti-ment. "You're not insane. Just upset."

She nods, and as she does, she's looking me over. Probably noticing that I'm blood-stained and my hair is crazy. Her brows narrow, but only for a moment, and then she's crying again. "My life is so messed up. You don't even know. First my fiancé broke things off and then I fell for my best guy friend. It was messed up—really messed up—but I've had a crush on him since like, the dawn of time, and he was in the middle of a really awful time and I just… I don't know." Her voice cracks.

"I think I just wanted to be invaluable to someone." She swallows, nodding as she holds my gaze. "He really needed me at the time, and I wanted to feel special." She sniffs and wipes her nose. "I let myself get carried away. And then I embarrassed myself. And now he's here, and I want to be his friend and be here for him but I'm not sure how I can." Tears drip off her chin and she wipes them out of her eyes. She glanced all about the room, then her eyes land on the shelf beside me. Her lips pucker, and she glanc-es to me, then back to the shelf.

"Oh my God, is that Cross Carlson's jacket?" The cry-ing starts again as she points a finger at me. "Are you his wife? Are you the biker chick he met in Mexico!"

I'm sure I must look like a deer in headlights. The pretty girl's eyes pop out, and she turns her back to me. "I can't believe I told you all that!" She wails. "I can't—Oh my God!"

"I'm not his wife." When I say that, she turns slowly around, and I get the feeling that whatever I say next is helping her off some kind of ledge. "I don't even know him," I say. And then the lie just goes from there. "I'm a nurse. I came in off-shift for a meeting with my boss and I got caught in the commotion surrounding, I guess your friend? Mr. Carlson. I helped them get him from the roof to the OR, and someone handed me this." I feel like I'm giving this girl a piece of my heart as I pass the jacket to her. "I'm hiding in this closet to avoid…my boss," I quickly lie. "He and I have this complicated thing…"

My heart is pounding and I feel like a lying sinner, but the girl isn't focused on me at all. "You saw Cross? Oh my God, how was he?"

I don't want to tell her. I'm being possessive of my knowledge, because at this point it may be the only thing I have.

"He was…" I fumble, then realize I can bypass my emotions by playing the role of a nurse. "Your friend had a gunshot wound, but I'm pretty sure it didn't hit anything vital. When they took him to the OR, the general consensus was that he would probably be fine."

"Oh my God." She covers her face, then seems to remember her chest and covers it with her other arm. "I'm so embarrassed that I freaked out like I did. It's just…I heard my friend got married to this random woman he met on this biker trip to Mexico. My other best friend is getting married, too, and..." She shrugs, and her face collapses like she's going to cry again.

All my possessive pseudo-animosity is gone, and suddenly it's like I remember how to be a woman. A normal, American woman...not a sex slave or a nun. I wrap my arms around her, and the woman's pretty face is pressed against my shoulder.

It's pitiful, because all I can think is that I'm happy I get to comfort someone Cross knows. Someone he cares about. I know he would like that.

I really shouldn't care.

After a minute, she pulls away. "Thank you," she says, and I can tell she's working hard to hid her embarrassment. She slips on the jacket and I smile. "See? No one will know about your shirt."

"Except my therapist." She laughs, a hollow little sound. "I think I need to find one, ASAP."

I shrug. "You don't seem too crazy to me."

"Maybe not," she sighs. "I'm definitely terrible at the boy-girl thing, though."

"Maybe you just haven't found the right boy." It sounds trite, but it makes my heart ache because I think of Cross. No son of Drake Carlson can ever be the right man for me.

The girl standing across from me bites her lip, then shakes her head—reminding me, in that moment, of someone years younger. "Not really," she says, as her eyes glitter with tears again. "I've started thinking there's just...no one."

I hug her again, this time one-armed. "That's not true.

There's someone for everyone."

She sighs. "My guy is probably a missionary on some tiny island somewhere."

This makes me laugh, and a second later she giggles. She has a cute-sounding giggle. As we smile, I can see why Cross likes her. Before I can wonder how much, the intercom hums on, and a woman's voice calls my name. Well, she says "Meredith Carlson. Please come to the Operating Room Intake Desk."

My lungs seize up, because the woman didn't say who was paging me—a nurse or the cops. Maybe I should just walk out. Hitchhike to Vegas. I could do that, couldn't I? It would suck, but I could do it.

The girl sniffs loudly. "I guess I can go meet the real..." She almost loses it. "His new wife," she finishes gamely. "I think maybe that means he's out of surgery now, and we can get an update."

I hold my breath. I hold it for so long I almost start to see stars. Then I make another choice—the choice not to leave quite yet, despite knowing Cross has people here for him. "Would you like me to walk you to the OR waiting area? You seem like you could use some company and I'd like to see how the patient is doing."

Cross's pretty friend smiles. "That'd be great."

She zips the jacket, igniting a sting of envy somewhere behind my breast bone, and we step into an over-bright hallway that smells of stale coffee and antiseptic.

I can't believe I'm doing this. Stepping out into these halls with nothing to shield me. No one to protect me. If the cartel is on my heels... If Cross killed Jesus's sister, Christina... If he *didn't*...

I'm a fool for not just leaving, but I can't seem to walk away.

All of a sudden I notice Cross's friend is looking at me, and I realize she doesn't know where she's going. I'm the 'nurse'. I'm supposed to be leading us.

"Oh, the OR waiting room. Sorry." I rub my eyes. "Long day."

Her gaze trails down my clothes, and her lips pinch together. "Are those dark stains from…"

I let my sorrow over all of this show on my face, and her expression matches mine.

"He's had a really rough time," she tells me as I lead us to the waiting area.

I don't want to hear this from her…but I do. "What happened to him?"

She sucks her perfect lip into her perfect mouth. "He got into a motorcycle wreck a couple of months ago. It's a really long story, but let's just say he had some enemies. One of them caught up with him and…it really is a long story, but it led to his wreck." She lowers her voice and moves her head a little closer to mine. "People think he wrecked because he was drunk. It kind of tarnished his reputation…not that he was thought of as a saint before." She sighs. "Anyway, after that he had a lot of health issues. He was in a coma, then he had a stroke. His parents are selfish, awful losers and they never came to visit him at all." Her shoulders rise and fall, like she's taking a deep, composing breath. "It just makes me so mad, you know. He's a good guy. He doesn't deserve what's going on."

I nod, feeling twenty things at once: the strongest of them are jealousy, want and loss. I'm not sure how much more Cross stuff I can stand to hear from this woman's mouth, so I ask a self-serving question. "Why was he down in Mexico?"

She shrugs. "That's the thing. I really don't know. My friend Liz said he was going to some motorcycle convention, but her fiancé Hunter is suspicious. After we got the call that Cross was here, we all jumped on a plane together and talked about it. I think it's even weirder because when we got here, another nurse told us Cross had arrived in the helicopter with a wife." Her hazel eyes widen. "A freaking *wife!*" She shakes her head, and I get the feeling she's trying not to get upset again.

"Have you met her yet?" I feel like a wolf in sheep's clothing, but I can't help myself.

The woman shakes her head. "I'm not sure I want to, either."

We walk in silence to the OR's waiting room, and as soon as I open the door, I wish I wasn't here. The place is filled with pretty, well-dressed people who I know at a glance are Cross's friends. There's a very familiar-looking guy dressed in slacks and a button-up; he's got a goatee and hair that is neither red nor blond nor brown, but some mix of all three. Beside him is a handsome guy in a baseball cap, blue jeans, and a worn-out-looking t-shirt; he's sitting in a plastic chair with his legs spread wide. He looks casual, but something about him just screams *wealth!* A pretty, dark-haired girl is latched onto his arm, practically sitting on top of him; that's how close their chairs are. Her eye-makeup is just as smeared as Barbie's. She's wearing skinny jeans, an over-sized white sweater, and charcoal Chucks, and she's got her eyes trained on some double-doors topped with a sign that says 'ICU'.

When I see that, my stomach twists.

I stand there, feeling like I just swallowed a ball of cotton. My blood-crusted clothes cling to me, and I think my heart is going to explode if I can't get my hands on Cross—right now.

And that's when I know: I have to leave. I'm too involved. I'm living in a fantasy.

I'm so grateful that I'm out of Mexico. I'm grateful for Cross's arms around me when I told him my story, even if at the moment I knew him as Evan. I'm sorry and grateful and confused at how he took two bullets for me...but I'm living in a fantasy. Whatever I think this is—it's not.

I don't even know this man.

And if I did know him, it would be wrong. So wrong and weird.

Whatever you think this is—it's not, I tell myself.

Tears start falling, but I keep on moving. This time, I'm not turning back, no matter how much I might want to.

CHAPTER THIRTY

CROSS

I WAKE UP with an IV in my hand and pull it out. I'm itchy, hot, and I feel like I'm floating. I know what this means. I know where I am, and I remember why. I also know I'm alone in this room. I can't see red-blonde hair, and I don't smell her, either.

The IV machine starts its beeping—*'put your IV back in, you fucker'*—and I decide I'm going to unplug it from the wall. The adjustable bed is sitting me up, and I don't really think about why that is before I grip the bed rail with my right hand and agony rips through my shoulder, so bad it leaves me gasping on my back. The lights on the ceiling are spinning like teacups. Teacups at the fair...right? Or is that Disney Land?

A nurse comes in, she's fussing with the machine. I can't make out what she's saying. I don't fucking care. I think the IV was in my left hand but she takes my right one and I'm dizzy but I know her game.

"You think...I can't...take it out with this...hand?" I try to raise my left.

She gives me a look I can't decipher. The room is way

too bright and she's all eyes—a creepy aberration all in white.

All in white…like a bride.

"Where's…my wife?"

"Your wife hasn't been here." Again, those eyes. They're big and green. Like ones I know. "…the police…" she's saying.

But I can't seem to follow. "What?"

"…your sister…"

I shut my eyes. I must be really out of it, 'cause I don't think I have a sister. I focus my eyes on her big ones and swallow past the soreness in my throat so I can croak, "Where's Meredith?"

"…get…sister, sir. Maybe she can…"

She turns to go, and I bat at my right hand with my left. "Turn this shit down. I can't…think."

I GUESS I pass out, because the next time I wake up, the halo around everything is dimmer and Lizzy is sitting in a chair beside my bed reading a magazine. I'm looking at her impassively, trying to get my brain to start working, when she jumps up and leans over me.

"You're awake!"

"…No shit."

Lizzy looks pretty and perky, and for some reason it's fucking annoying. I scowl at her. Don't mean to. My mouth just does it, and I'm too tired to think about why I shouldn't.

"Are you hurting? They've been—"

I shake my head, fighting the dizziness that makes the room seem to tilt a little. "I wanna...get out of here."

Her eyes, on me, are big and concerned. She bites her lip, looking around the room. There's a flower poster on one wall. "You're out of ICU and in a floor room now. They don't want to discharge you until tomorrow at the earliest."

I shut my eyes and sink back into my pillows. "Fuckin' ...stupid."

I think of Merri—I project her image onto the back of my lids. All I want is to get out of here and see her. Is that too much to ask?

I open my eyes again and unleash the full force of my misery on Lizzy. "The only thing I need from you is to find Meredith."

Lizzy looks surprised, then sad. She sits back down and scoots her chair closer to me. I wish she would scoot it back.

"Cross, about this Meredith... No one here seems to know who she is or where she is. We've looked, I'm sure you can believe that. We can't find her. And the police are here. They want to talk to you, but so far we've been able to keep you covered." There's a pause. I slit my eyes open and look at the stupid clouds somebody painted on the ceiling. "In case you can't tell already, they *had* to give you narcotics. I know you didn't want that, but your blood pressure was too high. Apparently they had to stitch your shoulder twice. It was the second time. No offense, but I think whatever they gave you is making you grumpy."

With some effort, I hold her gaze. "I'm not fucking grumpy."

"Okay."

I'm not. I just want Merri. Damnit, I want her so much I can hardly stand it. Where the fuck did she go? I sigh—a little louder than I meant to—and attempt to cover my face with my right hand. A shot of pain reminds me that I can't. I don't have a single fucking arm that I can use. I turn my head away from Lizzy and push my cheek into the pillow.

A second later, I hear her voice. "Cross...who is she? Are you really married?"

My eyes are rolling back into my head, but I don't want to go to sleep. I feel so...out of it. I lift my two-hundred-pound head and make it turn toward Lizzy. "Turn this stuff down, Liz. I don't want it anymore."

Instead of an ass, now I sound pathetic. Like I'm about to cry.

"I'll tell them, C."

I nod. My head feels hot and full. I need Lizzy to leave, but I'm too tired to tell her.

"Cross, who is Merri? Where did you meet her? ...If you're too tired, we can talk about it later."

I force my eyes open, though the effort makes me feel like passing out. "...won't tell?"

She shakes her head. "I promise. No one."

"Missy King," I croak.

I feel Lizzy's warm hand on my forearm. "Cross... Are you telling me you went to Mexico and found Missy King? And brought her back here?"

"Yes." The word's a gasp.

"So the wife story is a lie. You're not married to her."

I open my eyes. The light above the bed is bright—so bright. I can feel the fluorescent bulbs surging in time with my heartbeat. I look at Lizzy's face.

"I love her," I whisper.

Her eyes grow wide and I groan, "Go away."

When she shuts the door, I let a tear slip out.

FORTY-EIGHT HOURS LATER, Suri wheels me down to the lobby of the hospital, a brightly colored, sunny place decorated with big sunflower wall art. Hunter West is waiting with a car, while Lizzy takes care of my discharge paperwork. As she pushes me toward the automatic doors, the wheelchair hits a bump and I grunt a little. Suri gasps, "Oh my God, I'm so sorry!"

Since what I told Lizzy the day before yesterday, everyone is treating me like glass.

It was bad enough after I woke up from the coma, but this level of awkwardness and eggshell walking is maddening. This time, they don't just worry about my health. They worry about my sanity. They pity me. It's almost more than I can take.

The only reason I'm going to Love Inc. is because Lizzy begged me. She insists it's the most logical thing, to keep me safe from my father until I'm healed. I'm sure it's just so she and West can watch me, but she was so sincere I couldn't tell her no.

The automatic doors at the front of the hospital whisk open as we approach, and sunlight shines into my eyes. It's a hot day, hot and dry, and as soon as I inhale the outside air, I'm wrenched with worry over Merri.

Where is she? Why did she leave? Is she safe?

I guess I know she left because of who I really am, but in the middle of the night, as I lay awake with my shoulder throbbing, or got prodded awake by the fucking overzealous nurses, all I could think about is someone taking her from here while I was out. We're in El Paso, the cartel's front yard. What if she needs me?

I will never know.

I have a feeling deep down in my gut that Merri isn't coming back—and by now, I've had enough of these to trust it.

I'm looking at the blue sky when West steps into my line of sight, and I realize—a few seconds behind—that he just got out the side door of a limousine.

He nods at me, and tips his baseball cap. "How ya doing, kid?"

"Better than you, old shit."

This is our version of getting along.

West walks around to the rear of the limo, and I realize as Suri pushes me back that way that he's opening the trunk. What the fuck? "There's a bed in here," Suri says cheerily. "Lizzy got it for you."

Oh my fucking God. "It's a sex bed." I've seen a limo like this before, back in high school. They have little beds in the very back, and the only people who use them are teenagers on prom night.

West, still holding the door, gives me a scowl. "Don't let Lizzy hear you say that. It took her hours to find this, and she even went to a limousine store and bought you sheets."

I shut my eyes and take a few deep breaths. "I'll tell her thanks," I grit.

Suri makes a sighing sound, like she's sad that I don't like the limo. "You want some help in?"

I shake my head, but of course, that's bullshit. She and West know it is, so each one slides a hand under my arms, and I ease my ass out of the wheelchair like a fucking cripple. Up until today, the pain has been manageable, but I ripped off that pain patch they gave me in the bathroom just before we left, and it must have been strong, because I can already feel its absence in my screaming shoulder.

I'm dumped onto my left arm, and about that time Lizzy shows up, climbing into the limo and taking my head in her lap as they ease me onto a bunch of fluffy pillows. She gets me in a position she probably thinks will be comfortable, then comes around in front of me, where I can see her. Crouching on the bed with me, she lifts an eyebrow. "You hate this thing, don't you?"

I grit my teeth and shake my head, widening my eyes so maybe I look sincere.

"Don't lie to me. I knew you would hate it, but I did it anyway because I want you to be comfortable. When we get on the plane, you'll lie on the bed, and when we get to Love Inc., I'm going to make sure you get Marchant's suite."

Her take-charge tone makes my mouth twitch just a little. "Thank you...Mom." I shut my eyes, because I'm starting to see spots, and whisper the rest of what I have to say: "I'm not taking Marchant's room."

"Then you'll have Hunter's old room."

"Whatever you say...Mom."

I'm so damn tired, I just wish they would all leave— and they do, for a second, going around to the front and taking seats. But Lizzy and Suri sit on the row right in front of the bed, and the whole time we're driving to the airport, they keep turning around, to inspect me..

I'm shivering a little because the driver's not a careful guy—that or the road is shit. My shoulder is in agony.

I bite my lip—discreetly, I think, but I obviously fail, because Suri and Lizzy start to fuss like a couple of hens. I can't even turn over and face the wall and get some fucking privacy. With both arms fucked up, I can hardly move.

I shut my eyes as the whole damn car discusses my pain management. Whether I've pulled off my patch. Where I will sleep at the brothel. They come up with solutions for every problem they dream up, except the one that hurts the most.

Merri. Where is she?

I'll have to get used to not knowing.

CHAPTER THIRTY-ONE

Merri

I PULL THE plug at the bottom of the claw-footed tub, but I don't get out yet. I've got my hair piled on my head, and I'm up to my neck in the world's most fragrant lavender bubble bath. I lean against the tub's soft headrest and shut my eyes, figuring if I can mime a peaceful person, maybe I can be one, too.

Since I got here four days ago, I've had nothing to complain about. In fact, I've thanked God more than once for taking care of me. When I was getting off the elevator on the first floor of the hospital, trying not to have a messy breakdown before I made it outside, I saw the familiar-looking guy from upstairs, and I realized it was Marchant Radcliffe. Duh. I think when I looked straight at him, he looked at me, too—and in a matter of milliseconds, he had me ensconced in a little alcove full of leather chairs and magazines.

He said he recognized me from the governor's arm. He also said that after I disappeared, some of the girls who worked with their money to send a P.I. to San Luis to hunt for me. I almost cried when he told me that. That's how unexpected it was.

At first I didn't want to go with him, but he said he'd already chartered a jet for some urgent business anyway, so why didn't I go with him? I didn't trust him, so he offered to call Loveless for me. Once she offered to meet us at the airport and take me to the brothel in her car, I realized I wouldn't find better offers, so I got on Marchant's chartered plane.

The flight to Vegas was rough. I did Sudoku puzzles out of this little book I found in the back of one of the chairs, and as I worked, I let my hair hang down, so Marchant Radcliffe wouldn't see me cry. He stayed in the jet's small bedroom the whole time, though, so by the time we'd been off the ground for half an hour, I just put my head in my hands and let myself go.

A lot of my tears were for Cross—for *Evan*—but I was surprised to find how many other things are getting underneath my skin.

It's just so weird being back in the States. I push the bubbles around on the surface of the water, thinking about how many times I wished for this. How I really didn't think I'd ever be here. Not at Love Inc., of course—but in the States. Today, I used a whole big wad of toilet tissue for a Number One. I nearly clogged up the toilet. The wastefulness of it didn't bother me nearly as much as I'd thought it would. It was kind of nice.

The first day, when I stepped off the plane and into Loveless's adorable red Mini Cooper, I pointed the vents right at me and nearly purred. I rode in an air conditioned car with Jesus, but the clinic didn't have A.C. Just window fans.

One of the first things I did here was use the laptop Rachelle loaned me to look at a few Mexican news sites and blogs. Rachelle is Marchant's second-in-command, and she's been looking after me since Marchant took off on vacation. She's the one who told me Marchant wanted me to use his own suite. I thought that was insanely nice. Anyway, the news sites confirmed for me that the clinic is okay. That's about all I found, other than a very vague news story about some trouble at the border checkpoint we passed through. Sometimes the media is in the cartels' pockets, too.

Is it weird that I know all this? That I know, if they come for me, exactly how they will trace my footsteps? What they'll do to me?

Loveless says she thinks I should talk to the brothel's resident psychologist. So far, I've managed to put her off, but the truth is, I could maybe see the benefit in that. I'm not sure I'd want to be honest about everything, but it might be worth my time to go once or twice.

Maybe I could talk about Cross.

I curl my hand around a particularly glittery ball of bubbles and squish them. The crinkling sound they make doesn't give me any satisfaction, so I climb out of the tub and dry my body roughly.

Cross.

The man I left in ICU.

Son of my very own personal evil villain.

Cross Carlson. Evan. My fantasy.

Since coming here, I've dreamed about him every night. Not dreams—nightmares. While I know that leaving was the right thing to do, the practical thing, the only thing to do...I still feel horrible about it. Cross might have deceived me, but I deserted him. Which is worse?

My eyes burn, and I take a deep breath, releasing tension the way Sister Carolina taught me. I slip into a robe—one of several in Marchant Radcliffe's opulent bathroom closet—and sit in the window seat, which is big enough to be a twin bed. From my spot amidst an army of silk pillows, I can see acres of Love Inc.'s grounds. Pristine grass. Big, willowy trees. There's a gazebo, a labyrinth, and even a duck pond.

Today, the sky is blue. The sun is bright. I'm miles and miles away from Mexico, away from danger...and I'm miserable.

I wander over to the king-sized bed and flop down on the comforter. Within minutes of my arrival here, a housekeeper claimed all of Marchant's linens, leaving me with a fresh, deep green duvet, plus some beige silk sheets.

"Does he go on vacation and leave his room to strangers on a regular basis?" I asked her.

She smiled discreetly and said only, "Mr. Radcliffe is a thoughtful host."

Whatever that means.

Don't get me wrong: It's not that I'm not grateful, because I am. I'm very grateful. Loveless and I have been working out with some of the other girls in the escorts' gym, and everyone I've met so far has been absolutely wonderful—patient, discreet, and understanding, giving me the space I need to process things.

And I have, sort of. I've done a lot of thinking about my last year and a half. What it means to me. The parts I hate. The parts I miss. I've even thought a little about what happened right before I left Jesus. And thinking about it here, it doesn't feel as threatening as it once did. Maybe I can even work up enough nerve to tell the shrink about it.

It's been good being here, and I feel safe-ish. That much, I relish. But I miss Cross. I miss Evan. I miss the guy. It doesn't matter what I call him, who he is—I miss his freakin' face. All four days I've been here. I'm tired of missing him, I decide to find out when Marchant will be back from his vacation.

I have a fantasy, a terrible one I hate to admit, that Marchant's 'vacation' is really a trip back to El Paso. How insane would it be if Marchant was in on Cross's plans, and he chartered the jet just to whisk me off to somewhere safe. And now he's going to get Cross and Cross and I will meet up again here.

It's a fantasy…

I know that.

But after missing Cross like crazy for four days, I feel more willing to indulge in those—instead of less.

I've met two of his friends, and neither Marchant nor bra girl seemed like a Priscilla type. The girl said Cross didn't even tell his buddies where he was going when he went to Mexico. (Yes, I'm aware that makes the aforementioned fantasy scenario highly unlikely. So what?) I ask myself, in light of what I know, what are the odds that I'm actually in danger? Danger from Cross, I mean.

I tell myself they're very low.

I tell myself he doesn't like that perfect Barbie with the lacy bra.

I tell myself I'm not being an idiot. Not like before, with other guys.

This guy is different. At least that's what I tell myself. Then I put on the most comfortable outfit Loveless loaned me, spritz on some of the perfume that I found in Marchant's cabinet, and stride into the hall to take a more active role in my fate.

CROSS

I'M SITTING IN an Adirondack chair on the violently green lawn behind the English manor where Marchant and his women do their business. It's barely three o'clock, and I'm on my fourth screwdriver. There's an open bar just inside the back doors on the main floor, and the bartenders there have practically hunted me down to get me loaded.

It's pity, yeah—they've probably got orders to get the armless guy sloshed—but I don't really give a shit. Too tired.

It's fucking hot outside in Vegas, but my drink is cold, and I'm becoming too numb to notice or care much anyway. I've only been here a day and I'm already sick of it. I need to go back to Napa. I'm still here because something's going on with Lizzy. In my less self-absorbed moments, I can tell. Once I figure it out, I'll do whatever I can for her, but then I'm splitting. I can hear my nice, cold, lonely shop loft calling my name. When I get there, I won't have to talk to anyone or think about anything. Especially Merri.

Last night, Lizzy came to my room to try to get the

story. It's not my room—I got stuck in Hunter's old suite—but that didn't stop me from shutting the door on her. I guess the message wasn't clear enough, because Suri dropped by next, a little after nine o'clock. I pretended to be sleeping, but she had her own key. She came bearing a can of Sunkist. I wouldn't let her give me a sip of it, but I was secretly glad she brought a long straw and left the drink on one of the higher shelves of Hunter's entertainment center—one only a little lower than my head. Lifting my right arm is agony, and of course, the left one won't take orders.

I tell them I'm wearing the pain patches, but I'm not. In a way, the pain is good. It allows me to feel something that's not stuffed inside my fucking chest. It takes my mind off Merri. Already, I'm wondering how soon I can get back to my weight-lifting routine. If I can drive myself hard, this will get better. I just need to go home.

I have no idea where Merri is or what she's doing, and I have no idea what my father knows about what's happened in the last few days. He could do anything. I don't think he'd hurt me, but I don't really know. I know I want to hurt *him*. I might, too. But I'm also opening my shop and getting back to work. Not being able to use my right arm much is making me itchy to do things again, and one of them is work.

I stare out at the yard, shrugging my shoulder just enough to hurt. The wound is sore, but I think it's healing okay. I raise my arm, enjoying the pain as I take another gulp of my screwdriver. It makes my head feel cottony and warm, makes my chest feel full and heavy. Not so empty like it has been.

Yesterday Suri gave me back my jacket. Told me she got it from an off-duty nurse who was around when I came in.

"What'd she look like?" I asked.

Red hair. Had my blood all over her.

Yeah. Bet I know who that was.

Merri left. Got scared and fucking left.

I don't blame her, but it hurts.

I finish off the screwdriver. Make my way inside to get another one. Only when I'm at the bar, I hear myself ask for a vodka on the rocks. I drink it on my way back to my chair. Shit, this shit is strong. I kinda forgot. This must be why I used to drink so much. Have sex, too. Isn't that what I used to do? Fuck around?

I liked that, right?

I did.

Maybe I should go find someone to fuck.

I picture her green eyes and her long, wavy hair. I can't stop thinking of those huge tits. Her hands were always really soft. I liked her hands.

I look down at my hands. I should use them to beat the shit out of my father. One of them. But then he'd know. He would know I went to Mexico.

I think I need a refill. I stand up, and I see a fucking mirage, following Marchant toward the pond.

CHAPTER THIRTY-TWO

Merri

I WAS LOOKING for Rachelle when I ran into Marchant. Well, when I saw him. He didn't see me. He was walking away from the bar downstairs with a brown box underneath his arm. I kind of wondered if he might have taken to taking jobs himself, or maybe having sex with one of the girls, because he was wearing a black robe and black sleep pants. No shoes.

Weird, right?

Well then it gets weirder. I catch up to him maybe fifty feet behind the largest of the three mansions—the one where all the work happens and also the one where I'm staying in his suite. Because I'm feeling bold and a little desperate, and also because I'm super curious about why he's crossing the lawn dressed like Hugh Heffner, I call his name.

He spins around and strides to me, looking so intense that for a second I think he might hit me. Instead he grabs my forearm and snatches me closer. I try to twist my arm away, but his grip is tight.

"W-what are you doing?" My voice wobbles, and I try

to make myself relax. If I relax, there's a good chance he will, too, and then I'll snatch my arm away and run.

I look him over, noting the stubble on his cheeks, around his thicker goatee; also the way his red-blond-brown hair sticks up, like he's been running his fingers through it all day.

"What am I doing?" he asks. "I think the question is, what are *you* doing?"

I frown, and he lets go of my arm. It's a gentle release, as if he just forgot to keep holding it. "What do you mean, what am I—"

"You were following me," he interrupts. His grey eyes widen. "Don't tell me you're a fucking spy."

"A spy?" I shake my head. "A spy for who?" I look in-to his eyes, and they seem...ungrounded. Like Sean's used to get when he'd get really paranoid. But Sean was on drugs. Is Marchant Radcliffe doing drugs?

"You know who," he murmurs.

And then, without another word, he turns and stalks away. I stand there for a minute, trying to decide if I should follow him toward the pond or turn around. In the end, I decide to follow. If he's on drugs or drunk or something, I can probably get more information about Cross—and that's the reason I'm following him, after all. I don't know him, but I'm sure Loveless would have warned me if he was dangerous. Surely she would have, right? I pump my arms and feel grateful that I've got on leggings, sandals, and a flowing shirt.

I might be five-foot-three, but I'm a good sprinter. There's only a few feet of grass between us when I hear footfall behind me.

Now *that* has my heart pounding. Unlike one isolated incident of weirdness with Marchant, who is in all likelihood drunk or high or coked up, everything's going to get a lot weirder if that's someone running after *me*. It's the middle of a sunny day, in a semi-public place.

But still, my heart is hammering. That's definitely someone's footsteps. I work up the nerve to turn around, feeling a ridiculously powerful rush of déjà vu, a flash back to when I ran away from Jesus's place almost nine months ago.

I turn around, and there is Cross.

He looks confused, like someone has just flashed light into his eyes. His eyebrows come together, and I realize that he's panting; his broad shoulders are heaving. My gaze flies over him, and I can't help devouring him with my eyes. I eat up every inch, from the loose jeans hanging on his hips to the bulk of bandages I can see under his plain white undershirt. There's a scrape on his throat. One of his dark eyelashes has fallen on his cheek. There's new gauze wrapped around his left hand, where David shot him. His hair looks ruffled. There's stubble on his cheeks. His lips... They're even more perfect than I remembered.

"Merri—what the hell are you doing here?"

I look down at my borrowed sandals, because I'm not sure how to answer.

He sounds pissed. "Did Marchant bring you here?"

"Uh...yeah." I meet his eyes and find them guarded.

"You and him know each other?"

"No. I saw him at the hospital."

"He took you from the hospital."

I nod. My eyes tear, because I feel so guilty for leaving

him. My throat feels tight, so I can barely talk, but he's looking at me expectantly. "I didn't know that you were here," I whisper.

He tilts his head to the side, reminding me for a second of a curious dog. Then he sucks back a tired-sounding breath. "I'm surprised to see you, too."

I widen my watery eyes at him—a random thing I do sometimes when I'm not sure what to say—and he pushes his palm back through his hair. "Fuck."

I flinch at the word. "If you want me to go…"

"No, please." He nods at a bench under a willow tree out in front of us, and I start walking that way. He's moving more slowly than I am, and I slow. I steal glances at him as we cross the short distance, noting little things, like the motion of his throat as he swallows. The way he holds his right arm close to his chest. His face seems unguarded; has he been drinking? Another stealthy glance at his face shows me that he looks upset. I can't believe I haven't seen him in days. I want to know every single thing that's happened. All about the hospital. How he feels. I want to know who Evan really is. I want to know why Cross Carlson came and rescued me.

We reach the bench, and he lets me sit down first. He sits on the grass in front of me, sinking down clumsily.

"Are you okay?"

His eyes flick up to mine. "That's what you're gonna ask?" His voice is low. "You know my name, and that's your first question?"

I nod. I want to touch him so much my hands are shaking.

"Are *you* okay?" His eyes caress my face.

All of a sudden, it feels wrong to be seated on the bench, so far away from him, so I get down on the grass.

His gaze is all over me. Hungry. I imagine that instead of looking at me everywhere, he's licking me, and the thought makes me shiver.

"Are you?" he asks.again.

I nod. "I didn't really get hurt," I mumble.

His mouth twists, and I know he's waiting for me to ask.

"Why did you do it?" My voice is barely audible. I'm not sure I really want to know.

"Merri." He groans my name, and I smell vodka. His eyes are heavy—sad. "I came for you because I knew."

"What do you mean?"

"I found out about you—about what happened to you—almost a year ago." I watch his Adam's apple bob as I try to process what he's saying. "I could have told some-one…but I didn't."

"That's it? Are you serious?" I'm pretty sure my jaw is hanging open. Of all the things I expected him to say, this just isn't one of them. I'm not sure how I feel. Relieved that it's not something worse? Upset that he knew but didn't tell anyonwe?

He looks down at the grass, like he can't stand to look at me. I watch him roll his shoulder, but I'm not really see-ing him. I'm holding my breath.

"I tried to forget about it. I…didn't think that I could help." He shuts his eyes. "My father told Priscilla Heat and Jim Gunn that I knew, and I started being followed. I was… It was easier to forget." He swallows again, and when he speaks, his voice sounds hoarse. "I didn't want to know the details of his philandering. He's always done it. I just...hate it. I guess I didn't want to think that he could do that—what he did to you. That he was such a bad person."

I squeeze my eyes shut, trying to process all this. When I open them, I'm looking into Cross Carlson's face, and I can see Drake there—in the cheekbones; in the chin. "Was he a good father?" It's a weird question, but suddenly it's one I feel like I need answered.

Cross hangs his head. I watch a dry breeze ruffle his hair as he slowly shakes it. After a long moment, he looks back up at me, and I can tell he's not going to go into any more detail.

"I paid for my silence, in a way. Last November, Hunter West, the pro poker player, had a party at his vineyard out in Napa. That night, I got upset about something." His eyes come up to mine, then fall away. "I had a thing for my friend, West's fiancé. She wasn't then, but I did see her with West and I got really wasted."

Again, there's a silence, in which I lean forward.

"I was a dickhead to her, and then I left. I got on my bike, and some guy stopped me to ask about it. After he left I sped away, but I couldn't steer it. It didn't drive right."

I nod, because now what his friend told me in the hospital, about him having enemies, makes sense.

"I had the wreck, and I was in a coma for a while. And when I woke up, I remembered the guy who asked about my bike...and where I knew him from. It was Jim Gunn, my father's old body guard."

I can't breathe, much less respond, but it doesn't matter; Cross keeps talking. "My neck was all fucked up and I couldn't use my hand." He swallows and when he speaks again, his voice is thick. "I found out my parents moved me, while I was out. From this rehab place in Napa, where I'm from...to this other one, in L.A. Bad place," he exhales. "Bad track record for getting people out of comas. There was this therapy at the first place...the good place. And they didn't have it at this other."

He's quiet for a minute, and I watch him flex his jaw. The whole thing... It makes my throat feel tight. I want to hug him. I want to say something comforting, or reassuring, but the easiness between us down in Mexico is nowhere to be found.

Minutes pass. He's staring at the grass. I want to run, to scream, but instead I touch his hand and keep this painful conversation rolling. "Was it—the therapy the new place didn't have— was it therapy that could have brought you out of the coma?"

He nods once, briefly lifting his heavy-lashed eyes to mine. "It did...right before I got shipped off. It brought me kind of out." He rubs his lips together and seems to sink down between his broad shoulders. "I had the stroke on the transport over. I think I had a pain attack. Now, looking back on the weird memories I have..." He shakes his head. "They did a surgery there because my brain was swelling for no reason. Then I got an infection."

I'm about to ask about the infection when he shifts a little, leaning over like he might prop his right elbow on his knee—but he stops short and rolls his shoulder again. He makes a pained face. "My parents... didn't want to pay for the other place."

I can see how much this hurts him. "So they sent you to a place that wasn't good for what was wrong with you?"

His jaw pops, and again he's looking at the grass. The fingers of his right hand play in the blades as his eyes peek up at mine. And then ..just nothing. He won't even look back up at me—and I start to see why.

"I don't understand. Are you saying that he wanted you to...not wake up? Or that he didn't care?"

His blue eyes latch onto mine as he shrugs. "They never visited. Ever. My father called me only one time, right after I woke up, to tell me I was back in the good rehab because my best friend, Lizzy, sold herself, right here at Love Inc. That's how she got the money to have me moved back to a place where I would have a shot at getting better."

His eyes glitter as he tells me this, and I want desperately to take his hand.

"Were they always this way? Your parents?"

He shrugs, looking vacant. Bleak. "Maybe. When I was a kid, I just did what I should. It went well enough. I wasn't good in school," he murmurs. "I wasn't really...excellent at anything." He takes a deep breath, reaching up to rub his hair although the movement clearly hurts his shoulder; it makes him wince. He lowers the hand back to his lap and looks at me bitterly. "My mother is a famous interior designer. My father...well." He squeezes his eyes shut. "I tried to be...likable when I was younger. As I got older, I guess the burden was too much."

"The burden of what?"

"The burden of trying to be their son," he tells me bitterly. "One who couldn't finish college. One who wanted to work on motorcycles rather than go to school for business or law." I have a flash of memory of Cross working on the bike outside the house where we took shelter that first day on the run. "Then when I found out... When I got on my dad's computer one day and saw the e-mails about..." he swallows, "Missy King." He shakes his head, and I understand what he's implying.

"Your finding out just made everything with your family worse."

"It had nothing to do with you, Merri. My father...we just never bonded. I don't bond with people," he whispers.

"Yes you do."

Moving quickly, before I startle him away, I scoot close to him and wrap my arm around his back, lying my cheek against his unhurt left shoulder. I shut my eyes for a second, relishing the steady rhythm of his heartbeat.

I've really missed you. Those are the words that get hung up in my throat. What I actually say aloud is: "Why did you decide to come get me?"

Under my arm, his back stiffens. I pull away to give him space, lean back in the grass so I can see his face as he says, "In January, Priscilla kidnapped Lizzy and me and tried to sell us...to Guapo. Because of what we knew." He rubs his eyes, like just the memory is exhausting. "Hunter West came and saved the day, and that's how Priscilla and Jim Gunn got arrested. We were lucky, and I know we were. I couldn't stand to think you had gone through that and...not been found."

I'm reeling from the news that Priscilla and Jim Gunn actually did get busted, when another thought occurs to me—one that makes my stomach flip. "Do you still have the e-mails? The ones you found?"

He nods, and I wonder what they say about me. I try to picture his face when he first read them. What he was thinking, to do what he did. Was it guilt? I guess it was. He said he knew, but he didn't do anything. So he felt guilty. That's why he came.

Guilt. That's why he hauled me across the border.

Not because he loves you. Not because he likes you.

I cover my face with my hands and Cross is there, pulling me against his chest with his right arm.

"I'm so sorry, Merri."

I start to cry, and my thoughts are so jumbled, I'm not even sure what has set me off. Why can't he just be Evan? *I loved Evan. I was able to love him.* I think about giving Drake blow jobs, about being down on my knees in the brothel. I think about what happened with Jesus, at the end. I pull away from Cross's embrace to look at him, and I know he knows this about me. I sucked his dad's dick. I was desperate enough to be a whore, and in my lowest hour, I was.

Cross's lip is white from where he's biting it.

"You didn't care that you were rescuing a whore? Your father's mistress?"

"I don't know." He shrugs, looking uncomfortable. "I just thought that no one deserved what you got. And then I met you and I knew you didn't." He sighs. "Jesus, Merri. What are you thinking about all this? How do you feel?"

"I don't know what to think. I don't know how to feel. I care about you, Cross...but this is really hard." A tear spills down my cheek—just one hot, lone tear. My last shred of dignity. "I just...I don't think I can talk about this anymore with you."

I turn to go, hoping he'll let me.

CHAPTER THIRTY-THREE

$C\mathcal{ROSS}$

IT'S BECAUSE I'VE been drinking that I follow her. Even as I tromp along the pebble trail that leads to the pond, I know how wrong it is. Merri ran away from me. Going after her is like telling her I don't give a shit how she feels. But I just can't help myself.

I give her a minute or two lead and as I walk, I try to get my head on straight. I shouldn't have had so fucking much to drink. It's hard to figure out what to do, what to say, when I'm this wasted.

I'm being optimistic—foolishly so. I focus on how she said she cared about me, not the fact that she ran. If I remember right, she was pretty damn quiet about what I knew and what I didn't do about it. I know it has to bother her. It has to bother her that I'm my father's son. But maybe I can get her to overlook that.

I follow her toward the shiny circle of the pond, feeling like I want to throw myself at her feet and beg for forgiveness. I'm taking long strides, but Merri is running. I'm halfway around the pond before I start to close the gap between us. I focus on her bouncing, flowing hair and don't allow myself to think.

Out in front of us, on the right, behind a row of big oak trees, are a bunch of little cottages. She turns toward them. She cuts close to the first, but doesn't stop till the second, which is nestled a little farther back, and is surrounded by trees.

I follow around it, and find her sitting on her butt, her knees drawn up, her back against a quaint wooden door. She's not crying. She's just breathing hard.

When she sees me, she goes absolutely still.

Merri

I LOOK UP at his face and feel a vice around my heart. He's Drake Carlson's son. There's no way he can ever really care for me. Men aren't like that. They're territorial. He knows what I did with his father. Drake cheated on his wife, Derinda, and for at least a little while, I was the 'other woman'.

Tears fill my eyes, so he and the trees behind him are smeared, but I still can't look away. I feel my mouth tremble. I'm too upset to even be embarrassed.

Cross is watching me like he's watching his life pass before his eyes. Having him right here in front of me, looking at me that way, is too much at this moment. It's like I'm on one island and he's on another. I don't think the water that runs between us could ever dry up. Not unless one of us becomes someone else.

I wish I could. I wish we'd met some other way. I wish

he didn't know about my past.

I wipe my face with fingers that feel numb, and when I speak, the words sound thick and muffled. "What are you doing here?"

The expression on his face remains the same. Blank. Almost stoic. His eyes roll over me and then he looks away. "Can you tell that I've been drinking?" he asks softly.

I nod. I could smell it earlier.

"I've always been a rash drunk. Doing things I shouldn't." He sinks to the ground in front of me, making a face as he uses his right hand to balance. I lean forward, wishing I'd thought to help him.

He reaches out his right hand and takes my left one, threading my clammy fingers warmly through his stronger ones. He looks down at our hands.

"It makes me angry that he had you. It makes me angry because he didn't deserve you. No one does." He looks into my face. "Especially not me. I lied to you."

"That's true."

"I'm an asshole, Merri. I...didn't think I was, but now I know I always have been. I'm not brave like you are. When people started following me, I was afraid."

"Of course you were," I whisper. I bring our joined hands to my mouth so I can press a kiss on the back of his knuckles, because the least I can do is assuage his guilt. "Cross, you rode into Mexico, into cartel territory, alone, with only this." I squeeze the fingers of his right hand gently and look into his eyes. "Please don't ever think that you're not brave. I don't know of many people who would do something like that. Something so...selfless."

He shakes his head. "I wouldn't call it selfless. I couldn't live with the guilt anymore."

"It was still selfless," I say. "I've made bad choices, too, so I can't judge. And even if it did take you a year, I'm never going to feel anything but grateful toward you, promise. So we can go our own separate ways and as long as your dad never tracks me down or tries to hurt me, I'll be fine."

"I don't want to go separate ways."

His words feel like a stone thrown into the waters of my heart. I just sit there for a moment, unable to move or think. Cross's handsome face is blurry from my tears, but his voice is quiet and strong. "Meredith..." His hand around mine tightens. "I didn't expect to feel this way. I didn't want to. But I do. I know it's fu— it's weird, okay? It's crazy weird...because of my father mostly. But I want to be with you. I want to get to know you more."

I shake my head, pull my fingers from his and scoot away. I press myself against the door and whisper, "You should want to leave."

"There are reasons why I can't." He scoots toward me, thumbing my cheek. "And they are here—" he leans in close to kiss my temple— "and here—" his perfect lips find my mouth and taste it gently— "and here—" he says, kissing me just above my breasts.

He leans in close enough to steal the air out of my lungs and presses a kiss against my forehead. "And that's why I can't walk away, even though I know I should. My father might have found you first, but you were always mine."

He is all around me. I can smell him, feel the warmth

that radiates off him. I can feel his arm thread through my hair and then his mouth takes mine. The kisses start out soft and slow, excruciating. I'm shivering. But pretty soon they turn hungry. I'm pressed against the door and Cross is gently over me, smelling of vodka, breathing my name. The skin of his back is so soft and so warm. My hands are under his t-shirt, crawling up his hard, lean sides, blinded by lust until I feel the gauze.

I tug my mouth away from his and run my fingers through his hair. "I wish I had been there for you. I hate to think of you alone."

"I'm not alone right now."

His lips and tongue find mine, and we are lost again; the sum of us is skin and teeth and tongues. My greedy fingers find the button of his jeans and he is in my shirt, tearing the blouse, moving my bra, taking my breasts into his mouth.

I'm breathing so hard I'm nearly screaming when he moves off me, grabbing something from the ground beside us and rising up over my head. I see a flicker of blue eyes between his arms and he says, "Move, Merri."

I scramble up and hear the sound of breaking glass. Holy shit. He broke one of the glass panes on the door. He starts to stick his right arm through, and I yelp, "No!"

With a quick glance around me—there are only trees— I pull my shirt off and he wraps it around his arm before he reaches through the broken pane. He leans up a little and I watch his ass tighten through the sagging jeans as he works with the lock. The door swings open, and Cross grins.

"Come on, woman."

We're tangled up again the moment we crawl up on a

bed. Cross's mouth is magic, making the little cottage bed-room spin, tracing down my belly. I'm pulling on his hair, stroking his neck. I'm breathing hard and tugging down his jeans.

"Fuck, Merri."

Cross is lying on his side; we pull his jeans off togeth-er: one of his hands, both of mine, and I am stunned to see he's naked underneath. Mother Mary, he's so big and beau-tiful; just the sight of him makes me ache between my legs.

I push him gently back against the pillows and climb on top of him. I kiss his neck and stroke his thighs, and he groans, "Damn. Oh…damn."

He finds my lips with his and tugs at the top of my leggings.

"I'll help you."

But he's managed to get the leggings to my knees, and now he's stroking his fingers gently along the borders of my thong. I'm so wet I can barely straddle him without grinding my hips against his dick.

"I'll get these pants off." I draw away from him and pull them off, grateful for a chance to catch my breath. I'm too caught up in this. I feel like a teenager. For a second, as I pull the cottony leggings over my ankles, I think about being on my knees those other times, but then Cross leans up and strips off my thong.

He lays me on the pillows and crawls on top of me. He splays his right hand on my thigh, then walks it inward. When his fingers touch me there, I gasp. He smiles the sweetest little smile down on me. "You're beautiful," he says. He strokes me one more time. "Is this okay?"

I nod, and his head is lowering over me. I feel one finger glide inside and then his lips touch me. Oh God, his tongue. I'm warm and slick down there and he is stroking me. Stroking inside, lapping outside. It isn't long before I'm shaking violently, pressing my knees around his head and gasping his name.

His finger inside me is exquisite, stroking me just right, while his tongue glides down my center, teasing my most sensitive place, pushing me closer and closer to the edge till I can't breathe. I grab his left shoulder, sinking my nails into the muscle there. He licks me from top to bottom, curling his finger inside me, whispering, "God you're sexy," and it's his voice that does it: low and hoarse, it vibrates through me, sending me just over the edge.

As I shatter into pieces, I can hear him laughing. I hear him mutter, "Jesus Christ, that's sexy" and I can't believe I just did that with him. I can't believe how not weird it feels.

I draw my knees together, expecting to feel spent. Then I open my eyes, and there is Cross sitting, shirtless, on his knees with an enormous hard-on jutting up toward his beautiful abs. I look into his face, that face I've come to love so much, and his eyes are gleaming and I know—I know for sure—that I want to take this further.

"Cross, come here."

He palms himself, looking heavy-lidded and slightly predatory. His voice is soft, though; gentle. "You don't have to. It's not a trade."

I scramble up and clasp his left wrist. "I know, you crazy man. But I still want you."

This time it's me easing him down. I help him settle on the pillows, never breaking his hypnotic gaze as he settles on his back, with more weight on his left side than the right. I'm shaking as I situate myself between his legs.

His eyes are wide and glazed. He's breathing hard. He licks his gorgeous lips, and his right hand finds my knee and squeezes. "No pressure, Merri. I can finish this myself if you just lie beside me."

I shake my head. "I want to touch you." *Need* to touch him.

I was only going to touch him, but the moment my palm skates across his soft, thick head, finding him damp there, all I can think about is taking him inside my mouth. The idea makes me nervous, so I start by licking down his shaft. It's long and velvety and hard as steel; as I stroke him, my left hand gently cups his balls and Cross groans. His right hand strokes my shoulder as those blue eyes find mine. "Merri, are you sure?"

"Shhhh." I reach out and, smiling, shut his eyes. I stroke with my right hand and roll his balls with my left, and I want so much to take him inside my mouth, but I'm scared. Scared he'll push my head down. Scared it'll bring back memories I don't want.

I lean down and Cross strokes my cheek, and that's what lets me know that it will be okay. Cross is different. I wrap my mouth around his cock and squeeze my cheeks around it, and he nearly comes off the bed. "Merri. Oh my God." He groans my name again as he rocks gently into me, and I can tell by the way he's shaking that he's struggling to hold on.

I flick my tongue over the weeping slit at the top of his head and his hips jerk as I cup his tight balls. I take him deep inside my throat and keep things moving for a few more minutes. Then, when I'm sure he's wet enough, I pull him out. His eyes flip open and his hips lift automatically, but he doesn't grab for me or try to force me back.

While I work him with my hands again, I whisper, "Close your eyes."

With his hand cupping my knee, it feels so easy—doing what I want. Moving gently but quickly, so I don't lose all my nerve, I pull his length toward me a little, hold my breath, sit up a little, and sink down over him.

Cross's eyes fly open. *"Merri."*

His eyes squeeze shut and his mouth falls slightly open as I start to ride him.

"Merri. Oh God. Come … lay on me … so I can feel you." He leans his head back as I lift and plunge, lift and plunge, taking him deep inside me. My eyes are open as I wait for memories to surface, but I see his face, his eyes—grateful and surprised—and he's so lost to his lust that I feel safe.

Up and down, up and down, and when I sink down on him, he moans and shudders, grabs my ass. I speed up a little, moving with him in a rhythm that is only ours, and as he strokes my shoulder, I feel safe enough to give him what he asked for. I lean down over him, pressing my breasts against his chest and pumping him with the strength of my lower body. Kissing his throat as I gently stroke his hair and push and pull. His cock inside me is so big and hard, I'm on the cusp of orgasm already.

"Beautiful," he murmurs as he wraps my hair around his hand and shuts his eyes. "Fuck me, you're beautiful Merri."

Our lips meet for a long, open-mouthed kiss, and as his tongue strokes mine, his eyes fly open. He comes with a strangled moan and locks his arm around me. Somewhere far away, I think about moving off him quickly, but it's far away—because then I jerk on top of him, pulling his hair as I'm lost in my own release: so sweet and unexpected.

AFTERWARD, WE LIE there holding each other. Cross keeps kissing me: my cheeks, forehead, chin, mouth, throat. When he pulls away, the smile on his face is the sweetest thing I've ever seen. "That was amazing—what you did."

"You made it amazing," I murmur as I walk my fingers down his chiseled, scar-marked chest, below where the gauze covers his shoulder.

We lie there for a long time, while the sun sinks outside the window and the shadows crawl across the wall, and he just strokes my hair. I close my eyes and decide I'm happy with what happened. It helped me bury some old memories, and it was something I wanted to do with Cross, because despite the impossibility of our situation, I care about him—a lot.

He's wrapped around me, pressing his face into my chest, and I love holding him. I find my mind wandering, daydreaming about the two of us in our very own bed, and that's when the day starts crashing down around me.

What am I thinking?

A future with Cross Carlson can never be. Not just because of his father: for a lot of reasons. Reasons I will never tell him.

I've made a terrible mistake.

Abruptly, I pull away from him and force my body off the bed. Cross's eyes are wide. "Where are you going?"

I find my leggings and start to pull them on, looking down at what I'm doing, throwing him a glance as I search for my shirt. My heart is pounding hard, a warning of what I'm about to lose, but I never had it. Now the only thing to do is go.

Cross is up a few seconds after I am. I steal a glance and find his face is carefully neutral as he pulls his jeans on, then looks up at me, a breathtaking man in sexy jeans. He holds my gaze. "Where are we going?"

"Tell me the truth," I say, straightening my shirt as I attempt to bide my time; weaken the blow; shift the blame; *something*. "None of this is guilt? Really?"

His eyes widen like I've suggested he murders infants. "No, of course not."

"So it's lust?" I smooth my bra and torn shirt, then force myself to look back up at him. His mouth is open and he's wearing an expression that says it's a lot more complicated than lust. I know I can't stand to hear what he will say, so I cut him off. "Even if it's only lust, it can't go anywhere after this."

"Why not?" He looks annoyed, but I can already see through it. He's shocked; he's working his way to upset. I'm going to hurt him.

I need to make this sound logical—like it's not based on secrets and omissions from my past. I heave a deep breath and tuck my wayward hair behind my ears. "What if I want to write about my experience? What if I want to confront your father? How do you know he won't show up here right now?" I take a step back, bumping into a dresser, and Cross takes a small step toward me. The look on his face is enough to break my heart: so earnest, with something warm glowing in his pretty eyes.

"I don't," he says. "But I know that I'll protect you. I'll always try."

Always. He said 'always'. I pretend he doesn't mean it.

"You would turn in your own father?" I ask him.

He nods. "If that's what you want."

He looks so sincere, that I feel tears spring into my eyes. I want to throw something else at him, some other reason why this just can't work, but my throat is closed up tight. "I just don't understand," I cry. Oh yeah...I'm crying now. Crying wasn't in my plan, so I turn to face the wall.

Cross's hand touches my back, gentle as you would be with a baby, and before I can gather my defenses, he's turning me into his chest. He wraps his arms around me, and murmurs, "Talk to me. Tell me why you're upset."

I can only cry harder, because I can't answer that. I can't say anything to him. Or rather, I know I won't. I just stand there, relishing the comfort he's doling out like the selfish girl I always am, and I don't say anything at all. My mind is racing. Finally, I push away and look into his eyes. "Is it because you know I never had sex with any of them? With your father, with Jesus, with anybody else I didn't choose? Is that why you can...be with me?"

He frowns. "That helps," he says frankly, "but that's not why."

"Then why?" I whisper.

"I don't know." He rubs his hair, the motion sharp; frustrated. "Why are you here with me? Is it obligation? Pity?"

"No," I rasp. "I just...really like you." I should never have said it, but I couldn't seem to keep it in.

"That's how I feel," he says gently. "You're very lika-ble. And lickable." He touches his forehead to mine. "I just like you, Merri. Isn't that enough?"

I pull away from him and make some space, so there's no chance he'll touch me when I say this. "You don't know everything about me." My voice is shaking. I'm about to lose it, so I know I need to go. "You don't get it, Cross. Things have happened to me that can't unhappen." I choke on a sob. "I just don't get... How can you not judge me? What if I told you that I did have sex?"

His face goes slack. "With...who?"

"What if it was your father? It could have been Jesus or...damnit, anyone! Would it matter?" He shakes his head, and I raise my voice. "Tell me, would it matter?"

His face is so taut, so unhappy, that I feel a sweet wave of relief. This is it. He's going to walk away and I won't be to blame. It won't be my choice.

Instead, he strides forward and tips my face up so I'll have to look at him, and look at him I do. I do my best to memorize him. "Don't get me wrong," he whispers, "this is a surprise for me. I thought that I would care. Maybe I should care. But I'm finding that I don't. Because I want you so much, nothing else seems to matter." There's vul-nerability in his eyes, and I'm worried—terrified and elat-ed—over what he will say next. "Merri, I—"

"Don't say it!" I say shrilly.

And he gets it: that I'm telling him not to love me. I know he gets it, because his face crumples. His right hand drops down to his side and as he looks at me, his features harden, showing an instant of anger before settling on something that is terribly, wrenchingly sad.

"I don't say anything I don't mean," he says softly.

And that's a shame—because in another universe, maybe we end up together.

I step to him and kiss his sweet mouth one more time. "Thank you," I choke out. "Thank you so much, Cross." I kiss his jaw, and then I go.

CHAPTER THIRTY-FOUR

CROSS

I LIE THERE for a long time. On my back, staring at the ceiling. There's a fan that's going 'round and 'round. I try to follow it with my eyes and push my thoughts away, the way Akemi taught me. While my mind is empty, the room goes dark. Next time I notice where I am, my shoulder aches. I have to focus harder to stay empty.

Eventually I get tired of the effort.

Maybe I want to feel the pain.

I turn on my side so I can smell her in the sheets.

Merri. She was right here, only hours ago.

I curl over on my side and put my hand over my face. The ache inside my chest is crushing—much worse than my shoulder. I feel...broken. Almost like when I woke up from the coma.

I wonder if this will ever go away, and then I think *I don't want it to*. I'll take Merri any way I can have her.

I turn from side to side. Minutes feel like hours. I wonder where my shirt is. I wonder who she fucked. I wonder why I don't care—not at all. I think I know, but I keep the thought away.

I can feel my heartbeat in my shoulder.

Maybe I should go back to the brothel.

Outside, the air has cooled just a bit. I look around, in the grass around the house, but there is no sign of my shirt. I'm shutting the broken door, wondering if Merri will miss me, when I smell smoke. Dinner, I think. I turn toward the main house, and I see smoke, big, dark clouds of it, creeping like fingers between the trees.

Oh, fuck.

I hear screaming before I emerge from the trees, and when my boots hit the soft grass of the long, straight, English-style lawn, there is the brothel: glowing. The fire is contained to one back corner of the main building, but as I begin to run, I can already see it spreading. My heart skips a few beats. What if Merri's inside sleeping? What time is it?

I don't see the edge of the pond until I splash into it. I swerve the other way, blinking through the smoke.

Merri. I just need to get to Merri.

Terror fuels me, makes me faster. I'm past the pond. The smoke is thicker. It burns my lungs but I keep moving.

"MERRI!"

I'm still half a football field away from the mansion, but I can see shadowy figures in the smoke.

"*MERRI!*"

The figures are moving in a group, but I can see from here there's not that many of them. A dozen? Fewer? Where the fuck is Merri?

The blaze is growing. It has climbed up the left side of the mansion and is eating into the middle.

I pick up speed and try to prepare myself for the possibility of going in. I will, if I can't find her. And Lizzy and Suri.

Fuck—there's three of them. I'm near enough to the shadows now that I can see them grouped in a circle.

Someone must be hurt. Otherwise they would be moving farther back. Escaping the smoke that's so thick here, I'm wheezing.

Not Merri, I tell myself as I come up on them.

"MERRI!" She could be one of the onlookers. She would stick around if someone needed her.

I'm almost to them—maybe ten feet away—when the crowd splits up. One half headed toward the blaze, the other clump of figures moving toward me.

I'm confused. Are they firefighters?

And then, from a small distance, I hear her shrieking, "No!"

I can tell it's Merri because I've heard her voice in every intonation this past week. I'm sure it's her because the sound makes all my muscles tense.

"MERRI!" I run around the group in front of me, into smoke so thick I can't see a thing. "MERRI, WHERE ARE YOU?"

"No, Cross, NO!"

It sounds like she's moving farther away, but I can only see smoke and shadows, black against the brilliant glow of fire. I sprint forward, running into sparks now that are falling from the building, and I hear her shriek again.

With all my strength, I hurl myself into the flames, thinking that I'm running into fire when really the fire is somewhere above me. The first floor, right in front of me, is smoking like a chimney but not burning.

I'm gasping for air, trying to climb inside a broken window with only one working arm, when something grabs me hard from behind and I'm slammed onto the ground.

Before I can get my breath again, I hear a low laugh, and something sharp touches my throat. A second later, a large body drops down over mine.

I note a slew of Spanish words before I see the face, and when I see the face, I don't think it is real. The man sitting on my chest, holding a knife to my throat and leering at me through a cloud of black smoke… It's Jesus Cientos.

His blade draws blood. I can feel it run down my neck, onto my shoulders. He presses harder as he glares at me, and I know I'm dead. Then the knife is gone, and he's slapping me with both hands.

The slaps turn into punches. I try to fight, but he's got backup—several of his men emerge from the smoke and hold me down. Somewhere near the back of my consciousness, I can hear him giving orders. Talking about the house. The fire. The girl.

I'm trying so hard to stay conscious, I can barely translate.

"…convenient."

"…whore."

"…David."

"…explosives."

I shut my eyes and wonder: Where is Merri? I remember her voice fading as she neared the flames.

What if Merri's inside?

I'm opening my mouth to try and make some kind of deal when all of a sudden, all the weight is off me and I'm thrust up to my feet. My lungs are shit. I'm coughing and my knees won't work.

"Take him," someone says.

A stronger voice—one I think belongs to Jesus—says, "No. I want to make him watch."

For a couple of seconds, everyone around me is speaking Spanish: so many voices I can't translate, especially since I'm coughing out everything I just inhaled. Then something cold and hard is pressed into my neck and someone shoves me forward. We're marching into the smoke.

I can hear the roar of flames devouring the brothel, even if I can't see much. Then the smoke clears just a little, and it looks like we're in hell. I can barely make out bookshelves, partially charred and burning; over to my left, smoke is pouring from an area that I think might have been the bar. The walls are burning—or maybe that's the curtains. I don't know, because it's hard to think with so little oxygen. I'm coughing like crazy. The heat singes my skin, and I hold out my arms as the inferno around me starts to spin. I hope to Christ I don't pass out before we get to Merri.

I'm shoved once more before the gun pressed into my neck is slammed violently into my eye, and through the blood pouring down my cheek, I can see Jesus looking blurry and angry, framed by smoke. He says something about David. I think I say I'm sorry. I just want to stay on my feet until they take me to Merri.

I pass out for a minute I guess, because when I wake up, we're standing in front of a burning staircase. I'm irritated. Why are we here? And that's when I hear Merri screaming.

Merri

WHEN I SEE Cross, I start screaming again. I can't help it. Maybe screaming will help hasten my end, because as soon as I start, I black out and fall down to my knees. I grab onto the railing when the black spots clear enough so I can see. I just want to make sure he's gone now—that I really am hallucinating.

But when I glance into the inferno of the main floor, there he is: bleeding from the head and being hauled toward the stairs on Tito's back.

"NO, NO, NO! No...*no!*" I flop against the railing, pulling my hair over my mouth because maybe it will filter some of the smoke. I end up clutching at my hair and shaking, unable to move. I really don't think I can breathe this time. I can hear my lungs trying and the sound is terrifying.

"Cross." I start to sob. If I'm going to die, I want to feel his arms around me one more time. And then suddenly, I do. I can feel his body behind mine; over the roar of the fire, I can barely hear him whispering my name.

I hear screaming from somewhere: angry yelling. I can make out 'David' and the Spanish word for whore. Cross grunts like he's been hurt, and I can hear the fire crunching through things around us. It's so hot.

"Cross," I hiss, "I'm sorry."

I can't think straight enough to remember what for, but with the hand that's not chained to the statue, I grasp around for him, finding something I think is his shirt and holding on.

"Merri...I've got to get your hand out of this thing." I

feel him tugging on my bruised and bleeding hand, the one clasped in the cuff, and I can't help but whimper.

"I'm sorry," he chokes. "I'm so sorry, sweetheart."

And then my hand is ripped apart. I'm screaming, screaming, screaming. Then I'm floating through the flames.

CROSS

I BREAK MERRI'S hand—*on purpose*. Before she even gets a scream out, her body goes limp.

I throw her over my agonized right shoulder, holding onto her by her legs as I move through smoke and flames. I try to remember which hand it was: the left or right? Was it her dominant hand? Did I break it in a way that spares her three middle fingers, or will the whole hand be fucked up— like mine?

I'm so dizzy, the problem of her hand is magnified, so it seems more tragic than the fact that we're midway down the stairs and fire is *everywhere*. There's no way we can pass through that. No fucking way.

I can barely tell which direction is up, but I can feel the stair rail with my left hip, and that's how I get us back up to the second floor—by pressing my hip against rail as I struggle up the stairs. When the smoke is too thick for me to breathe, I lean against the railing, praying to God and the Virgin that it doesn't crumple underneath the weight of us. The prayer must have worked, because I make it back up- stairs with Merri still over my shoulder. I can hear her groaning, talking nonsense, but I ignore her.

I need to think.

I find a window—big and vertical—but it's covered with a film of smoke so I can't see how far it is to the backyard. I turn a circle, but all I see down the hall on either side is flames.

I lean my left shoulder against the wall, worrying about the smoke Merri is breathing, and then there's a boom from somewhere and the floor shakes. The ceiling to our right, above the hall that way, has caved in, and fire is rushing toward us like a tidal wave.

I need to do something, but all of a sudden I'm paralyzed because I'm about to die. And it never seemed right, it never seemed real before, because it seemed like it would be too much. That I'd be cheated out of too much. But now I've met Merri. I have Merri with me, and I'm pulling her down my chest so I can feel her face in the crook of my arm, and I'm damn near crying because I wanted something better for us both.

Merri says, "Cross..." and something else, but I can't tell what. Her eyes close. I look around me one more time, but it's an inferno. The only way out is this big, smutty window. I rub a circle on one of the panes and use my limp left hand to make a haphazard cross before I look outside. And when I do, I see the glittering green-blue water of a lit-up swimming pool.

RIGHT BEFORE WE jumped out, I heard gunfire. Turns out it was Marchant. After running through the building, trying to get all the staff out, he split off from the EMTs and firefighters in the front of the building—where evacuees had gathered—and ran around to the back, where he used his burned hands to push back a thin slab of concrete below which a pool was hiding. He said he thought it would prevent the fire from spreading, at least behind the building.

Usually the concrete was pulled back via remote, but somehow he got the thing to slide, so of the 100-someodd feet of rectangular swimming pool in the deck behind the brothel, I had about thirty to jump into.

Lucky for Merri and me, the Carlsons have always had a pool, and more than once in high school, Lizzy and I jumped out the second-story window of the pool house into the deep end. I knew I needed to get a running start and overshoot it some. I hardly remember doing it, but I know I considered throwing Merri down first, and I discarded that idea because I was worried that she couldn't swim. Her body was limp, so I jumped with her.

I remember being worried we would hit cement or yard instead, and I remember that at first I thought we had. That's how bad the impact hurt my burned skin. I remember thrusting Merri up toward the surface as I choked on chlorinated water.

And that's it. That's where our story ends, at least in my memory.

CHAPTER THIRTY-FIVE

CROSS

I'M IN AND out of consciousness for two days at University Medical Center, which, so far, is three days fewer than Merri. I'm a big pain in the ass and get myself discharged early, the third day after admission, just as long as I promise to stay off my fractured ankle and let the ICU nurses coming in and out of Merri's room put an oxygen mask on my face a few times a day. Apparently my lungs are still fried to shit, but I'm told they'll heal if I suck back this bitter-tasting breathing treatment. I'm glad to do it if I can sit by Merri's bed and watch her sleep.

While I like being near her, holding her uninjured hand and playing with her hair, seeing her like this sucks. She was in the brothel longer than I was, and because she was at the top of the stairs, she inhaled a bunch of smoke. No one knows how long it'll take her lungs to heal, and until the doctors feel satisfied with her progress, they're keeping her sedated, on a ventilator.

Yeah—can you fucking believe that? Someone else is in the bed and I'm in one of these dinky plastic chairs. It takes me about two minutes to realize how much I prefer being the one in the bed.

I drive the nurses crazy with my questions, and the only thing that gives me any peace is that they're required to answer me. Lizzy had Merri's fake passport in her purse, still hanging around from when I was in the hospital in El Paso, and when the fire started, Lizzy and Hunter were heading out to dinner—so she had her purse. So far, I've used my husbandly rights to micromanage Merri's sedatives; to demand that she get lip gloss to help heal her chapped lips; to play music from my iPod for her; and to decline a visit from the all-faith minister and select, instead, the hospital's Catholic priest to do occasional blessings.

I'm allowed in the ICU almost all the time, and during the two hours they do shift change, usually the nurses let me chill here anyway—on account of my fucked up lungs. I need to rest.

By the second night, thanks to the sympathies of a nice, elderly nurse named Martha, I've got my very own cot right by Merri's bed. When Martha steps behind the wall to monitor Merri and the other patients via camera, I push it close to Merri's bed so I can hold her hand through the metal bars.

The days crawl by. Six days turn into seven before the head pulmonologist starts weaning Merri's ventilator. She does well, so the next day they cut it down even more, and with it her sedatives. That night, she opens her eyes smiles at me. Then she notices the tube in her throat and starts to cry big, silent tears that rip me up. By the time they take the damn thing out the next day at noon, I'm feeling cagey and helpless. Worried about what will happen when she and I finally talk.

I've had a lot of time to think, but I still don't understand what happened that day in the cottage after we had sex. How she kept acting like she didn't get why I would want her and then she implied that maybe she had sex with my dad. It was like she *wanted* to make me say I didn't want her. Because when I told her it didn't matter, that didn't make her happy. It made her leave.

When it's late at night and I'm lying in my cot, listening to the machines around her bed, the only conclusion I can ever reach is that she just doesn't want me, and she was using all the other shit as a means to make me not want her.

This is why, on the evening of the day that they removed her breathing tube, I'm hanging out in the cafeteria rather than the ICU, while the nurses do some X-rays on her lungs to see if she's able to move to a room outside the ICU.

I'm on my second plate of bland potatoes and plastic chicken when a dude about my age, in a long white coat, stops at my booth.

He's got dark skin; short, curly hair; and the most serious-looking face I've ever seen in my life. I'm on my feet before I swallow the chicken in my mouth, because I'm scared to shit that something's happened to Merri.

The guy steps back, holding out both hands. "Hey, man. I mean no harm."

"Did something?"

He frowns, then a look of realization spreads across his face and he shakes his head. "I'm sorry. I didn't mean to alarm you. I'm here about you. You are Cross Carlson?"

I feel my breath catch in my throat, and I look the guy over, wondering if he was sent here to fuck with me.

He smiles, revealing straight white teeth. "Well, are you?"

I rub my face. "Yeah. Why?"

He takes a seat across from me and extends his hand again. "My name is Dr. Marty Grantham and I know you as Case Study C from an article published last month in the journal *Neurology*. You injured your neck in a motorcycle accident, correct?"

I frown, glancing at the clock behind him on the wall. In just a few minutes, they'll probably be done with Merri, and I want to be back in the ICU.

I flick my gaze to him. "Yeah, I fu— I screwed it up. You a neurosurgeon?"

"Orthopedics—and neurosurgery."

"Okay."

I stand up and grab my tray, and the guy follows me to the garbage cans, where I scrape the food off my plate and stack my tray atop a bunch of others. When I turn to head into the hall, he folds his arms.

"Look, Mr. Carlson, I don't want to waste your time, but I was wondering, has anyone suggested to you that removing the metal caging around your vertebrae and using a simple chicken bone procedure instead could alleviate the pressure on your damaged nerves and alleviate some of the symptoms you're experiencing in your arm and hand?"

I blink, then frown, then shake my head.

"Where are you going? Why don't you let me walk you back, and I'll tell you what I have in mind."

IT'S NOT UNTIL the next day that I know there's something wrong. Merri's awake—they don't have her sedated anymore—and I'm familiar enough with her pulse ox and other monitors to know when she's sleeping... But she won't open her eyes and talk to me.

She doesn't want me here. I know it. But I just can't leave.

Merri

I KNOW I can talk now, but my throat hurts so much, I don't even consider it until the lights are dimmed for the night and I know Cross is somewhere in the room. Before I speak, I turn my head just a little to the side so I can see him. He's shirtless in what look like scrubs, and in the faint glow of his cell phone, I can see the beautiful contours of his chest and shoulders.

When my gaze rolls over his face, hot tears fill my eyes. That's how much I've missed him, even though I know he's probably been here the whole time.

I want to talk to him, but I'm not sure what to say, so I just lie there and watch him. I try to focus on his handsome face, but too often my mind takes me back to the night Jesus found me in the labyrinth. The way he pushed that knife into my throat and grabbed my breasts so hard he surely left bruises.

"You're my wife," he hissed into my face. "Why did you think that you could leave me?"

I was so, so shocked, I didn't even plead for my life as Jesus held a gun to my head and said it was for David. I think he was about to shoot me when he noticed the smoke in the sky. He smiled, and I remembered that devious face from before, when he was about to do something terrible; it made me shiver.

He dragged me out of the labyrinth and to the back of the mansion, where a couple of his underlings were waiting. People were pouring from the building, which was burning on the left side. I tried to scream for help, but Jesus clamped a hand over my face. There was so much panic, no one even noticed us.

Jesus pushed me up against the burning building and he tried to rip my pants off. I was still wearing Loveless's leggings, though, and they were made of spandex, so they wouldn't rip. I could tell by the way he breathed that he was still very much wounded. He hadn't died, but he probably almost had.

He kept trying to get me to tell him I was sorry, but I know Jesus. I knew that if I did, he'd kill me on the spot. When someone apologizes to Jesus, he uses it to justify whatever awful thing he wants to do; they must be guilty, because they said 'sorry'. I had my eyes shut, praying for it to end quickly, when I heard Cross's voice. I guess I must have flinched or something, because right around then, Jesus left and some of the others pulled me into the burning building.

The weirdest thing about it was, I never felt real fear. I panicked, of course, when they started pulling me up the stairs and the smoke was so thick I couldn't breathe, but there wasn't that bone-deep fear of death. All I wanted was for everyone else to make it out alive. I guess, in my mind, I've been tied up with Jesus for so long, I always kind of knew that it would end badly.

It's the main reason I couldn't be with Cross—or anyone.

I lie there on the hospital bed thinking about Cross, thinking of what I can say to him to make everything okay. But there's nothing, so on my last night in the ICU, I can't bring myself to say a word.

Sometime in the wee hours, I hear Cross murmuring into the phone. He sounds unhappy. My nurse—the older woman with the nice blue eyes—comes in, and I think she shoos him out. He comes back a few minutes later and gets back on his cot and I can feel him moving close to me. I hold my breath then, wanting his touch as much as I know I shouldn't, but all he does is rest his forehead on the bars of my bed and breathe.

I still can't bring myself to move or speak.

Morning comes—I know this only because the lights come on—and everyone in my room is excited. I'm doing better. Requiring less oxygen through these plastic tubes in my nose. They're moving me to a regular room.

I leave my eyes shut, pretending that I'm resting, but really I just want to know if Cross will stay or go. I'm out of danger now. Maybe he won't feel obligated to stay.

It's not lost on me at all, as they wheel my bed through halls and into elevators, that I'm in Cross's position. The exact same position that I left him in, in El Paso. It's also not lost on me that I don't hear his voice or see his body through my half-shut lids.

A FULL DAY passes. I'm alone in my room. The nurses come and go, and it's all that I can do to force myself to speak to them. I know my body is healing, but I feel dead inside.

I'm napping when my door creaks. I slit my eyes open, because it feels too early in the afternoon for another vitals check. I turn my head a little, and my breath lodges inside my battered lungs. Before I can start to breathe properly again, Cross is at my bedside. He's leaning down and pressing his face into my hair.

"I missed you." He kisses my forehead and pulls a chair beside my bed, and while I lie there with my eyes shut, with my heart pounding, he just talks…like this is normal. He tells me about his parents, first.

"I had to leave because my mom came into town. Sometime while I was down in Mexico, she decided to leave him. My dad."

My eyes are still shut. Cross takes my hand and starts tracing my fingers, the way I did one time to his.

"She's kind of pissed off. At everyone. She doesn't want the house in Napa anymore, she said, so she gave me all the keys. Apparently my dad's been gone a week already." I hear him shift, and I can sense that he's leaned forward, closer to my bed. The railing on my hospital bed is folded down now, and I imagine I can feel the heat of his body through my blankets.

"Last night, at the hotel, I called my dad. I told him you've been evaluated by a psychiatrist here and that you've told 'her' what happened to you. I told him that you're not sure what you want to do yet, but at least he knows if he were to want to..." Cross pauses. Sighs. "If he were to come after you or some shit, at least he knows he'd be the first suspect. And Merri—" he squeezes my unhurt right hand— "I don't think he'd ever do that. I just wanted you to feel safe."

Silence fills the room, and that's when the tears start flowing. I didn't plan to cry, but my body doesn't ask permission. Cross does what I sense he will and leans down to wrap his arm around me. When he does, I lean into his neck and cry, "I'm married to Jesus!"

It's the only way I can tell him, I guess. Like jumping into cold water, I just have to do it.

I feel his body stiffen, and I cry a little harder as I wait for him to pull away. Instead he gets in bed with me, curling over sideways so he doesn't crowd me. After a minute or two of my crying and his arm holding tightly to me, he whispers, "Meredith, Jesus is dead."

And then I'm crying so much harder, because it doesn't matter. That's not the only reason I can't be with Cross.

"Meredith... Meredith. Please don't cry. Talk to me." He's whispering into my throat and playing with my hair, and I'm sobbing so hard a nurse peeks in.

"Is there a problem here? Sir," she says, "you need to give the patient space."

"I'm fine," I sob out. "He's fine."

Cross murmurs something to her; I can't hear, because I'm too lost in my sobbing, but I think she leaves, and then he's saying, "Merri, please don't cry. It's over. I swear baby, everything's going to be okay." He turns my shoulders

ELLA JAMES

slightly, so I'm facing him a little more, and he puts both
arms around my back, rubbing soothing circles with his
right hand until I'm able to stop gasping. I keep my head
against his chest, because I don't want to see the look on
his face.

I wonder how he really feels about me, knowing I was
married to Jesus. He's a nice guy, so he's going to be nice,
but I'm sure inside he's appalled. Anyone would be, especially if they knew the whole story.

I look back up at Cross and am almost surprised to find
him speaking. He's saying something about the fire and:
"Marchant killed him, baby. He and the fuckers with him
tried to exit out the front, and that's where everybody had
evacuated. Marchant had a gun, and he recognized Jesus."

A shudder ripples through me, and he actually says, "I
hope you're not upset."

I whisper, "No. Of course not. I'm...glad."

Cross nods. "That's what I thought." He smoothes my
hair back, and for a long time we just sit there, clinging to
each other. I can feel his gaze on me, but I still can't bring
myself to look into his eyes.

His fingers stroke my forehead. "How's the hand?"

I'm not sure what he means until I look down and abruptly remember my left hand is in a cast. Tears fill my
eyes again, and I shrug. "I don't know. It hurts."

"I'm sorry." His forehead touches mine. "I'm so sorry
that I hurt you."

"You...?" And then I remember being chained to that
statue thing; the smoke; and Cross. "Oh my God, that was
you who got me out! It wasn't a firefighter."

He smiles, but it's a sad one. "Nope."

"Cross...wow. Just...wow, and thank you." I lean up and kiss him on the cheek, and if it's possible, his smile gets even sadder.

"You don't owe me anything, Merri."

There's a long silence, during which I still cling to him. Even with Jesus dead...I shouldn't be clinging to Cross. Not considering the bomb that I'm about to drop on him.

I shut my eyes and hold it in. I really want a few more minutes with him.

"I know I don't owe you anything." I lay my head against my pillow, close my eyes, and enjoy the feeling of his arm around me. The familiar scent of him. Everything about this man I've come to love will have to be remembered, because in a second, I know he'll leave. Even someone like Cross couldn't ignore what I've been holding back.

I keep telling myself I'll say it in a minute, but I let many of them go by.

Cross doesn't speak, and neither do I, and when a nurse comes in the room to check my temperature, she doesn't ask him to move, so we don't have to separate.

He's lying on his left side with his right arm draped gently over me, his face buried in my hair, and it feels perfect, which is how I know I have to tell him now.

My voice trembles. "Cross—" I glance over at him and find his blue eyes rapt. "I need to tell you something else. Remember what I said back at that cottage?"

He nods. His face blurs from my tears, my voice cracks as I whisper, "I had sex with Jesus." I squeeze my eyes shut, and before he can jump up or say something that hurts too much, I add: "He made me!"

Maybe that's the worst part—the fact that I've been used like that—but I don't think so. Jesus was a vile person, a violent killer, and regardless of how good he was to me for most of the time I was with him... "He forced me to marry him, and he forced me to have sex."

I draw my knees up, pushing Cross away a little, and cover my face with my hand as I cry.

"Tell me about it." Cross is holding onto me, and even though I swore I'd never tell anyone, I open up my mouth and let the words pour out.

"It was after we were...oh God, I can't even say it. Married. A rumor got started. That he was gay," I say tearily. "He was upset and so...he forced me to have sex with him...in front of other people." There were lots of them: a whole room. "And it wasn't just once, it was..." I gasp, struggling to get air, and Cross pulls me to his chest, holding onto the back of my head like he's afraid someone will come take me away. He leans me back against the pillows and presses his finger on the oxygen tubing as he looks into my eyes.

"Damnit, Merri—I'm sorry. I'm so sorry."

I nod, just focus on breathing, and when I get myself together, Cross pulls me tight against him again. "Merri," he whispers into my hair, "why didn't you tell me sooner?"

"I don't know," I sob. "I guess I was...ashamed!"

"You have nothing to be ashamed of." He pulls away from me and looks into my eyes; his blue ones look like steel. "Nothing, Merri. You were a fucking— fracking victim. Nothing else."

"But I'm ashamed of *that*!"

"What could you have done?" he asks me. "Were you

bigger than Jesus? Could you have fought him?"

I shake my head; the tears are still pouring. "Things like this don't happen to good people who live the life they should."

He strokes my forehead, gently pushing my hair back. "If they happened to you, baby, then they definitely do."

I avert my eyes to the blanket and voice one of my deepest, most difficult feelings about what happened. "I feel like it only happened for one night, and other men and women—other sex slaves—have it so much worse. How can I complain?"

He grips my shoulder. "Because what happened to you was horrible. That's why." He sighs, and I notice that his eyes are wet. "I hope when we get out of here you'll go talk to a shrink."

For some reason, the statement makes me laugh. "I'm not going by myself."

He threads his fingers through mine. "Then I'll go with you."

I rake my gaze down his body, looking for a sign that he's upset; disgusted. Searching myself for a feeling of regret. I've carried this secret for almost ten months, and every day, it's strangled me. I'm shocked to find that now, I just feel warm.

"Are you sure you're not...upset," I whisper.

His dark brows arch. "About what you told me?"

Tears wet my eyes again; I nod, struggling to keep my gaze on him.

"Hell yes, I'm upset." He takes my hand in his and looks into my eyes. "Merri, I'm upset for *you*."

Tears drip down my face again, but I don't bother trying to stop them this time. They feel good almost. And even though I'm still scared about what Cross might really think, I'm glad I told him. As if to demonstrate that I'm wrong—that he really doesn't think I'm damaged or disgusting—he pulls me to his chest and lets me cry.

He doesn't say anything. He doesn't tell me not to.

I'm not sure how long I go, but I know when I'm finished, I feel lighter. *Tons* lighter. With a shaky hand, I shift my body on the mattress, angling myself so I'm looking right at him. I look him over, from his handsome face down to the splint on his right ankle. I didn't even notice that before.

"Are you okay?" I squeeze his fingers. "You hurt your foot?"

He nods. "It's just a minor fracture."

"What about your lungs and stuff?"

"Got a little fracked, but I've been discharged. I was better off than you..." He sounds hoarse. "I didn't get there as fast as I wanted to."

And I'm surprised—no, shocked—to see his eyes glitter with tears.

Reaching up with our joined hands, I stroke his neck. "You got there soon enough—on both counts." And I can see in his sad eyes that he knows what I'm saying: I'm talking about Mexico, too. I pull him close to me. "You got there just in time. I promise."

I'm surprised to find it doesn't feel like I'm telling a lie. Tonight, at least, with Cross right here beside me, I feel like I'll be okay.

I nuzzle his cheek and bring him down beside me on the bed. So I can kiss his hair and catch up on loving him.

EPILOGUE

Merri

WE SPEND THE night wrapped in each other. When the nurses come to check my temperature and blood pressure, they work around Cross. I like to think that they can tell how much we need this. When the sun comes up, shining brilliant pink on the windows of some of the buildings around ours, I'm lying between Cross's legs, my back against his chest, and his arms are wrapped around my waist. His left hand rests under my casted one. He can't hold it, of course, and I can barely move my fingers without pain, but I like our hands beside each other.

Yeah. It's that kind of thing. Like a high school crush. But so much better.

We spend the morning just talking. We turn around so we're facing each other, and in a low voice, so no monitors or cameras can hear me, I tell him more than I ever thought I would tell anyone about my time in Mexico. I cry sometimes, but Cross is always there with me, so it's not half as hard as I'd imagined it would be.

I think I'm getting discharged in a day or two. My lungs will be weak for a while, but my team of pulmonologists thinks that they'll recover in the next few months.

In the meantime, I'm posing as Cross Carlson's wife.

"I would make it official," he whispers at one point, when he's got his face hidden in my neck. I freeze, and he nuzzles me, then pulls away, so I can see his eyes. "No pressure. I'm not in a hurry. I just wanted you to know how I feel."

And I don't know what to say. My eyes are wide and I think my mouth is open.

Cross laughs. "You're as bad as I am?"

I can barely speak. "What do you mean?"

"The idea of marriage usually terrifies me. And I promise you, I'm not proposing."

I search his face, and when I see that he's being sincere—he doesn't really want to get married either—I laugh. I try to smile, but it comes out sad. "My last marriage kind of sucked."

"I know." He's not smiling at all. He takes my hand and kisses my ring finger, blazing through me with those bright blue eyes. "I'm gonna make that up to you one day. But for now you wanna just stick with the passport?"

"Is that my official non-commitment commitment?"

He nods.

I smile. "Then yeah, let's stick with that."

We're joking when really, there's a lot to figure out. Not just who I am or where I've been, but where I'm going. Where we're going. I think we're both serious about the shrink, and I know that part won't be fun. But I have a feeling we're also both serious about the passport. About our commitment to each other, whatever it is.

We're holding hands again when a doctor comes in. This one, I don't recognize. I sit up straighter, expecting to talk about my lungs, but the guy's looking at Cross.

"How are you, man?"

Cross looks at me, then at the doctor. "I'm good."

The guy looks us both over, then he smiles. "That's good. I heard you guys were headed out, was wondering if you'd like to do some of your pre-op stuff before you go."

My heart stops. "Pre-op?"

The doctor raises his eyebrows at Cross. "You haven't told your wife about our plan?"

I open my mouth to say, I'm not his wife, but Cross just shakes his head. "Not yet. But I will. And on the pre-op, can I give you a call in a little while?"

The doctor nods, looking from me to Cross and back to me. "Of course." He hands Cross his card, and I try not to feel afraid.

CROSS

WE SPEND THE afternoon talking about the procedure Dr. Grantham wants to do, and when Merri is discharged the next morning, we walk together to the outpatient center to do blood work and schedule the surgery.

A week later, I'm back in one of those ugly ass hospital gowns before the sun is even up. They give me something to swallow to start the 'relaxation process', and I take it even though I don't want to.

Merri lies her head against my shoulder as we wait, on

a stretcher in a dreary little room, for them to come get me.

"How are you feeling?" she whispers after we pass some time in silence.

I squeeze her hand. "Sleepy."

"Go to sleep." She strokes my hair. I close my eyes, or maybe they close on their own. I can still feel her. Still smell her. I murmur, "I can't."

"Why not?"

"I don't want to leave you."

I hear her smiling, even though I can't see. "I'll be here when you get back. Promise."

And later on, I find that she is.

ABOUT ELLA

ELLA JAMES IS A Colorado author who writes teen and adult romance. She is happily married to a man who knows how to wield a red pen, and together they are raising two children under three who will probably grow up believing everyone's parents go to war over the placement of a comma.

Ella's books have been listed on numerous Amazon bestseller lists; two were listed among Amazon's Top 100 Young Adult Ebooks of 2012.

To find out more about Ella's projects and get dates on upcoming releases, find her on Facebook at *facebook.com/ellajamesauthorpage* and follow her blog, *www.ellajamesbooks.com*. Questions or comments? Tweet her at *author_ellaj* or e-mail her at *ella_f_james@ymail.com*

OTHER TITLES BY ELLA JAMES

STAINED SERIES
Stained
Stolen
Chosen
Exalted

HERE TRILOGY
Here
Trapped

LOVE, INC. SERIES
Selling Scarlett
Taming Cross
Unmaking Marchant

www.ingramcontent.com/pod-product-compliance
Lightning Source LLC
Chambersburg PA
CBHW030436270626
47155CB00023B/2619